Ron Rash is the author of the prizewinning novels *One Foot in Eden* and *Saints at the River,* as well as the collection *Chemistry and Other Stories.* He is the recipient of an O. Henry Award and the James Still Award from the Fellowship of Southern Writers. For *Saints at the River,* he received the 2004 Weatherford Award for Fiction, the Southern Book Critics Circle Award for best novel, and the 2005 SEBA Best Book Award for Fiction. Rash holds the John Parris Chair in Appalachian Studies at Western Carolina University.

Additional Praise for *The World Made Straight*

"Ron Rash writes some of the most memorable novels of this young century, and brings to the task a poet's love of language and a short-storyist's sense of gripping plots. His third novel, *The World Made Straight* . . . establishes Rash as a major writer. . . . No writer since the late Larry Brown has handled the raw grit of country people as truthfully as Rash. His knowledge of his own Appalachian past, which extends back into the mid-1700s, with his keen observation of people in Oconee County, South Carolina, where he lives, and Cullowhee, North Carolina, where he teaches, enables him to craft fiction that is at once uplifting, harrowing, and unforgettable." —*The News & Observer*

"Part melancholy historical novel and part high-voltage thriller, this third novel from the talented Rash will appeal to readers who like their suspense done with literary flair." —*Booklist*

"The strength of Rash's descriptions, the shards of philosophy, the well-rounded characterizations, join the reader and the characters in mutual longing for what the characters don't have and desperately need. . . . Rash paints the beauty of the mountains vividly. The sun flooding over the rims turning the black valleys gold, the speckled trout flashing in the water, are visions Rash makes sing to the reader. . . . Rash creates a forceful reality, and his skill and style establish him as a powerful writer. He ties shadowy past and harsh present with a vine as strong and pervasive as kudzu." —*The Post and Courier* (Charleston)

"Ron Rash writes so well about real people, people one paycheck short of extinction, that you care what happens to his characters in every clause. In *The World Made Straight,* he shows how much trouble a poor ol' boy can get in, just trying to catch a fish or two. Even in this novel, his words sound like poetry."
—Rick Bragg, author of *All Over but the Shoutin'* and *Ava's Man*

"Finely wrought . . . vivid."   —*Publishers Weekly*

"A powerful, and at times hair-raising, story of historical loss and recovery. . . . Steeped in the rich language and lyricism of Appalachia that has won Rash national acclaim as a poet, *The World Made Straight* joins Toni Morrison's *Song of Solomon* as an important lyric page-turner for our times; an American masterpiece about the power of unresolved history to shatter, subvert, and ultimately heal our heartbreaking attempts to understand our identities and own times. . . . An enormously moving novel that will be read, discussed, and grappled with beyond the rest of our lives."
—*The Bloomsbury Review*

"Some of his magic comes from the tales of home he tells. Some of his magic comes from words themselves and the love a poet has for words, especially for the vocabulary of home."
—*The State* (Columbia)

"Poets' novels tend to be finely wrought, pretty failures—or worse. Ron Rash, a justly admired poet, is an exhilarating exception."
—*Los Angeles Times Book Review*

"A convincing portrayal of Southern life . . . Rash's prose demonstrates a deep understanding of the characters and their dialect."

—Library Journal

"Immensely powerful."   *—Asheville Citizen-Times*

"In *The World Made Straight*, Rash—like his Southern Gothic ancestors William Faulkner and Flannery O'Connor—offers readers a powerful story about families and individuals troubled by subtle evils, persistent violence, malignant fear, and the relentless encroachment of the past upon the present."   *—BookPage*

"Deft, intelligent, crisp, sensual, and lyrical, *The World Made Straight* is the best work yet by a wonderful writer. This is why we read books: to encounter a great story told well."

—Rick Bass, author of The Lives of Rocks

"This is the third novel by Ron Rash that has brought my life to a grinding halt—but to praise Rash simply as a powerful storyteller would be to overlook his gifts as a profoundly ethical writer and, at the same time, a poet with a fine and tender eye for the beauty of nature. What I love and admire most of all about this book, however, is its fierce confrontation of a human dilemma that has sparked too many of the world's most violent tragedies: the burning question of just how much allegiance we owe family and community, including the ghosts from our past."

—Julia Glass, author of Three Junes

"Rash writes with beauty and simplicity, understanding his characters with a poet's eye and heart and telling their tale with a poet's tongue."   *—William Gay, author of Provinces of Night*

THE
WORLD
MADE
STRAIGHT

RON RASH

PICADOR

HENRY HOLT AND COMPANY

NEW YORK

www.picadorusa.com

Picador® is a U.S. registered trademark and is used by
Henry Holt and Company under license from Pan Books Limited.

For information on Picador Reading Group Guides,
as well as ordering, please contact Picador.
Phone: 646-307-5629
Fax: 212-253-9627
E-mail: readinggroupguides@picadorusa.com

A version of chapter one appeared in a slightly different form in
The Kenyan Review and *The O. Henry Prize Stories 2005*.

Designed by Kelly S. Too

Library of Congress Cataloging-in-Publication Data

Rash, Ron, date.
   The world made straight / Ron Rash.
      p. cm.
   ISBN-13: 978-0-312-42660-6
   ISBN-10: 0-312-42660-7
   1. Teenage boys—Fiction. 2. United States—History—Civil War, 1861–1865—
Influence—Fiction. 3. Marijuana industry—Fiction. 4. City and town life—Fiction.
5. Male friendship—Fiction. 6. North Carolina—Fiction. 7. Massacres—Fiction. 8.
Violence—Fiction. I. Title.

PS3568.A698W67 2006
813'.54—dc22

2005050304

First published in the United States by Henry Holt and Company

D 20 19 18 17 16 15 14 13 12 11

For my son, James

But not yet have we solved the incantation of this whiteness, and learned why it appeals with such power to the soul; and more strange and far more portentous—why, as we have seen, it is at once the most meaning symbol of spiritual things, nay, the very veil of the Christian's Deity; and yet should be as it is, the intensifying agent in things the most appalling to mankind.

Moby-Dick

PART ONE

August 5, 1850

Lansford Hawkins, age 48.
Complaint: Fevered, headache.
Diagnosis: Coriza. Consulted Wood's Theory and Practice of
  Medicine.
Treatment: Dover's Powder. At patient's insistence cupped
  sixteen ounces of blood from left arm to remove morbific
  matter. Rest in bed two days.
Fee: Fifty cents. Paid in cash.

Clementine Crockett, age 58.
Complaint: Locked bowels.
Diagnosis: Same.
Treatment: Blue mass.
Fee: Fifty cents. Paid with twenty pounds flour.

P.M.

Summoned to Shelton Farm.
Maggie Shelton, age 25.
Complaint: Uterine bleeding. Seventh month with child.
Diagnosis: Physical exertings inducing early labor. Consulted
  Meigs's Females and Their Diseases.
Treatment: Tincture valerian to relieve spasmodic tendency. Bed
  rest for week. No field work until month after child born. Black
  haw tea twice daily to lessen bleeding. Bloodstone for same
  though dubious of effectingness.
Fee: Two dollars. Paid with venison, two dozen eggs delivered
  next time in town.

ONE

Travis came upon the marijuana plants while fishing Caney Creek. It was a Saturday, the first week of August, and after helping his father sucker tobacco all morning he'd had the rest of the day for himself. He'd changed into his fishing clothes and driven three miles of dirt road to the French Broad. Travis drove fast, the rod and reel clattering in the truck bed, red dust rising in his wake. The Marlin .22 slid on its makeshift gun rack with each hard curve. He had the windows down, and if the radio worked he would have had it blasting. The truck was a '66 Ford, battered from a dozen years of farm use. Travis had paid a neighbor five hundred dollars for it three months earlier.

He parked by the bridge and walked upriver toward where Caney Creek entered. Afternoon light slanted over Divide Mountain and tinged the water the deep gold of curing tobacco. A fish leaped in the shallows, but Travis's spinning rod was broken down and even if it hadn't been he wouldn't have bothered to cast. Nothing swam in the French Broad he could sell, only hatchery-bred rainbows and browns, some small-mouth, and catfish. The old men who fished the river stayed in one place for hours, motionless as the stumps and rocks they sat on. Travis liked to keep moving, and he fished where even the younger fishermen wouldn't go.

In forty minutes he was half a mile up Caney Creek, the rod still in two pieces. There were trout in this lower section, browns and rainbows that had worked their way up from the river, but Old Man Jenkins would not buy them. The gorge narrowed to a thirty-foot wall of water and rock, below it the creek's deepest pool. This was the place where everyone else turned back, but Travis waded through waist-high water to reach the waterfall's right side. Then he began climbing, the rod clasped in his left palm as his fingers used juts and fissures for leverage and resting places.

When he got to the top he fitted the rod sections together and threaded monofilament through the guides. He was about to tie on the silver Panther Martin spinner when a tapping began above him. Travis spotted the yellowhammer thirty feet up in the hickory and immediately wished he had his .22 with him. He scanned the woods for a dead tree or old fence post where the bird's nest might be. A flytier in Marshall paid two dollars if you brought him a yellowhammer or wood duck, a nickel for a single good feather, and Travis needed every dollar and nickel he could get if he was going to get his truck insurance paid this month.

The only fish this far up were what fishing books and magazines called brook trout, though Travis had never heard Old Man Jenkins or anyone else call them a name other than speck-led trout. Jenkins swore they tasted better than any brown or rainbow and paid Travis fifty cents apiece no matter how small. Old Man Jenkins ate them head and all, like sardines.

Mountain laurel slapped his face and arms, and he scraped his hands and elbows climbing rocks there was no other way around. Water was the only path now. Travis thought of his daddy back at the farmhouse and smiled. The old man had told him never to fish places like this alone, because a broken leg or rattlesnake bite could get a body graveyard dead before someone found you. That was about the only kind of talk he'd ever heard from the old man, Travis thought as he tested his knot, always being put down about something—how fast he drove, who he hung out with. Nothing but a bother from the day he was born. Puny and sickly as a baby and nothing but trouble since. That's what his father had said to his junior high principal, like it was Travis's fault he wasn't stout as his daddy, and like the old man hadn't raised all sorts of hell when he himself was young.

The only places with enough water to hold fish were the pools, some no bigger than a washtub. Travis flicked the spin-ner into the front of each pool and reeled soon as it hit the sur-face, the spinner moving through the water like a slow bright bullet. In every third or fourth pool a small orange-finned trout came flopping onto the bank, treble hook snagged in its mouth. Travis slapped the speckleds' heads against a rock and felt the fish shudder in his hand and die. If he missed a strike, he cast again into the same pool. Unlike brown and rainbows, speckleds would hit twice, sometimes even three times. Old Man Jenkins had said when he was a boy most every stream in Madison County was thick as gnats with speckleds, but they'd been too easy caught and soon fished out, which was why now you had to go to the back of beyond to find them.

EIGHT TROUT WEIGHTED THE BACK OF HIS FISHING VEST WHEN Travis passed the NO TRESPASSING sign nailed aslant a pin oak tree. The sign was as scabbed with rust as the decade-old car tag nailed on his family's barn, and he paid it no more heed now than when he'd first seen it a month ago. He knew he was on Toomey land, and he knew the stories. How Carlton Toomey once used his thumb to gouge a man's eye out in a bar fight and another time opened a man's face from ear to mouth with a broken beer bottle. Stories about events Travis's daddy had witnessed before he'd got right with the Lord. But Travis had heard other things. About how Carlton Toomey and his son were too lazy and hard-drinking to hold steady jobs. Travis's daddy claimed the Toomeys poached bears on national forest land. They cut off the paws and gutted out the gallbladders because folks in China paid good money to make potions from them. The Toomeys left the meat to rot, too sorry even to cut a few hams off the bears' flanks. Anybody that trifling wouldn't bother walking the hundred yards between farmhouse and creek to watch for trespassers.

Travis waded on upstream, going farther than he'd ever been before. He caught more speckleds, and soon seven dollars' worth bulged the back of his fishing vest. Enough money for gas and to help pay his insurance, and though it wasn't near the money he'd been making at Pay-Lo bagging groceries, at least he could do this alone, not fussed at by some old hag of a store manager with nothing better to do than watch his every move, then fire him just because he was late a few times.

He came to where the creek forked and it was there he saw a sudden high greening a few yards above him on the left. He stepped from the water and climbed the bank to make sure it was what he thought. The plants were staked like tomatoes and set in rows like tobacco or corn. They were worth money, a lot of money, because Travis knew how much his friend Shank paid for an ounce of good pot and this wasn't ounces but pounds.

He heard something behind him and turned, ready to drop the rod and reel and make a run for it. On the other side of the creek a gray squirrel scrambled up the thick bark of a black-jack oak. Travis told himself there was no reason to get all feather-legged, that nobody would have seen him coming up the creek.

He let his eyes scan what lay beyond the plants. A woodshed concealed the marijuana from anyone at the farmhouse or the dirt drive that petered out at the porch steps. Animal hides stalled mid-climb on the shed's graying boards. Coon and fox, in the center a bear, their limbs spread as though even in death they were still trying to escape. Nailed up there like a warning, Travis thought.

He looked past the shed and didn't see anything moving, not even a cow or chicken. Nothing but some open ground and then a stand of tulip poplar. He rubbed a pot leaf between his finger and thumb, and it felt like money, a lot more money than he'd ever make at a grocery store. He looked around one more time before taking out his pocketknife and cutting down five plants. The stalks had a twiney toughness like rope.

That was the easy part. Dragging them a mile down the creek was a chore, especially while trying to keep the leaves and buds from being stripped off. When he got to the river he hid the marijuana in the underbrush and walked the trail to make sure no one was fishing. Then he carried the plants to the road edge, stashed them in the gully, and got the truck.

When the last plants lay in the truck bed, he wiped his face with his hand. Blood and sweat wet his palm. Travis looked in the side mirror and saw a thin red line where mountain laurel had slapped his cheek. The cut made him look tougher, more dangerous, and he wished it had slashed him deeper, enough to leave a scar. He dumped his catch into the ditch, the trout stiff and glaze-eyed. He wouldn't be delivering Old Man Jenkins any speckleds this evening.

Travis drove home with the plants hidden under willow branches and feed sacks. He planned to stay only long enough to get a shower and put on clean clothes, but as he was about to leave his father stopped him.

"We haven't ate yet."

"I'll get something in town," Travis replied.

"No. Your momma's fixing supper right now, and she's got the table set for three."

"I ain't got time. Shank's expecting me."

"You'll make time, boy," his father said. "Else you and that truck can stay in for the evening."

—

IT WAS SIX-THIRTY BEFORE TRAVIS TURNED INTO THE ABAN-doned Gulf station and parked window to window beside Shank's Plymouth Wildebeast.

"You won't believe what I got in the back of this truck."

Shank grinned.

"It's not the old prune-faced bitch that fired you, is it?"

"No, this here is worth something. Get out and I'll show you."

They walked around to the truck bed and Shank peered in.

"I didn't know there to be a big market for willow branches and feed sacks."

Travis looked around to see if anyone was watching, then pulled back enough of a sack so Travis could see some leaves.

"I got five of them," Travis said.

"Holy shit. Where'd that come from?"

"Found it when I was fishing."

Travis pulled the sack back over the plant.

"Reckon I better start doing my fishing with you," Shank said. "It's for sure I been going to the wrong places." Shank leaned against the tailgate. "What are you going to do with it? I know you ain't about to smoke it yourself."

"Sell it, if I can figure out who'll buy it."

"I bet Leonard Shuler would," Shank said. "Probably give you good money for it too."

"He don't know me though. I'm not one of his potheads like you."

"Well, we'll just have to go and get you all introduced,"

Shank said. "Let me lock my car and me and you will go pay him a visit."

"How about we go over to Dink Shackleford's first and get some beer."

"Leonard's got beer," Shank said, "and his ain't piss-warm like what we got last time at Dink's."

They drove out of Marshall, following 25 North. A pink, dreamy glow tinged the air. Rose-light evenings, Travis's mother had called them. The carburetor coughed and gasped as the pickup struggled up High Rock Ridge. Travis figured soon enough he'd have money for a carburetor kit, maybe even get the whole damn engine rebuilt.

"You're in for a treat, meeting Leonard," Shank said. "There's not another like him, leastways in this county."

"Wasn't he a teacher somewhere up north?"

"Yeah, but they kicked his ass out."

"What for," Travis asked, "taking money during home-room for dope instead of lunch?"

Shank laughed.

"I wouldn't put it past him, but the way I heard it he shot some fellow."

"Kill him?"

"No, but he wasn't trying to. If he had that man would have been dead before he hit the ground."

"I heard tell he's a good shot."

"He's way beyond good," Shank said. "He can hit a chigger's ass with that pistol of his."

After a mile they turned off the blacktop and onto a dirt road. On both sides what had once been pasture sprouted with scrub pine and broom sedge. They passed a deserted farm-house, and the road withered to no better than a logger's skid trail. Trees thickened, a few silver-trunked river birch like slats of caught light among the darker hardwoods. The land made a deep seesaw and the woods opened into a small meadow, at the center a battered green and white trailer, its back windows painted black. Parked beside the trailer was a Buick LeSabre, front fender crumpled, rusty tailpipe held in place with a clothes hanger. Two large big-shouldered dogs scrambled out from under the trailer, barking furiously, brindle hair hackled behind their necks.

"Those damn dogs are Plott hounds," Travis said, rolling his window up higher.

Shank laughed.

"They're all bark and bristle," Shank said. "Them two wouldn't fight a tomcat, much less a bear."

The trailer door opened and a man wearing nothing but a frayed pair of khaki shorts stepped out, his brown eyes blink-ing like some creature unused to light. He yelled at the dogs and they slunk back under the trailer.

The man was no taller than Travis. Blond, stringy hair touched his shoulders, something not quite a beard and not quite stubble on his face. Older than Travis had figured, at least in his mid-thirties. But it was more than the creases in the brow that told Travis this. It was the way the man's shoulders drooped and arms hung—like taut, invisible ropes were at-tached to both his wrists and pulling toward the ground.

"That's Leonard?"

"Yeah," Shank said. "The one and only."

"He don't look like much."

"Well, he'll fool you that way. There's a lot more to him than you'd think. Like I said, you ought to see that son-of-a-bitch shoot a gun. He shot both that yankee's shoulders in the exact same place. They say you could of put a level on those two holes and the bubble would of stayed plumb."

"That sounds like a crock of shit to me," Travis said. He lit a cigarette, felt the warm smoke fill his lungs. Smoking cigarettes was the one thing his old man didn't nag him about. Afraid it would cut into his sales profits, Travis figured.

"If you'd seen him shooting at the fair last year you'd not think so," Shank said.

Leonard walked over to Travis's window, but he spoke to Shank.

"Who's this you got with you?"

"Travis Shelton."

"Shelton," Leonard said, pronouncing the name slowly as he looked at Travis. "You from the Laurel?"

Leonard's eyes were a deep gray, the same color as the birds old folks called mountain witch doves. Travis had once heard the best marksmen most always had gray eyes and wondered why that might be so.

"No," Travis said. "But my daddy grew up there."

Leonard nodded in a manner that seemed to say he'd figured as much. He stared at Travis a few moments before speaking, as though he'd seen Travis before and was trying to haul up in his mind exactly where.

"You vouch for this guy?" Leonard asked Shank.

"Hell, yeah," Shank said. "Me and Travis been best buddies since first grade."

Leonard stepped back from the car.

"I got beer and pills but just a few nickel bags if you've come for pot," Leonard said. "Supplies are low until people start to harvest."

"Well, we come at a good time then." Shank turned to Travis. "Let's show Leonard what you brought him."

Travis and Shank got out. Travis pulled back the branches and feed sacks.

"Where'd you get that?" Leonard asked.

"Found it," Travis said.

"Found it, did you. And you figured finders keepers."

"Yeah," said Travis.

"Looks like you dragged it through every briar patch and laurel slick between here and the county line," Leonard said.

"There's plenty of buds left," Shank said, lifting one of the stalks so Leonard could see it better.

"What you give me for it?" Travis asked.

Leonard lifted a stalk himself, rubbed the leaves the same way Travis had seen tobacco buyers do before the market's opening bell rang.

"Fifty dollars."

"You're trying to cheat me," Travis said. "I'll find somebody else to buy it."

As soon as he spoke he wished he hadn't. Travis was about to say that he reckoned fifty dollars would be fine but Leonard spoke first.

"I'll give you sixty dollars, and I'll give you even more if you bring me some that doesn't look like it's been run through a hay bine."

"OK," Travis said, surprised at Leonard but more surprised at himself, how tough he'd sounded. He tried not to smile as he thought of telling guys back in Marshall that he'd called Leonard Shuler a cheater to his face and Leonard hadn't done a damn thing about it but offer more money.

Leonard pulled a roll of bills from his pocket, peeled off three twenties, and handed them to Travis.

"I was figuring you might add a couple of beers, maybe some quaaludes or a joint," Shank said.

Leonard nodded toward the meadow's far corner.

"Put them over there in those tall weeds next to my tomatoes. Then come inside if you've got a notion to."

Travis and Shank lifted the plants from the truck bed and laid them where Leonard said. As they approached the door Travis watched where the Plotts had vanished under the trailer. He didn't lift his eyes until he reached the steps. Inside, it took Travis's vision a few moments to adjust, because the only light came from a TV screen. Strings of unlit Christmas lights ran across the walls and over door eaves like bad wiring. A dusty couch slouched against the back wall. In the corner Leonard sat in a fake-leather recliner patched with black electrician's tape. A stereo system filled a cabinet and the music coming from the speakers didn't have guitars or words. Beside it stood two shoddily built bookshelves teetering with albums and books. What held Travis's attention lay on a cherrywood gun rack above the couch.

Travis had seen a Model 70 Winchester only in catalogs. The checkering was done by hand, the walnut so polished and smooth it seemed to Travis he looked deep into the wood, almost through the wood, as he might look through a jar filled with sourwood honey. Shank saw him staring at the rifle and grinned.

"That's nothing like the peashooter you got, is it?" Shank said. "That's a real rifle, a Winchester Seventy."

Shank turned to Leonard.

"Let him have a look at that pistol."

Shank nodded at a small table next to Leonard's chair. Behind the lamp Travis saw the tip of a barrel.

"Let him hold that sweetheart in his hand," Shank said.

"I don't think so," Leonard said.

"Come on, Leonard. Just let him hold it. We're not talking about shooting."

Leonard looked put out with them both. He lifted the pistol from the table and emptied bullets from the cylinder into his palm, then handed it to Shank.

Shank held the pistol a few moments and passed it to Travis. Travis knew the gun was composed of springs and screws and sheet metal, but it felt more solid than that, as if smithed from a single piece of case-hardened steel. The white grips had a rich blueing to them that looked, like the Winchester's stock, almost liquid. The Colt of the company's name was etched on the receiver.

"It's a forty-five," Shank said. "There's no better pistol a man can buy, is there Leonard?"

"Show-and-tell is over for today," Leonard said, and held

his hand out for the pistol. He took the weapon and placed it back behind the lamp. Travis stepped closer to the gun rack, his eyes not on the Winchester but what lay beneath it, a long-handled piece of metal with a dinner-plate-sized disk on one end.

"What's that thing?" Travis asked.

"A metal detector," Leonard said.

"You looking for buried treasure?"

"No," Leonard said. "A guy wanted some dope and came up a few bucks short. It was collateral."

"What do you do with it?"

"He used it to hunt Civil War relics."

Travis looked more closely at the machine. He thought it might be fun to try, kind of like fishing in the ground instead of water.

"You use it much?"

"I've found some dimes and quarters on the riverbank."

Leonard sat back down in the recliner. He nodded at the couch. "You can stand there like fence posts if you like, but if not that couch ought to hold both of you."

A woman came from the back room and stood in the foyer between the living room and kitchen. She wore cut-off jeans and a halter top, her legs and arms thin but cantaloupe-sized bulges beneath the halter. Her hair was blond but Travis could see the dark roots. She was sunburned and splotches of pink underskin made her look wormy and mangy. Like some stray dog around a garbage dump, Travis thought. Except for her face. Hard-looking, as if the sun had dried up any softness there once was, but pretty—high cheekbones and full lips, dark-brown eyes. If she wasn't all scabbed up she'd be near beautiful, Travis figured.

"How about getting Shank and his buddy here a couple of beers, Dena," Leonard said.

"Get them your ownself," the woman said. She took a Coke from the refrigerator and disappeared again into the back room.

Leonard shook his head but said nothing as he got up. He brought back two cans of Budweiser and a sandwich bag filled with pot and rolling papers. He handed the beers to Travis and Shank and sat down in the chair. Travis was thirsty and drank quickly as he watched Leonard carefully shake pot out of the baggie and onto the paper. Leonard licked the paper and twisted both ends.

"Here," he said, and handed the marijuana to Shank.

Shank lit the joint, the orange tip brightening as he inhaled. Shank offered the joint back but Leonard declined.

"All these times I've been out here I never seen you mellow out and take a toke," Shank said. "Why is that?"

"I'm not a very mellow guy." Leonard nodded at Travis. "Looks like your buddy isn't either."

"He's just scared his daddy would find out."

"That ain't so," Travis said. "I just like a beer buzz better."

He lifted the beer to his lips and drank until the can was empty, then squeezed the can's middle. The cool metal popped and creaked as it folded inward.

"I'd like me another one."

"Quite the drinker, aren't you," Leonard said. "Just make

sure you don't overdo it. I don't want you passed out and pissing my couch."

Travis stood and for a moment felt off plumb, maybe because he'd drunk the beer so fast. When the world steadied he got the beer from the refrigerator and sat back down. He looked at the TV, some kind of Western, but without the sound he couldn't tell what was happening. He drank the second beer quick as the first.

Shank had his eyes closed.

"Man, I'm feeling so good," Shank said. "If we had us some real music on that stereo things would be perfect."

"Real music," Leonard said, and smiled, but Travis knew he was only smiling to himself.

Travis studied the man who sat in the recliner, trying to figure out what it was that made Leonard Shuler a man you didn't want to mess with. Leonard looked soft, Travis thought, pale and soft like bread dough. Just because a man had a couple of bear dogs and a hotshot pistol didn't make him such a badass. He thought about his own daddy and Carlton Toomey, big men who didn't need to talk loud because they could clear out a room with just a hard look. Travis wondered if anyone would ever call him a badass and wished again that he didn't take after his mother, so thin-boned.

"So what is this shit you're listening to, Leonard?" Shank asked.

"It's called *Appalachian Spring*. It's by Copland."

"Never heard of them," Shank said.

Leonard looked amused.

"Are you sure? They used to be the warm-up act for Lynyrd Skynyrd."

"Well, it still sucks," Shank said.

"That's probably because you fail to empathize with his view of the region," Leonard said.

"Empa what?" Shank said.

"Empathize," Leonard said.

"I don't know what you're talking about," Shank said. "All I know is I'd rather tie a bunch of cats together by their tails and hear them squall."

Travis knew Leonard was putting down not just Shank but him also, talking over him like he was stupid. It made Travis think of his teachers at the high school, teachers who used sentences with big words against him when he gave them trouble, trying to tangle him up in a laurel slick of language. Figuring he hadn't read nothing but what they made him read, never used a dictionary to look up a word he didn't know.

Travis got up and made his way to the refrigerator, damned if he was going to ask permission. He pulled the metal tab off the beer but didn't go back to the couch. He went down the hallway to find the bathroom.

He almost had to walk slantways because of the makeshift shelves lining the narrow hallway. They were tall as Travis and each shelf sagged under the weight of books of various sizes and shapes, more books than Travis had seen anywhere outside a library. There was a bookshelf in the bathroom as well. He read the titles as he pissed, all unfamiliar to him. But some looked interesting. When he stepped back into the hallway, he saw the bedroom door was open. The woman sat up in the bed reading a magazine. Travis walked into the room.

The woman laid down the magazine.

"What the hell do you want?"

Travis grinned.

"What you offering?"

Even buzzed on beer he knew it was a stupid thing to say. Ever since he'd got to Leonard's his mouth had been like a faucet he couldn't shut off.

The woman's brown eyes stared at him like he was nothing more than a sack of manure somebody had dumped on the floor.

"I ain't offering you anything," she said. "Even if I was, a little peckerhead like you wouldn't know what to do with it."

The woman looked toward the open door.

"Leonard," she shouted.

Leonard appeared at the doorway.

"It's past time to get your Cub Scout meeting over," she said.

Leonard nodded at Travis.

"I believe you boys have overstayed your welcome."

"I was getting ready to leave anyhow," Travis said. He turned toward the door and the can slipped from his hand, spilling beer on the bed.

"Nothing but a little peckerhead," the woman repeated.

In a few moments he and Shank were outside. The last rind of sun embered on Brushy Mountain. Cicadas had started their racket in the trees and lightning bugs rode an invisible current over the grass. Travis tried to catch one, but when he opened his hand it held nothing but air. He tried again and felt a soft tickling in his palm.

"You get more plants, come again," Leonard said from the steps.

"I was hoping you'd show us some of that fancy shooting of yours," Shank said.

"Not this evening," Leonard said.

Travis loosened his fingers. The lightning bug seemed not so much to fly as float out of his hand. In a few moments it was one tiny flicker among many, like a star returned to its constellation.

"Good night," Leonard said, turning to go back inside the trailer.

"Empathy means you can feel what other people are feeling," Travis said.

Leonard's hand was on the door handle but he paused and looked at Travis. He nodded and went inside.

"Boy, you're in high cotton now," Shank said as they drove toward Marshall. "Sixty damn dollars. That'll pay your truck insurance for two months."

"I figured to give you ten," Travis said, "for hooking me up with Leonard."

"No, I got a good buzz. That's payment enough."

Travis drifted onto the shoulder and for a moment one tire was on asphalt and the other on dirt and grass. He swerved back onto the road.

"You better let me drive," Shank said. "I was hoping to stay out of the emergency room tonight."

"I'm all right," Travis said, but he slowed down, thinking

about what the old man would do if he wrecked or got stopped for drunk driving. Better off if I got killed outright, he figured.

"Are you going to get some more plants?" Shank asked.

"I expect I will."

"Well, if you do, be careful. Whoever planted it's not likely to appreciate you thinning their crop out for them."

TRAVIS WENT BACK THE NEXT SATURDAY, TWO FLAT-WOVEN cabbage sacks stuffed into his belt. After he'd been fired from the Pay-Lo, he'd about given up on paying the insurance on his truck, but now things had changed. He had what was pretty damn near a money tree and all he had to do was get its leaves to Leonard Shuler. An honest-to-god money tree if there was ever such a thing, he kept thinking to himself when he got a little scared.

He climbed the waterfall, the trip up easier without a rod and reel. Once he passed the NO TRESPASSING sign, he moved slower, quieter. From the far bank's underbrush a warbler sang a refrain of three slow notes and three quick ones, the song echoing into the scattering of tamarack trees rising there. Travis's mother had once told him the bird was saying *pleased pleased pleased to meetcha.*

Soon cinnamon ferns brushed like huge green feathers against his legs, thick enough to hide a copperhead or satin-back. But he kept his eyes raised, watching upstream for the glimpse of a shirt, a movement on a bank. I bet Carlton Toomey didn't even plant it, Travis told himself, probably somebody who figured the Toomeys were too sorry to notice pot growing on their land.

When he came to where the plants were, he got on all fours and crawled up the bank, raising his head like a soldier in a trench. A Confederate flag brightened his tee-shirt, and he wished he'd had the good sense to wear something less visible. Might as well have a damn bull's-eye on his chest. He scanned the tree line across the field and saw no one. Travis told himself even if someone hid in the tulip poplars they could never get to him before he was long gone down the creek.

Travis cut the stalks just below the last leaves. Six plants filled up the sacks. He thought about cutting more, taking what he had to the truck and coming back to get the rest, but figured that was too risky. On his return Travis didn't see anyone on the river trail. If he had and they'd asked what was in the sacks, he'd have said galax.

When Travis pulled up to the trailer, Leonard was watering the tomatoes. He unlatched the tailgate and waited for Leonard to finish. Less than a mile away, the granite north face of Price Mountain jutted up beyond the pasture. Afternoon heat haze made the mountain appear to expand and contract as if breathing. *God's like these hills,* Preacher Caldwell had said one Sunday, *high enough up to see everything that goes on.* It ain't like stealing a cash crop like tobacco where a man's shed some real sweat, Travis reminded himself, for marijuana was little more bother than a few seeds dropped in the ground. Taking the pot plants was just the same as picking up windfall apples—less so because those that grew it had broken the law themselves. That was the way to think about it, Travis decided.

"How come you grow your own tomatoes but not your own pot?" Travis asked when Leonard laid down his hose and came over.

"Because I'm a low-risk kind of guy. It's getting too chancy unless you have a place way back in some hollow."

One of the Plotts nudged Leonard's leg and Leonard scratched the dog's head. The dog closed its watery brown eyes, seemed about to fall asleep. Not very fierce for a bear dog, Travis thought.

"Where's Shank?" Leonard said. "I thought you two were partners."

"I don't need a partner," Travis said. He lifted the first sack from the truck bed, pulled out each stalk carefully so as not to tear off any leaves and buds. He placed the plants on the ground between them. It was a good feeling, knowing everything on his end was done. A lot like when he and the old man unloaded tobacco at the auction barn. Even his daddy would be in a good mood as they laid their crop on the worn market-house floor.

As Travis emptied the second sack he imagined the old man's reaction if he knew what Travis was doing. Probably have a fit, Travis figured, though some part of his daddy, the part that had been near an outlaw when he was Travis's age, would surely admire the pluck of what his boy had done, even if he never said so. Travis nodded at his harvest.

"That's one hundred and twenty dollars' worth at the least," he said.

Leonard stepped closer and studied the plants a few moments. He pulled the billfold from his pocket and handed Travis five twenty-dollar bills. Leonard hesitated, then added four fives.

Travis stuffed the bills into his pocket but did not get back in the truck.

"What?" Leonard finally said.

"I figured you to ask me in for a beer."

"I don't think so. I don't much want to play host this afternoon."

"You don't think I'm good enough to set foot in that roachy old trailer of yours."

Leonard settled his eyes on Travis.

"You get your hackles up pretty quick, don't you?"

Travis did his best to match Leonard's steady gaze.

"I'm not afraid of you," Travis said.

Leonard shifted his gaze lower and to the right as though someone sat in a chair beside Travis. Someone who took Travis's words no more seriously than Leonard did.

"After the world has its way with you a few years, it'll knock some of the strut out of you," Leonard said, no longer smiling. "If you live that long."

A part of Travis wanted to clamp a hand over his own mouth, keep it there till he was back in Marshall. He had the uneasy feeling that Leonard knew things about him, things so deep inside that Travis himself hadn't figured them out, and every time he opened his mouth Leonard knew more.

"I ain't wanting your advice," Travis said. "I just want some beer."

"One beer," Leonard said, and they walked into the trailer. While Leonard got the beers Travis went down the hall to the bathroom. The bedroom door was shut and he hoped it stayed so. If the woman came out she'd surely have some more sass words for him. When he came back Leonard sat in the leather recliner, a beer in each hand. He handed one to Travis. Travis sat on the couch and pulled the tab. He still didn't much care for the taste, but the beer was cold and felt good as it slid down his throat.

"You got a lot of books," Travis said, nodding toward the shelves.

"Keeps me from being ignorant," Leonard said.

"I've known plenty of teachers without any sense," Travis said. "They didn't even know how to change their own car tire."

Leonard leaned back a little deeper in the chair.

"Stupidity and ignorance aren't the same thing. You can't cure someone of stupidity. Somebody like yourself that's merely ignorant there might be hope for."

"What reason you got to say I'm ignorant?"

"That tee-shirt you're wearing, for one thing. If you'd worn it up here in the 1860s it could have gotten you killed, and by your own blood kin."

Travis had drunk only half his beer but Leonard's words were as hard to grasp as wisps of ground fog.

"You trying to say my family was yankees?"

"No, at least not in the geographical sense. They just didn't see any reason to side with the slave owners."

"So they weren't on either side?"

"They had a side. Nobody had the luxury of staying out of it up here. Most places they'd fight a battle and move on, but once war came it didn't leave Madison County."

Travis took a last swallow and set the empty can at his feet. He wondered if the older man was just messing with him, like when Shank had asked about the music. But it didn't seem that way. Leonard looked to be serious.

"You go out to Shelton Laurel much?" Leonard asked.

"Just for family reunions when I was a kid."

"And your kin never talked about what happened in 1863 or said anything about Bloody Madison?"

"What's Bloody Madison?"

"The name this county went by during the Civil War."

Travis thought back to church homecomings and family reunions in the Laurel. Most of the talk, at least among the men, had been about tobacco. But not all of it.

"Sometimes my daddy and uncle talked about kin that got killed in Shelton Laurel during the war, but I always figured the yankees had done it."

The Plotts began barking, and a few moments later Travis saw a red Camaro rumble up to the trailer, its back wheels jacked up, white racing stripe on the hood. Two men with long black hair got out. One threw a cigarette butt on the ground and didn't bother to grind it out with his boot heel. They stood beside the car, both doors open, the engine catching and coughing. When Leonard didn't come out, the driver leaned into the car and blew the horn. Both dogs barked furiously but stayed near the trailer.

Leonard lifted himself wearily from the chair. He went to

the kitchen and came back with two plastic baggies filled with pills. The car horn blew again.

"The worst thing the nineteen sixties did to this country was introduce drugs to rednecks," Leonard said. He laid the baggies on the coffee table and went to the refrigerator.

"You don't seem to much mind taking their money," Travis said.

Leonard's lips creased into a tight smile.

"True enough," he said, taking another beer from the refrigerator. "Here," he said, holding the can out to Travis. "A farewell present. It's best if you don't come around here anymore."

"What if I get you some more plants?"

"I don't think you better try to do that," Leonard said. "Whoever's pot that is will be harvesting in the next few days. You better not be anywhere near when they're doing it either."

Travis left the couch and stepped into the kitchen. The first faint buzz from the alcohol made his scalp tingle.

"I ain't scared," Travis said.

"Well, maybe you should be in this instance."

Leonard's words were soft, barely audible over the roar of the Camaro. He wasn't talking down to him the way the teachers or his father might. For a moment Travis thought he saw something like concern flicker in Leonard's eyes. Then it was gone.

"But what if I do get more?" Travis asked as he reached for the beer. Leonard did not release his grip on the can.

"Same price, but if you want any beer you'll have to pay bootleg price like your buddies."

THE NEXT DAY AFTER LUNCH, TRAVIS TOOK OFF HIS CHURCH clothes and put on a green tee-shirt and a pair of cutoffs instead of regular jeans. That meant more scrapes and scratches but he'd be able to run faster if needed. The day was hot and humid, and when he parked by the bridge the only people on the river were a man and two boys swimming near the far bank. By the time Travis reached the creek, his tee-shirt was soggy and sweat stung his eyes.

Upstream, trees blocked most of the sun and the water he waded cooled him off. At the waterfall, an otter slid into the pool. Travis watched its body surge through the water as straight and sleek as a torpedo before disappearing under the bank. He wondered how much otter pelts brought and figured come winter it might be worth finding out, maybe set out a rabbit gum and bait it with a dead trout. He knelt and cupped his hand to drink, the pool's water so cold it hurt his teeth.

He climbed the left side of the falls, then made his way upstream to the sign. If someone waited for him, Travis believed that by now the person would have figured out he came up the creek, so he left it and climbed the ridge into the woods. He followed the sound of water until he'd gone far enough and came down the slope deliberate and quiet, stopping every few yards to listen.

He was almost to the creek when something rustled to his left in the underbrush. Travis did not move until he heard *pleased pleased pleased to meetcha* rising from the web of sweetbrier and scrub oak. When he stepped onto the sandy bank, he looked upstream and down before crossing.

The marijuana was still there, every bit as tall as the corn Travis and his daddy had planted in early April. He pulled the sacks from his belt and walked toward the closest plant, his eyes on the trees across the field. The ground gave slightly beneath his right foot. He heard a click, then the sound of metal striking bone. Pain flamed up his leg like a quick fuse, consumed his whole body. The sun slid sideways and the ground tilted as well and slapped up against the side of his face.

When he came to, his head lay inches from a pot plant. This ain't nothing but a bad dream, he told himself, thinking if he believed hard enough that might make it true. He used his forearm to lift his head and look at the leg. The leg twisted slightly and pain slugged him like a tire iron. The world darkened for a few moments before slowly lighting back up. He looked at his foot and immediately wished he hadn't. The trap's jaws clenched his leg just above the ankle. Blood soaked his tennis shoe and Travis feared if he looked too long he'd see the white nakedness of bone. Don't look at it anymore until you have to, he told himself, and laid his head back on the ground.

His face was turned toward the west now, and he guessed midafternoon from the sun's angle. Maybe it ain't that bad, he thought. Maybe if I just lay here awhile it'll ease up some and I can get the trap off. He kept still as possible, taking shallow breaths. A soft humming rose inside his head, like a mud dauber had crawled deep into his ear and gotten stuck. But it wasn't a bad sound. It reminded Travis of when his mother sang him to sleep when he was a child. He could hear the creek and its sound merged with the sound inside his head. Did trout hear water? he wondered. That was a crazy sort of thought and he tried to think of something that made sense.

He remembered what Old Man Jenkins had said about how just one man could pretty much fish out a stream of speckled trout if he took a notion to. Travis wondered how many speckled trout he'd be able to catch out of Caney Creek before they were all gone. He wondered if after he did he'd be able to find another way-back trickle of water that held them. He tried to imagine that stream, imagine he was there right now fishing it.

He must have passed out again, because when he opened his eyes the sun hovered just above the tree line. The humming in his head was gone and when he tested the leg, pain flamed up every bit as fierce as before. He wondered how long it would be until his parents got worried and how long it would take after that before someone found his truck and folks began searching. Tomorrow at the earliest, he figured, and even then they'd search the river before looking anywhere else.

Travis lifted his head a few inches and shouted toward the woods. No one called back. Being so close to the ground muffled his voice, so he used a forearm to raise himself a little higher and shout again.

I'm going to have to sit up, he told himself, and just the thought of doing so made bile rise into his throat. He took deliberate breaths and used both arms to lift himself. Pain smashed against his body and the world drained of color until all of what surrounded him was shaded a deep blue. He leaned back on the ground, sweat popping out on his face and arms like blisters. Everything was moving farther away, the sky and trees and plants, as though he were being slowly lowered into a well. He shivered and wondered why he hadn't brought a sweatshirt or jacket with him.

Two men came out of the woods, and seeing them somehow cleared his head for a few moments, brought the world's color and proximity back. They walked toward him with no more hurry than men come to check their plants for cutworms. Travis knew the big man in front was Carlton Toomey and the man trailing him his son. He couldn't remember the son's name but had seen him in town. What he remembered was the son had been away from the county for nearly a decade, and some said he'd been in the Marines and others said prison and some said both, though you wouldn't know it from his long brown hair, the bright bead necklace around his neck. The younger man wore a dirty white tee-shirt and jeans, the older man blue coveralls with no shirt underneath. Grease coated their hands and arms.

They stood above him but did not speak or look at him. Carlton Toomey jerked a red rag from his back pocket and rubbed his hands and wrists. The son stared at the woods across the creek. Travis wondered if they weren't there at all, were just some imagining in his head.

"My leg's hurt," Travis said, figuring if they spoke back they must be real.

"I reckon it is," Carlton Toomey said, looking at him now. "I reckon it's near about cut clear off."

The younger man spoke.

"What we going to do?"

Carlton Toomey did not answer, instead eased himself onto the ground beside the boy. They were almost eye level now.

"Who's your people?"

"My daddy's Harvey Shelton."

"You ain't much more than ass and elbows, boy. I'd have thought what Harvey Shelton sired to be stouter. You must favor your mother." Carlton Toomey nodded his head and smiled. "Me and your daddy used to drink some together, but that was back when he was sowing his wild oats. He still farming tobacco?"

"Yes sir."

"The best days of tobacco men is behind them. I planted my share of burley, made decent money for a while. But that tit has done gone dry. How much your daddy make last year, six–seven thousand?"

Travis tried to remember, but the numbers would not line up in his head. His brain seemed tangled in cobwebs.

"He'd make as much sitting on his ass and collecting welfare. If you're going to make a go of it in these mountains today you got to find another way."

Carlton Toomey stuffed the rag in his back pocket.

"I've done that, but your daddy's too stubborn to change. Always has been. Stubborn as a white oak stump. But you've figured it out, else you'd not have stole my plants in the first place."

"I reckon I need me a doctor," Travis said. He was feeling better, knowing the older man was there beside him. His leg didn't hurt nearly as much now as before, and he told himself he could probably walk on it if he had to once the Toomeys got the trap off.

"The best thing to do is put him down there below the falls," the son said. "They'll figure him to fallen and drowned himself."

Carlton Toomey looked up.

"I think we done used up our allotment of accidental drownings around here. It'd likely be more than just Crockett nosing around if there was another."

Toomey looked back at Travis. He spoke slowly, his voice soft.

"Coming back up here a second time took some guts. Even if I'd figured out you was the one I'd have let it go, just for the feistiness of your doing it. But coming a third time was down-right stupid, and greedy. It ain't like you're some shit-britches young'un. You're old enough to know better."

"I'm sorry," Travis said.

Carlton Toomey reached out his hand and gently brushed some of the dirt off Travis's face.

"I know you are, son, just like every other poor son-of-a-bitch that's got his ass in a sling he can't get out of."

Travis knew he was forgetting something, something important he needed to tell Carlton Toomey. He squeezed his eyes shut a few moments to think harder. It finally came to him.

"I reckon you better get me to the doctor," Travis said.

"We got to harvest these plants first," the older Toomey replied. "What if we was to take you down to the hospital and folks started wondering why we'd set a bear trap. They might figure there's something up here we wanted to keep folks from poking around and finding."

Carlton Toomey's words started to blur and swirl in Travis's mind. They were hard to hold in place long enough to make sense. He tried to remember what had brought him this far up the creek. Travis finally thought of something he could say in just a few words.

"Could you get that trap off my foot?"

"Sure," Toomey said. He slid over a few feet to reach the trap, then looked up at his son.

"Step on that lever, Hubert, and I'll get his leg out."

The younger man stepped closer. Travis stared hard at the beads. They were red and yellow and black, a dime-sized silver peace sign clipped on the necklace as well. Hubert raised his head as he pressed and afternoon sun glanced the silver, momentarily blinding Travis. The pain rose up his leg again but it seemed less a part of him now, the way an aching tooth he'd had last fall felt after a needle of Novocain. Travis kept staring at the beads, because they were the only thing now that hadn't been drained of color. There was a name for those beads. He almost remembered but then the name slipped free like a balloon let go, rising steadily farther and farther away.

"That's got it," Carlton Toomey said and slowly raised Travis's leg, placed it on the ground beside the trap. Toomey used spit and his rag to wipe blood from the wound.

"What's your given name, son?" he asked.

"Travis."

"This ain't near bad as it looks, Travis," Toomey said. "I

don't think that trap even put a gouge in the leg bone. Probably didn't tear up any ligaments or tendons either. You're just a pint low in the blood department. That's the thing what's making you foggyheaded."

"Now what?" the son said.

"Go call Dooley and tell him we'll be bringing him plants sooner than we thought. Bring back them machetes and we'll get this done." He paused. "Give me that hawkbill of yours."

Hubert took the knife from his pocket and handed it to his father.

"What you going to do to him?" Hubert asked.

"What's got to be done," the elder Toomey said. "Now go on and get those damn machetes."

Hubert started walking toward the farmhouse.

"I'm sorry I have to do this, son," Carlton said.

The knife blade made a clicking sound as it locked into place. Travis squeezed his eyes shut. For a few moments the only sound was the gurgle of the creek, and he remembered how it was the speckled trout that had brought him here. He remembered how you could not see the orange fins and red flank spots but only the dark backs in the rippling water. And how it was only when they lay gasping on the green bank moss that you realized how bright and pretty they were.

August 12, 1852

A.M.

Summoned to Franklin Farm.
Nance Franklin, age 34.
Complaint: Female bleeding.
Diagnosis: Excessive uterine haemorrhage.
Treatment: Tincture of valerian. Black haw tea. Cold cloths
  applied to abdomen.

Twelve P.M.
Haemorrhage lessening. Continue to apply cloths and minister
  with valerian, black haw tea.

One P.M.
Bleeding arrested. Pallor improved. Pulse firm.
Treatment: Bed rest for week. Dose of Dover's Powder once
  daily. Black haw tea twice daily.
Fee: Four dollars. Days work repairing my roof by two
  oldest sons.

P.M.

Dewy Morton, age 10.
Complaint: Arm hurt in fall from barn loft.
Diagnosis: Fracture of tibia, left arm.
Treatment: Laudanum to set arm.
Splint, cloth sling. Wear four weeks.
Return to confirm salutory mending.
Fee: One dollar, twenty-five cents.
  Paid with shoeing of horse.

Royce McCall, age 31.

Complaint: Fits, frothing at mouth.

Diagnosis: Epilepsy.

Treatment: Half-dram solution of iodine and iodide potash twice daily. Avoid excessive agitations of body and mind.

Note: Next time in Asheville order Dunglison's Treatise on Special Pathology and Therapeutics.

Fee: One dollar. Paid with eight pounds butter.

Attended lecture in Asheville by Doctor Justice on Botanic Medicine. Confirmed my views on eschewing cupping and blistering of patients and felicitous use of plants. Must devote further study to injurious symptoms of mineral preparations.

TWO

When he woke there was so little light he thought it must be night. The inside of his mouth felt tacked over with sandpaper. His ankle and head throbbed and his mind was stirred up like murky water. But it soon began to clear. Travis heard at first what he thought his own heart but soon realized the sound was the ticking of a clock. His eyes began adjusting to the dim light and he found himself in a room. He lay in a bed and a frayed quilt covered him to his neck, above a bare yellow lightbulb. Venetian blinds allowed in a few dim, motey stripes of sun. Enough to realize it was not full dark but early evening.

Travis raised up on his elbows and the leg caught fire, not just where the trap had bit into his leg but lower. He remembered feeling the knife blade settle not on his throat but his heel. Carlton Toomey had worked almost delicately, using a slow, sawing motion. At first it hadn't hurt enough to override the pain from the trap. Then he'd felt the Achilles tendon snap apart like a thick rubber band. Travis didn't remember anything after that.

A voice came from the room's far corner.

"I'd not try to move much."

Travis looked toward the voice, trying not to move anything below his neck.

Carlton Toomey sat in a ladderback chair, dressed in the same work clothes he'd had on earlier. Travis remembered more quickly now, scattered images and thoughts put back in proper sequence. He remembered scaling the falls, the click of the trap, everything up to the moment he'd passed out the last time.

Travis's throat was so dry his voice was nothing more than an unintelligible raspy whisper.

Carlton Toomey left the room and came back with a quart jar filled with water. Hubert came in the room as well and leaned in an easygoing way against the wall. Hubert had changed into jeans and a flannel shirt with its sleeves hacked just below the shoulders. He still wore the beads. Love beads, that's what they're called, Travis thought.

"Here," Carlton Toomey said, and lifted Travis's head.

Travis sipped until the glass was empty. Water had no taste, most folks claimed, but Travis knew if they'd been thirsty as he was they'd know that it did. Not like anything else you'd ever tasted, not like that at all, but the clear, cool tang he'd smelled in deep, mossy woods after a long rain. The water helped him think better, maybe because one bodily alarm bell had been stilled. The pain in his head and leg seemed to pull back a bit as well.

"Hate I had to take that knife to your foot," Toomey said, "but we got to be certain sure you don't forget there's a price to be paid for stealing. I'm of a mind you got off easy. There's places in this world they'd have cut your hand off."

"I need to get to the doctor," Travis said.

Carlton nodded.

"That's where we're soon enough headed. But some things got to be made clear first about what you're going to say when we get there."

"You're gonna regret this," Hubert said. "We best put him below the falls. It ain't too late."

"We're not doing that," Carlton Toomey said, "so shut up about it." He turned back to Travis. "The quicker we get some things clear the sooner we go to the hospital. If we dodder around here too long that ankle likely could get infected, especially with a rusty old trap germing it up. They might have to chop that leg of yours plumb off. You hear me?"

"Yes sir." Travis wanted to say more but the pain made it hard to talk.

"You're going to tell whatever busybody wants to know that you fell climbing the falls. Not a word about that trap neither. You never was on my land and you never saw no pot plants. The only reason we showed up was you yelling for help. You understand?"

"Yes sir," he said again.

Hubert stepped closer to the bed. He was a big man, though

not as big as his father. His nose had been broken, maybe more than once, enough that it swerved to the right, making his whole face appear misaligned. He looked at Travis as though he were nothing more than a groundhog or possum they'd caught.

"He ain't going to do it, Daddy. Soon as he gets to that hospital he'll be testifying like a damn tent-revival preacher."

"He'll do like we tell him," Carlton Toomey said. "Travis here is smart. Smart enough to outslick us twice, smart enough to keep his mouth shut now."

"I won't tell," Travis said, and he was suddenly more afraid than he'd been before, because he remembered the hawkbill's blade, how for a moment he thought that blade was going to slit his throat. "I swear it, Mr. Toomey."

"Then tell it back at me what you're going to say when we get there."

Travis told how he'd fallen trying to climb the falls, how the Toomeys had found him. The words came hard, and a skim of sweat covered his face when he'd finished.

"One other thing," Carlton Toomey said. "Who'd you sell them plants to?"

He didn't bother to hesitate or lie.

"Leonard Shuler."

"He know where you got them from?"

"No sir."

"Didn't go out of his way to ask, I bet," Hubert said to his father.

Carlton nodded, his eyes on Travis.

"Satisfied him to act like them plants fell out of the sky, and you just shackling along with nothing more to do than stretch your arms out and catch them." Carlton turned the glass in his hand, the same way he might test a doorknob. "That seems to be more and more a problem around here," he said, "people thinking anything they happen across is theirs for the taking."

Travis shifted his leg slightly.

"My leg's hurting bad," he said.

"It's likely to hurt more when we start moving you," Carlton said. He turned to his son. "We best get to it."

The two men lifted Travis from the bed and the pain returned, reverberating through his body until they laid him in the car's backseat. He knew the men had been working on this vehicle, not the green pickup, because the hood was still up. For a few moments Travis had a terrible fear that it would not start, that the Toomeys would have to do more repairs while he waited in the backseat. But Carlton Toomey slammed the hood shut and got in.

"Take the truck and get them plants down to Dooley," he told his son before cranking the engine. "We'll meet back here."

"What about the pills?"

Carlton Toomey nodded at a paper bag in the floorboard.

"I'll take care of that," Carlton Toomey said. "I know someone obliged to take them off our hands."

They bumped out of the yard and onto a dirt road leading to the two-lane.

"It won't be long now," Toomey said, but it seemed forever to Travis because the fire in his leg hadn't dimmed much since they'd laid him in the car. What Carlton Toomey had said about the bear trap's rusty steel worried him. Old Man Jenkins had once told about a man up near Flag Pond who'd gotten lockjaw from rusty barbed wire. The man had lost his ability to swallow and drowned from a cup of water his wife poured down his throat.

Travis raised his head slightly, spoke to the back of Toomey's head.

"Make sure they give me a tetanus shot," Travis said, gasping the last word as they hit another bump.

Carlton Toomey's dark eyes appeared in the driver's mirror. The eyes seemed disembodied, as if they'd slipped free from the face.

"I'll try and remember to do that," the big man said. His gaze returned to the road but he continued speaking. "There's probably near a million ways a man can die, but I reckon not many would outworse your throat clamping shut on you."

They were in Marshall before either spoke again.

"You ain't forgot what you're to say?"

"No sir," Travis said.

He felt the car turn a last time and stop, then hands eased him out of the backseat. He opened his eyes to be sure those hands did not belong to one of the Toomeys. Two men dressed in white laid him on a gurney as Carlton Toomey's face loomed over him a last time, close enough that he could smell tobacco and onion.

"See, I told you I'd get you here," Toomey said softly. "I kept my word and you best keep yours."

Then the gurney was rolling and Carlton Toomey's face fell away like something unlodged by a current. Rectangles of flu-

orescent light passed above Travis and he felt like he was looking out a train window, a train moving away from Toomey,
and because of that he could close his eyes now and not imagine a gleaming knife blade about to slit his throat.

CARLTON TOOMEY ARRIVED AT THE TRAILER JUST AS DARKNESS
made its final ascent up from the coves and ridges to the tree
line. He didn't blow the horn, just cut off the engine and
waited. Leonard was surprised the older man knew where he
lived, for they'd always done their transactions at the
Toomeys' farmhouse. I don't make house calls, Carlton had
once told him.

"You caused me a whole passel of trouble today, professor," Toomey said. The sobriquet was one Leonard had never
cared for. He'd told Carlton he'd never been a professor and
was not a teacher of any kind anymore, but the elder Toomey
continued to use the title, always with a little extra emphasis
on the word.

"What do you mean?" Leonard asked.

"Your pot supplier ain't a very good middleman. He has this
interesting notion that he don't have to pay them who growed
it. He just struts up on my land and picks it like it's no more
than blackberries."

Today had been the hottest of the summer, the trailer near
unbearable except for the cold beers Leonard had been drinking since midafternoon, so a few moments passed as he filtered
Carlton Toomey's words through the alcohol.

"I didn't know you were growing. I wouldn't have bought

from him if I'd known it was yours," Leonard said, telling the truth, because Carlton Toomey was not a man you wanted to cross.

"And it never entered your mind to ask where he was getting it?"

Leonard's bare feet stood on ground that, like the trailer, still retained the day's heat. No moon was out, and the stars had yet to pitch their tents and spark their small fires. He could barely see Toomey though their faces were no more than a yard apart. He'd never realized how much darker night could be in the mountains until he'd left them, seen nights in the Carolina piedmont and the Midwest. It seemed as if the coal-dark core of the mountains flowed out on nights like this, rose all the way up to the floor of the sky.

Toomey laughed softly.

"I'd likely as not have asked either. Kind of like looking a gift horse in the mouth."

A light came on as Toomey opened the glove compartment and removed a crinkled paper bag.

"Planting that crop was Hubert's idea. Young folks go out in the world and come back with all sorts of notions. Got that pot-growing idea from the hippies, like they'd know anything about how to make do in the world. Too bad that boy missed Vietnam. That would have shown him the real what's-what. Anyway, I told him we'd try our hand at growing this year and see the worth of it. I still figure us to make a profit but there's been more bother than I'd counted on. I've a mind to just stick to these pills."

Toomey offered the paper bag to Leonard.

"Brought you some black beauties and some 747s. A hundred will cover it."

"I haven't sold what I bought from you last week," Leonard said.

Toomey let his elbow settle on the window's lower frame, the bag in abeyance between him and Leonard. He shook the bag, the capsules making a dry rattling sound as they clicked against each other.

"Never hurts to stock up. Besides, after buying pot stole from me I'd think you right eager to prove we're still partners. Matter of fact, if I was you I'd probably add another twenty to boot just to show it was all a misunderstanding. That or one of them Plotts. It's getting pretty damn obvious I need me a guard dog."

Carlton shook the bag again.

"That's the sound of extra profits, professor."

But the dry rattling sound brought to mind something else, what Leonard had heard one morning years ago in a brush pile. He'd looked closer through the tangle of sticks and spotted the triangular head and thick coiled body. What he'd heard that morning and heard again tonight was a warning. Leonard removed five twenties and two tens from his billfold, handed them to Toomey, and took the bag.

"Thank you," Toomey said, vigilantly folding the bills before placing them in his shirt pocket. "Glad all this is behind us. The rest of these chuckleheads I deal with can't figure their way out of a one-door shithouse, so it's nice to deal with a man with some smarts about him. That's why I done business with you in the first place. Needed the intellectual stimulation. Been good for you too. Leastways you ain't clerking in a Seven-Eleven no more."

"Yes," Leonard agreed. "It's been good."

Carlton chuckled. "I'll never forget the day I come to that store to check you out. The way I was talking to them farmers you figured me for just another simple no-sense hayseed, didn't you?"

"I don't think I ever figured you for simple," Leonard said. But he knew the older man was partly right. Others loitered in the store that day and Toomey had joined their conversation about hunting and tobacco, Carlton's diction and grammar mimicking the other men's, making it easy to believe he was no different from those men. But once the others left, Toomey had winked at Leonard conspiratorially, then talked about Jimmy Carter's economic policy fifteen minutes before offering to expand Leonard's side business to quaaludes and uppers. Carlton had refrained from using colloquial language or subject-verb errors during that conversation. Just to show you this one time that I do know the King's English, the big man had said.

Carlton placed his hands on the steering wheel and leaned his head slightly forward, as if Leonard's words had pressed a heavy weight onto his back.

"No, I sure ain't simple," he said. "Some folks blame me for every meanness done in this county, from selling heroin to stealing kids' lollipops. Say I even killed my wife. Others say only a child of God could sing gospel the way I do. I guess I'm somewheres betwixt and between, like any another man."

Carlton gestured toward the bills in his pocket.

"There's some fellows who'd have bowed up their backs

about a matter like this. Men like that just keep on being stupid till they get themselves in a real bad fix, like it did that boy."

Carlton Toomey paused, seemed to be waiting for Leonard to ask about the "bad fix" Travis had gotten into. But Leonard said nothing.

The trailer's front room lit up with a gray muted glow. Voices came from the television.

"Still with you, is she," Carlton said. "That girl's like a mule following a carrot on a stick. Show her some pills and she'll go anywhere. Of course she does put a dent in your profit margin."

Toomey cranked the truck but let the engine idle.

"Not that I blame you. She's been rode hard but there's some pretty left in her yet. Everything has a price, I reckon." Toomey paused. "Listen at me. I'm pontificating like I'm the teacher, not you."

"I'm not a teacher anymore," Leonard said.

Carlton Toomey turned on the headlights and put the truck in gear.

"It's been a damn long day. I need to get back to the house and make sure that boy of mine done what I told him. He takes after his momma in the brains department, but ain't that ever the way of it."

Toomey backed up the truck a few feet and turned around. The pickup's taillights disappeared into the trees. Leonard stood outside a few minutes. He'd warned the boy not to go back and Travis hadn't listened. Something had happened. But whatever that something was wasn't his concern. The boy had stirred up all sorts of things deep inside Leonard that he'd thought safely locked in the past. He'd probably never see Travis again, and that was for the best.

When he went inside, Dena was on the couch watching TV, clothed only in panties and a halter top. She'd lain out in the sun that afternoon and her skin had a pink tinge.

"You need a air conditioner for this trailer," she said, her voice slurred by the quaaludes.

He looked at her face. Carlton Toomey had been right. There was, despite all the pills and booze, the scars and two knocked-out teeth, some pretty left in her. High cheekbones, delicate nose, and sensuous lips. The morning after he'd brought her back from the Ponderosa, Leonard had awakened to the smell of coffee. He'd walked into the kitchen where Dena had set the table with two plates and a pair of mismatched forks, paper towels as napkins. On each plate was a single piece of buttered toast. It looked like something a child might have done, a child who'd witnessed such domesticity only in a movie or a book. When he'd asked if she was ready to go home, she'd said there was no home, just a back room she rented from a quarrelsome old woman. She'd lingered at the breakfast table, then tried to coax him back into bed. The morning and her hangover accentuated her dry jaundiced pallor as though the nicotine in the cigarettes she smoked had tinted her skin. The plastic and wire where two of her front teeth should have been was more evident as well in the morning's unflinching light. Before leaving she'd taken a decade-old photograph from her billfold, one that showed a woman of undeniable beauty. Recognize me? she'd challenged, not putting the photo away until he'd nodded yes.

"You could buy us a couple of those window units, for God's sake. I got you enough new business to afford it." Dena slumped deeper into the couch, weary from the effort of speaking two whole sentences.

"I could afford a lot more things if you weren't eating my pills like they were jellybeans," Leonard responded. He couldn't help but wish that they did have a window unit, because hot as it was he wouldn't sleep well tonight.

"Anyway, you owe me a gift," Dena said, her eyes still on the TV.

"How do you figure that?"

"It's our anniversary, sweetheart. This time last July's when we first met."

Leonard retrieved another beer from the refrigerator and left her on the couch, knowing he'd find her there in the morning. He undressed and turned on the bedroom's ceiling fan, noticing the watermark on the ceiling as he did so. He went to the closet and pushed aside the thick leather-bound ledgers one at a time to reach the picture album in the far back corner. Leonard briefly contemplated taking down the 1848 ledger as well. He lay in bed, the album propped on his stomach as he turned the pages slowly, counting the pictures. Fifty-seven, and only two in Illinois.

Kera had believed they had no choice but to go. Two high-school teachers finding jobs in one county was hard enough, much less at the same school. Every morning for four years, they'd each driven thirty minutes away from their apartment in Asheville to opposite sides of the county. In Illinois they would work at the same school. There would be more time to be with their child, with each other. Less stress as well, fewer arguments fueled by that stress. The problem was the long commutes, Kera argued, but Leonard believed the long commutes, like the sleep-deprived year when Emily's ears and lungs had been welcoming harbors for infection, had not created but revealed fissures in their marriage, fissures that would be all the more apparent in a landscape where nothing remained hidden. He'd finally agreed to go, but Kera noted his sullenness. An English teacher, she'd accused him of living in the passive voice, letting others make choices so if things went wrong he didn't have to bear the blame.

The hottest day of the year, the radio announcer had predicted as they'd started the all-day drive to Illinois. He and Kera had been up past midnight loading the U-Haul, already exhausted come daybreak as they buckled Emily in her car seat and headed north. An hour out of Asheville Leonard and Kera were already bickering, about when to stop and feed Emily, which radio station to listen to. The Ford Fairlane struggled in the higher mountains. As they approached the eastern continental divide, the orange and white trailer swayed and dragged behind them like an anchor someone forgot to raise. The temperature gauge rose, and it seemed the mountains and summer day had collaborated to keep them from getting out of North Carolina. Leonard cut off the air conditioner. They rolled windows down but Emily still whined she was hot. Kera told him to turn the air-conditioning back on, but Leonard was afraid the car would overheat. When Emily began to cry, Kera reached over and punched the ON button herself.

They had almost made it. EASTERN CONTINENTAL DIVIDE,

½ MILE, a blue-and-white sign proclaimed. The temperature indicator wavered like a compass needle in the red part of the gauge but the car kept moving, and their continued ascent seemed a small miracle that might harbinger the possibility of even greater ones. For a few moments Leonard believed luck might stroll into their lives and announce itself, that he would be wrong about the car overheating, maybe wrong about some other things as well. He was about to reach for Kera's hand when the radiator hose burst.

He'd managed to pull the car onto the shoulder, then hitch-hiked across the mountain, leaving Kera and Emily by the roadside. He returned two hours later in a tow truck. Kera and Emily waited where he'd left them, both dehydrated and sunburned. The driver chained the car and trailer to his truck, and the four of them had crammed into the front seat, crossing the divide like a family fleeing a fire or flood.

They'd waited inside the hot, grimy service station for the radiator hose to be replaced. Emily hunched in Kera's lap, whimpering from her sunburn. No door dimmed the racket between office and garage. When a rivet gun battered their ears Emily pressed her bent forearms to the sides of her head and shrieked.

You're glad this happened, Kera said, then carried Emily across the street to a café. On the cinder-block wall opposite where Leonard sat, a nail crookedly hung a photograph of a father and son fishing from a wooden bridge. Under this bucolic scene the coming days of August were numbered and lined up like rows of boxcars, headed for a future he told himself had been derailed by a five-dollar piece of black rubber.

Leonard opened his eyes and stared at the watermark last week's downpour had formed on the trailer's ceiling. The stain had reminded him of something for days but only now did he recognize that what he saw above him evoked the rhinoceros-head outline of Australia.

September 12, 1856

Joe Woods, age 58.
Complaint: Sore back.
Diagnosis: Lumbago.
Treatment: Heated poultice applied to afflicted area first thing
  in morning and before bed. Sassafras tea three times daily.
  Refused to cup afflicted region despite patient's insistence.
Fee: One dollar. Paid in cash.

Ruth McKinney, age 6.
Complaint: Earache.
Diagnosis: Inflammation of inner passage of right ear.
Treatment: Rabbit tobacco vapors blown in afflicted ear. Two
  drops castor oil in afflicted ear. Repeat both treatments three
  times daily for three days. Have child sleep with right ear on
  warmed pillow.
Fee: One dollar. Paid with half sack of salt.

Summoned to Revis Farm.
Billy Revis, age 28.
Complaint: Left arm mangled by threshing machine. Violent
  bleeding.
Diagnosis: Severed artery. Ineffectual tourniquet. In Articule
  Mortis.
Treatment: Cauterized artery. Sealed with hot tar. Lead acetate
  to arrest further discharge.

One P.M.

Some recovery but pulse dismal. Chalky pallor.

Four P.M.

*Pallor improved. Pulse full. Left family with sanguine
assurances of recovery.*
*Treatment: Fomentations to balm pain. No exertions for three
days. Rare beef every meal for next week.*
*Fee: Four dollars. Paid with one dollar cash. Fifteen pounds
tobacco at harvest.*

THREE

It was the second afternoon when Lori Triplett came to Travis's room, dressed not in white like the nurses but in a pink and white striped skirt and blouse. Girls at the high school who wore these outfits called themselves Candy Stripers. Travis knew they did something at the hospital but wasn't sure exactly what. Shank called them candy strippers.

Travis had been feigning sleep, because until now no one who came through the door had brought anything good. The doctor had dismissed his waterfall story, saying he'd heard more convincing lies from first-graders and if he had the time he'd get the sheriff and find out what really happened. His daddy was no better. He'd driven Travis's truck back from the bridge and found the six-pack stowed in the cab. The old man spent his first visit lecturing about the beer and Travis's climbing the waterfall. His mother sat in the corner while his daddy went at him for half an hour. The next time his parents came all the old man talked about was how much the hospital bill would be. You're seventeen years old, boy, his father had said. When I was your age I was making my way alone in the world. If you don't straighten out real quick you'll be on your own too.

So when he heard footsteps approaching Travis closed his eyes, hoping whoever it was would think him asleep and leave. But this time it was Lori Triplett, a blue plastic watering can in her hand. She was from Antioch, the far upper part of the county, so they'd been in school together only since ninth grade. Travis didn't know much about her. The girls and boys from Antioch tended to keep to themselves. They ate at the same lunch tables and sat together at assemblies and ball games.

He'd paid some notice to her though. Hard not to with her red hair and green eyes, skin white and smooth as porcelain. Tall as well, five-eight probably. Travis thought her pretty and had once told Shank as much, though Shank said she didn't have enough up top to suit him. Shank had added that Antioch girls were a hard lot. His older brother had dated one and come in one night scratched up like he'd lost a ten-round fight with a bobcat. After she got through with him she'd took to his car seats with a butcher knife, Shank had said. All that just because he was fifteen minutes late.

But Lori had never seemed that kind of girl, even less so now as he watched her water the plants. Besides homeroom, she'd been in two of Travis's classes. She always sat in the back, head down like she might not be paying attention, yet she always knew the answer when called upon, knew it quick without a stammer. Smart, he knew that, but not in a show-offy way like the snobby town kids.

Lori turned from the window. Sunlight slanting through the glass burnished her hair, making it shine like a new penny. Her eyes met his for a moment and then stared at the watering can as if to remind herself why she was there.

"We've been in homeroom together," Travis said.

Lori raised her eyes. Maybe it was because he had never looked at them so carefully, but now he saw how distinctive their color was, the soft cool green of a luna moth. Travis looked away first this time. Those eyes made his whole body feel light. Like swinging out on a muscadine vine and letting go, he thought. That moment you hung above the river, waiting to fall.

"I know that," she said.

"My name's Travis, Travis Shelton."

"I know that too."

Something almost a smile softened her face.

"Anything I can get you before I go?"

"You ain't got a cigarette, do you?"

"I don't smoke, and you shouldn't either," Lori said.

The feistiness of her reply surprised him. He'd never much cared for other folks' advice, but before it had come from his parents and teachers and Preacher Caldwell, not someone his own age and as pretty as Lori Triplett.

Travis searched for something else to say as Lori walked toward the door.

"Do you get paid for doing this?" he asked.

She paused in the doorway.

"No."

"Then why do it?"

"I'm going to A-B Tech next year to become a nursing assistant," Lori said. "I wanted to know what it was like first."

Travis didn't want her to go. Except for Shank she was the only person he'd been glad to see since waking from the operation. But words fled out of reach. He made a solemn vow that next time he'd have a whole peck of questions for her.

She lingered by his doorway a few moments.

"I'll see you tomorrow," she said.

After Lori left he thought of the high school library's big unabridged dictionary and how it was filled with thousands and thousands of words but he couldn't find half a dozen to make a sentence, had just sat there in the bed like there'd been a C-clamp on his tongue. Unlike Shank, he never seemed to know what to say to girls. The one time he'd acted like he had, at Leonard's trailer, he'd made a jackass of himself. What he knew about was fishing and engines and farming tobacco, some other things he'd read. None of these things seemed of much interest to girls.

An orderly brought supper, and two hours later the night nurse gave Travis a red pill to help him sleep. Then she'd asked if he needed to go to the bathroom. This nurse was older than the one who'd come the previous night. Her gray hair was balled on the back of her head tight as a fist, and it seemed to tug her mouth into a tight-lipped frown.

"I guess you'll need me to help," she said irritably, as if she couldn't see his lower right leg looked like it belonged to a mummy. Instead of getting a male orderly or a bedpan like the other nurse, she'd helped him to the bathroom herself and hadn't even looked away, just watched Travis make water like she didn't trust him to hit the bowl. Travis swore to piss in his water glass before he ever asked her help again.

THE NEXT MORNING PASSED EVEN SLOWER THAN THE PREVIOUS two. There was nothing on TV but game shows and the only thing to read was a Bible. He asked the nurse if she could get him some magazines and she brought back some year-old copies of *National Geographic*. One had an article on Civil War battlefields and Travis remembered what Leonard had said about Sheltons siding with the Union. He wondered if there were books about what happened in Madison County during the Civil War.

Late morning the doctor read the chart and checked Travis's foot, not seeming to care much when he turned the ankle and Travis winced. You'll be going home tomorrow morning, he told Travis, but that was nothing to get excited about. It just meant being stuck in his own bed instead of the hospital's. Besides, at home the old man wouldn't have to wait for visiting hours to light into him. Probably lay a pallet on my floor just so he can bad-mouth me last thing at night and first thing come morning, Travis figured.

The clock hands moved as if coated with tobacco resin. But it wasn't just boredom that made time crawl. He was waiting for Lori. To help pass the time, he rummaged through his mind as he might a woodshed, searching for something long ago put away. Travis remembered one thing, something that happened in homeroom their sophomore year. It had been the Friday before Christmas break. During the last period students went to their homerooms for a "party," though it was nothing but soft drinks and stale cookies. Slick Abernathy, the principal, had shown up at the door and handed Lori a full grocery bag. Soon as it was in her hands she'd sat back down while everyone else milled around the room. There was one detail more though, just at the edge of memory. Then it came to him. Lori had used only her right hand to eat and drink. The left gripped the grocery bag so no one could look inside.

He ate his lunch and had two more thermometers shoved in his mouth before Lori appeared. She brought not just her watering can but also a backpack.

"I went to the library to get you something to read, but I wasn't certain what you'd like."

She lifted three books from the backpack, let him see the titles: *For Whom the Bell Tolls* by Ernest Hemingway, *Call of the Wild* by Jack London, and *The Last of the Mohicans* by James Fenimore Cooper. He'd read the first two, so he took *The Last of the Mohicans*, though he had serious doubts if someone with the middle name Fenimore could write anything he'd much care for.

"The doctor says I'll be going home in the morning," Travis said. "How will I get it back to you?"

"Give the book to the nurse and I'll get it from her."

This time he made sure Lori stayed awhile, filling silences with questions he'd stacked in his mind like square bales in a barn loft. He learned more about her plans to get a CNA and found out she worked mornings and evenings at Carter's Café.

She had an older sister and a younger brother, and her mother worked at the yarn mill in Marshall. When he asked about her father, she said he'd left three years ago. She didn't offer the where to and why.

"What are you going to do when you get out of high school?" she asked when he struggled for more words to keep her in the room.

Travis wanted to sidle around the question, but Lori wouldn't allow it.

"I'm not sure," he finally said, not mentioning he'd quit school three weeks before last year's term ended.

"You could probably do a lot of different things," Lori said. She picked up the backpack. "I guess I better get to the other rooms."

"Too bad you won't be here in the morning. I like talking to you."

"I'll see you at school in a few weeks," Lori said. "Maybe we'll be in homeroom again, like in tenth grade."

"Maybe we could do something before then." Travis spoke the words quickly, afraid if he didn't they would hang on his tongue and he'd swallow them.

"I'd like that," Lori said.

"Can I have your phone number?"

She blushed slightly but kept her eyes steady on his.

"We don't have a phone."

"Can I call you at work?"

"Yes," Lori said, and took a blue pen from her apron. She looked for a piece of paper but there was only the ivory colored hospital chart.

"Write it on my hand," Travis said.

He laid his open palm on the aluminum rail. Lori's left hand gripped his wrist, the firmness surprising him. The pen tickled as she wrote the numbers.

"Don't forget and wash it off," she said, a playfulness in her voice he hadn't heard before.

"I'll not do that," Travis said, making a fist as though afraid the numbers might slip away.

When the nurse came in later he asked her to write the number on a card and put it in his billfold. That night as he drifted toward sleep he remembered Lori's fingers and thumb as they enclosed his wrist, how good that felt. Travis wondered if her fingers had measured how much her touch speeded up his heart.

July 14, 1857

Nail Hinson, age 6.
Complaint: Copperhead bite.
Diagnosis: Non-envenomed snakebite. Corn snake? No fang
  marks or noxious swelling.
Treatment: Moistened tobacco applied to soothe pain.
Fee: One dollar. To be paid with two peck of apples at harvest.

Georgina Singleton, age 10.
Return in regard to July 11 complaint of puniness and diagnosis
  of whipworms.
Treatment: Two drams tobacco seed, whiskey, turpentine at
  bedtime for three nights.
Wool rag soaked in heated turpentine on stomach each morning.
Response: Voided fifty-seven worms. Continue treatment two
  more nights.
Fee: None.

Levi Peek, age 35.
Complaint: Vomiting blood.
Diagnosis: Hematemesis.
Treatment: Alum and yellow root tonic before meals. No
  drinking of any spirits for month.
Fee: One dollar. Paid with four pecks of chestnuts.

P.M.

James Shelton, age 28.
Return in regard to broken leg set on June 20.
Wear splint ten more days.
Fee: No charge.

Ten P.M.
Summoned to Winchester Farm.
Ellie Winchester, age 19.
Complaint: Remittent fever three days. Abdominal pain.
Shivering. Fifth day after childbirth.
Diagnosis: Puerperal fever due to rupture and infection of
fundus uteri. Lochia excessive.
Treatment: Camphor. Boneset tea but patient too distressed to
drink. Cold poultices to forehead. Sent husband to office to
fetch Meigs's Treatise on Obstetrics.

Twelve A.M.
Fever unabated. Galloping pulse. Violent shivering. Patient
cannot bear touch of poultices on abdomen. Infection ravenous
with resultant purulent uterine fluid. Meigs's consultation of
no profit. Two drams of laudanum. Dose of Dover's Powder.
Husband told patient In Articule Mortis.

One A.M.
Fever unabated. Galloping pulse. Two drams of laudanum.
One Twenty A.M.
Patient deceased. Husband inconsolable, as would any man
brought to such a pass. More distressing the cries of the infant,
despite the wet nurse's attempt to suckle, as though the infant
fathomed its loss.
Fee: None.

FOUR

Leonard woke slowly, a dull pain pressing like thumbs against the back of his eyes. Dena lay beside him. The covers were off and he could see the pink splotches where her skin had peeled. He'd told her to wear sunscreen, not to stay out so long. She might just as well have lain down in a skillet.

Still asleep, Dena raised an arm across her face as if fending off a blow. He saw again the pink centipede-shaped welt. She had never told him what caused that scar, just as she'd never explained her missing front teeth. But she'd told him enough about her life for him to know neither had been an accident. The arm fell to her side as she shifted onto her back. She'd wanted to make love the previous night, and an alcohol-induced ardor had made him receptive. But her skin felt like that of a shedding reptile. Her bridge soaked in a water glass by the bed, and when she'd pressed her lips to his, her mouth caved in like a sinkhole, sucking him into its dark void. He'd had to imagine another woman. Another room, another bed. Kera had once told him that during the Renaissance sex was believed to be a little death. It seemed so to him now, but in a way nothing like the swooning ecstasy depicted in sixteenth-century poetry.

When he'd dropped Dena off in Marshall that morning thirteen months ago, Leonard thought he'd gotten rid of her, but two days later she'd been on the trailer steps, everything she possessed inside a battered suitcase and dark-green trash bag. Just like that, expecting to be taken in simply because she was there.

And now the boy reappearing eight days ago. Other people living in the country had abandoned cats and dogs show up at their doors. Leonard had women and children. Even when he put them out, they kept coming back. He'd asked Dena once why she'd believed he would let her stay. Because you don't like being alone, she'd said. You wish you did, but you don't.

Leonard stared at the ceiling a few more moments and then got up. He pulled on a pair of jeans, a V-neck tee-shirt once white but now soiled to the gray of used dishwater. The five- and ten-dollar bills from yesterday's sales lay on top of the chest of drawers, and he stuffed them in his front pocket. He searched in the closet for the book Travis had asked about and found it. Before going into the kitchen to make coffee he took down the 1859 ledger. Leonard read the December 21 entry, then put the ledger back on the closet shelf and went into the front room.

The boy slept on the couch, shirtless but still in his jeans, a ragged quilt draped over his waist and chest. A wind-up alarm clock ticked below him on the floor, its hands on eight and five. Travis had brought time into the trailer with him, not just the clock but a wristwatch as well. In the corner two cardboard boxes overspilled with the rest of his belongings. Leonard had told him he could stay a week, long enough to find another place. Or get homesick and go home, as Leonard had believed would happen. Now that week had passed and apparently Travis had no more intention of leaving than Dena.

The boy shuddered, pulled his knees close to his chest. Even in sleep trying to protect himself, just as Dena had. Leonard wondered if what the boy dreamed was more memory than illusion. Travis had had a lot of the starch taken out of him since the first time Leonard met him. The Toomeys were responsible for that.

The smell of coffee soon filled the trailer. Its dense rich odor always reminded Leonard of the time he'd needed a clock and a watch. The dogs rustled under the trailer, making their first whines for food. Purebred Plott hounds, bear dogs worth a thousand dollars easy, the man who'd settled a two-hundred-dollar drug debt with them claimed. They were pups then and Leonard had planned to place a For Sale ad in the Marshall paper, but he'd never gotten around to it.

He poured a cup of coffee and went outside to feed the Plotts and hide the money. When he'd done these things he sat on the steps as morning made its slow lean into the valley—sunlight grabbing hold of the treetops and sliding down the sycamore and birch trunks, which threw the light back, almost a reflection. Then the sun eased into the pasture, a slow unfurling that lit up dew beads on the grass and the spiderwebs. A pair of goldfinches flashed across the meadow like yellow sparks flung out from the morning's bright becoming.

I got nowhere else to go, Travis had said when Leonard stood on these same steps and tried to turn the boy away. Travis had taken a wad of five- and one-dollar bills from his front pocket and offered them to Leonard. I ain't asking to stay free. I got my job back at the store, so I can pay you twenty a week, he had said, a last flicker of pride in his voice. Leonard had stuffed the bills in his pocket, then stepped aside so Travis could come into the trailer. For all Leonard knew the boy had been driving around the county for hours, searching for a place of refuge. Having damn little luck finding one if he'd had to settle for a rusting hulk of tin inhabited by a bootlegger and drug peddler. Luck. Not a word Leonard had heard much growing up, because the word implied chance, randomness. Never a sparrow falls from the sky but God knows it, Preacher Rankin had said Sunday mornings as he waved a Bible before them as if fanning a fire. Nor a drop of rain nor even the wind stirring the most slightsome leaf.

They got to you early with all that otherworldly mumbo jumbo and you just can't shed it, Kera once told him. She'd blamed his Pentecostal upbringing, but Leonard suspected such beliefs came as much from the mountains themselves, their brooding presence and unyielding shadows. Shades, his Grandfather Shuler had always called ghosts, as if created by the mountains' light-starved ridges and coves.

His family's far pasture had bordered church property, and one of Leonard's earliest chores was walking the pasture after a storm to gather up wreaths, styrofoam crosses, whatever else belonged on the barbed wire's other side. He was taught to place the grave ornaments back into the cemetery with respect, not thrown or kicked but ever so carefully set down. Because it mattered, not just to those above the ground but those in it. Leonard remembered his hand crossing that boundary between living and dead, easing through the barbed wire the grave litter he'd gathered, one wreath or cross at a time, laying each gently on the plush green grass, and how he'd feared something on the other side might grip his wrist, announce its presence.

But nothing ever had. The dead in the cemetery had stayed dead. But now Travis Shelton had suddenly reappeared on his doorstep, expecting to be sheltered, protected. It was as if, three decades later, Leonard's hand had slipped through the cemetery's barbed wire and felt something brush against his skin.

Travis's alarm still hadn't gone off, so in a few minutes Leonard went inside, stood close to where the boy slept. Travis was trying to grow a mustache, but the fine blond hairs on his upper lip reminded Leonard of wisps on a baby's head. The bruise on the boy's left cheek was a mere dull-yellow tinge now, nothing like last week when purple stained his face like a birthmark. That first night he'd shown up, Travis had told Leonard about his father slapping him. The boy also volunteered what had really happened to his foot. Probably nothing more than an attempt to gain sympathy, Leonard suspected. No good could come from the boy being here, especially if Carlton Toomey found out, which was why Leonard had driven to the Toomeys' farmhouse last night to get his monthly quota of pills early.

He spoke the boy's name, and Travis's eyes opened.

"Your alarm didn't go off," Leonard said.

"Ain't it Sunday?"

"I guess so," Leonard said, though he wasn't sure since no calendar hung on the trailer wall.

Travis raised to a sitting position and brushed the long blond hair from his gray eyes. The boy's face was all jut and angle, as though the features had been outlined but not yet filled in. A lanky build but strength in the shoulders and arms, the muscles wiry and tough like wisteria vines. He'd probably grow another inch or two in height, Leonard figured, maybe reach six feet.

If he lived that long. After their first encounter, Leonard had written Travis off as just another smirking loud-mouthed punk, no different from the majority of adolescents he had dealings with. Casualties of his own prideful recklessness, they ran vehicles into trees and bridge abutments, crippled themselves in rock quarries, got knifed or shot in roadhouse parking lots. Easy enough to argue that Leonard performed a public service by selling them alcohol and drugs, merely speeding up the process of natural selection.

But Travis had shown him something besides arrogance and recklessness. The boy wanted to know things. His first night in the trailer Travis had asked for the book with the Shelton Laurel chapter. Leonard hadn't felt like searching through the boxes filling the bedroom closet, so the boy had pulled a thick tome about Gettysburg off the shelves instead. Travis had finished that volume last night and asked again about the other book.

"The book with the Shelton Laurel chapter, that's it on the coffee table," Leonard said.

Travis sat on the couch and opened the big brown hardback to the chapter Leonard had marked. Thirty minutes passed before he looked up for anything other than a word to be defined.

"So they just shot them like dogs," the boy said.

"The lucky ones. The rest got bayoneted."

"Why'd they kill a twelve-year-old?"

"Because a nit makes a louse, or so one of the soldiers stated." Leonard paused. "You know that saying?"

"I heard my daddy use it," Travis said, "but I never knew exactly what it meant."

"A nit is a louse's immature offspring. The soldier was saying kill the offspring before they get big enough to kill you."

"Sounds like you know more about it than is in this book," Travis said. He closed the book slowly, carefully, respecting not just the physical book but its contents, Leonard believed. "They just left them in that ditch to rot?"

"Yes," Leonard said. "It was their own kin who buried them the next day."

The boy slipped on his shirt and stood up, left leg bearing most of the weight. He ate a bowl of cereal while Leonard drank a second cup of coffee. Travis ate quickly, his head down, free arm cradling the bowl.

"I want to go see where it happened, where they buried them afterward," Travis said when he'd finished. "I want to go this morning."

Leonard heard Dena walk up the hall to the bathroom, the warped linoleum crackling beneath her as if she traversed a pond's thawing ice. He believed that one day the whole floor would give way and the trailer fold in on itself like a squeezed accordion. But the rent was cheap, eighty dollars a month, the landlord nothing more than an address in central Florida. In a few moments pipes whistled and the shower came on.

"It's hard to find unless you know what you're looking for," Leonard said.

"But you know where it is?"

"Yes."

Travis got up and rooted around in the boxes that served as his chest of drawers. He came back with a pen and a spiral-bound notebook, laid them on the table between him and Leonard.

"Then draw me a map," Travis said.

"Even with a map you still might not find the grave site."

"Draw it and I'll figure out where it is," Travis said, pushing the notebook and pen closer to Leonard.

Leonard took a long swallow and felt the last of the coffee warm his throat. The boy was impatient. Leonard saw it in his hurry to grow up, in the way he drove, even the way he ate breakfast, as if expecting the bowl to be snatched away at any moment. Impulsive as well, and that combination had nearly gotten him killed by Carlton Toomey.

"I'll go with you," Leonard said. "Just give me a few minutes to shower and dress."

"Can we take that metal detector?"

"Not much use to. The fellow I got it from said he'd swept that site pretty good."

"I'd still like to try."

"Then stick it in the truck and get a shovel as well," Leonard said, and went to the bathroom Dena had just vacated. The mirror was clouded with condensation, water on the floor because once again she hadn't pulled the curtain into the tub. Speeding up the rot in the flooring, not giving a damn if the floor gave way beneath her. Leonard rubbed the mirror's center with his hand, the image of himself clear for a moment, then slowly fading as if receding farther into the mirror, the mirror soon cloudy as before. He remembered the day his Grandfather Candler had died. His grandmother had stopped the mantel clock's ticking, its hands suspended at eleven and five, the time of her husband's death. Every mirror in the farmhouse was covered as well, because mirrors were portals through which the new dead could return to the place they'd once lived. Kera was right. They had gotten to him early.

December 21, 1859

Sophie Holifield, age 79.
Complaint: Aches and swollen joints.
Diagnosis: Rheumatism.
Treatment: Poultice of warmed ginseng applied to bothersome
  joints. Three teaspoons of clover honey every night. One-hour
  soak in baths at Hot Springs soon as weather permits.
Fee: One dollar and a quarter. Paid with peach pie.

Naomi Lewis, age 22.
Complaint: Sore eyes.
Diagnosis: Optical inflammation due to handling mistletoe.
Treatment: Wash made of infusion of goldenseal root in cold
  water. Use twice daily.
Fee: One dollar and a quarter. Paid with cash.
Note: Consulted Barton's Collections Towards a Media Medica.
  Try to obtain cayenne powder next trip to Asheville.

P.M.

Summoned to Shelton Farm.
David Shelton, age eight.
Symptoms: Fever and chills. Galloping pulse. Strawberry
  tongue. Rash on neck and tongue. Agitated speech.
  Imaginings.
Diagnosis: Scarlet fever.
Treatment: Sponged with water and vinegar. Two spoons of
  laudanum. Had patient drink cold well water. Moved bed
  farther from hearth.

Nine P.M.

*Galloping pulse. Fever high. Patient agitated, talking his
   imaginings. Prepared family for possible dismal reckoning.
   Prayers. Mother in much consternation. Continued sponging
   but little effect. Boneset tea alternated with cold water.*

Ten P.M.
Packed snow on patient's forehead and chest.

Twelve A.M.
*Pulse fuller but fever still high. Two spoons of laudanum.
   Continue to pack snow on chest and forehead.*

Three A.M.
*Fever quietened. Pulse not as tense. Family sent to bed with
   assurances. Snow packs ceased. Continue to sponge with water
   every thirty minutes. Patient less agitated, able to sleep with
   no irksome dreams or imaginings.*

Six A.M.
*Fever lessened. No sweats. Continue to sponge every thirty
   minutes.*

Ten A.M.
Pulse full. Fever abated. Sleeps finely now.

Two P.M.
Patient awake and taking broth.
*Prescription: Stay in bed three days. Continue broth. Keep away
   from drafts.*
Boneset tea three times a day.
Fee: Five dollars. Paid with five laying bantams and cured ham.

FIVE

Travis and Leonard rode northward with the windows down. They took Highway 25 and turned on 208, following Laurel Fork as the valley narrowed. Soon the air blowing in through the windows grew cooler and less humid. The stream ran on the left beyond the guardrails, the water a white rush and plunge occasionally slowed by deep pools the old folks called blue holes. Travis knew some huge hook-jawed browns had been pulled from these pools, caught with minnows or bass plugs by older men who'd fish a month to get one wrist-snapping strike.

By the time they entered Shelton Laurel the stream was diminished enough that Travis could easily jump it, no bigger than the creek that had led him to Carlton Toomey's pot plants, the place he went back to so often in his dreams. He was always caught in the bear trap, but when he shouted for help it wasn't the Toomeys who showed up but a dark shape-shifting presence. Only when the presence spoke did it solidify to become his father, who claimed caught in a bear trap was exactly where a no-account son like Travis deserved to be.

They now passed tobacco fields whose rows rippled out over bottomland in lush waves. The plants were healthy, their leaves bright green like lamb's ear, stalks tall and straight and not riven. No blue mold or yellow spots. Travis knew if he touched these leaves he'd feel the same cool leathery dampness he'd felt eight days ago in his family's tobacco field.

The old man hadn't let it go, the beer in the cab, the hospital bill. The grocery store manager had felt sorry for him and given Travis his old job back. He'd worked his usual forty-five hours there, but his daddy demanded twenty hours a week on the farm as well. Travis had done that extra work, suckering and topping tobacco in the fields every evening even though he'd bagged groceries all day and his aching Achilles tendon needed to be propped up and iced. To help pay hospital costs, the old man claimed, but Travis knew it was more to punish him, the same way his daddy had once done their black-and-tan when it killed a chicken, rubbing the dog's face in the rotting carcass every day till the chicken was nothing but mush and bones.

Then things had become even worse. One evening his hoe hit a yellow jacket nest. The insects boiled out of the ground and swirled a stinging halo around his head. Travis jerked off his cap, swatting at them as he stumbled across the rows fast as his game leg would take him, stung seven times before he was out of their range. The poison raised white welts on his arm and face and neck. The old man had spit a plug of Beechnut from his mouth, then dabbed the wet tobacco on each sting to draw the venom, all the while acting put out with him, like Travis had done it on purpose. You ought to have been looking better, boy, his father had said. Your damn hoe would have hit them as well, Travis had mumbled softly, but not soft enough.

He'd seen it coming, his daddy's right hand flattening, raised like he was taking an oath before the hand came forward, slapping him so hard it felt like he'd been hit by a two-by-four. The blow sent him to the ground, where he lay sprawled across a tobacco plant. Long as you live under my roof I'll not abide your back sass, his daddy had told him.

His mother had stood on the porch the whole time he packed the truck, trying to talk him out of leaving, downright begging him. But all the old man said was Travis would be back in a week. You ain't got enough man in you to go it alone, his daddy had said.

Travis shifted gears as the land rose sharply. He imagined the old man looking out the farmhouse window for over a week now for a pickup that wasn't coming, because Travis had more sand in him than his daddy supposed. Travis imagined more—his daddy out in the fields alone and realizing how much of the farmwork Travis had done, his daddy stove up with regret about slapping him and wishing Travis would come home so he could apologize.

"You can tell we're getting close," Leonard said, staring out the passenger window.

Travis looked out and saw nothing other than a tractor working a cornfield.

"Look at the mailboxes," Leonard said.

At first Travis didn't understand. Some were new and silvery, some little more than rusting cylinders nailed to leaning locust posts. Then he saw the name Shelton. Saw it again and then again, each mailbox looming clear a moment then whisking away as the next rushed into view. Like a fast-turning calendar, Travis thought, but with one unchanging word instead of months and days.

"Your kin, I suppose," Leonard said.

"I guess so," Travis said, and remembered something he'd been meaning to ask Leonard.

"One summer when I was a kid we had a family reunion at my great-grandmother's house. Her clock hadn't been changed for daylight savings time, and I remember one of my uncles saying her doing that was because of the Civil War."

"Roosevelt time," Leonard said. "That's what they called it because Roosevelt started daylight savings time. Lincoln Republicans like your great-grandmother didn't want to go along with a Democrat's idea."

"She was remembering what happened in Shelton Laurel in 1863?"

"Yes," Leonard said.

They passed a store, its gas pumps reminding Travis of old-timey diving bells, then a white clapboard church and a field some farmer had let go, full of chickweed and bull thistles. A sure sign the soil had gone poor from overgrazing, his daddy always said, claiming any farmer sorry enough to let his pasture get in such shape wasn't worthy of farming a hog lot.

"Turn there," Leonard said, pointing up the road at a shotgun-frame house on the right.

Travis turned and bumped up a washout that passed close to the house before ending abruptly.

"They don't mind us parking here?"

"No, they're used to people coming."

Leonard lifted the metal detector and shovel from the truck bed. Travis took the shovel, letting it dangle at his side like a rifle as they followed a faint trail through a stand of white oak. The trail slanted downward and Travis shifted more weight to his left leg, set the right foot down carefully as though afraid of a stump hole. He iced the Achilles tendon every night, did the exercises the nurse had shown him, but it still nagged like a bad tooth. Farther down honeysuckle sweetened the air, a smell that reminded Travis of Lori's perfume.

She was in church this morning with the rest of her family. Not too far from here, Travis knew, eight miles at the most by road, less if you had a way to cut across Roundtop Ridge. She wanted him to go to church with her, and he would, maybe next Sunday. He'd have to get up early but it'd be worth it just to have an extra hour with Lori, to sit beside her and smell her perfume, feel her hand touching his as they shared a hymnal. He liked the way Lori always reached for his hand when they were together, how that made him feel he was protecting her.

Soon the land leveled out and they stepped onto hardtop, a broad meadow on the road's other side. A steel historical marker stood nearby. Travis read the placard and then went into the meadow. He tried to envision it, not the killing but afterward. Late January after a blizzard, the book had said. Snow pinked by blood. The dead half buried. Travis couldn't imagine thirteen bodies, that was too much, so he thought only of the youngest, David Shelton.

Maybe it was because the sun hovered high overhead now, but the meadow was intense with light, its pallor distilled, insistent, almost as if the place radiated something of itself from within. Travis wondered if the meadow would feel the same if he didn't know what happened here.

Leonard came up and stood beside him.

"You know a place is haunted when it feels more real than you are," Leonard said.

As soon as Leonard said those words, Travis knew that was what he felt, not just now but over the years when he'd turned up arrowheads while plowing. Rubbing off the layers of dirt, he'd always had the bothersome notion the arrowheads were alive, like caddis flies inside their thick casings. He'd tried to make sense of the notion that time didn't so much pass as *layer over things,* as if under the world's surface the past was still occurring. Travis had never spoken of this feeling because it was something you couldn't explain or show, like how to tie a fishing knot or check tobacco for black shank. But just because it was inside you didn't mean it wasn't real. And now he felt it here, more than even when he'd held those arrowheads.

"You believe in ghosts?" Travis asked.

"When I'm in this meadow I almost do," Leonard said. He nodded at the marker. "It ought to feel even more that way to you. It's your family's blood that got spilled here."

Travis walked toward the creek, his hands brushing hip-high broom sedge whose coppery color shone in the meadow's gathered light. Grasshoppers leaped stalk to stalk in brown and green arcs, the biggest ones whirring as their wings spread like paper fans. The creek ran thin and muted, a low gurgle where it rubbed over rocks. The morning of the massacre it would have been even quieter, the creek muffled under ice, no metallic chatter of cicadas in the high branches. Not much color either, gray sky and everything below it coated white. At least until the killing started. Travis tried to imagine what he'd read—David Shelton shot in both arms, his father and three brothers lying dead around him, the last Shelton still alive in that meadow speaking his last words: *I forgive you all this—I can get well. Let me go home to my mother and sisters.*

Twelve years old.

Travis thought of himself at twelve and when he'd been most scared. Probably sitting in the principal's office waiting for his daddy to show up. He and Shank had put a green snake in their homeroom teacher's desk, causing Mrs. Debo a near heart attack. Mr. Ketner had threatened everything short of the electric chair, but it was only when the principal called their parents that Travis became afraid. Whatever Mr. Ketner did, his daddy would do far worse with a belt. But knowing somebody was going to shoot you. He couldn't imagine how terrifying that was. But as quick as Travis thought that he remembered Carlton Toomey opening his hawkbill, the soft click as the blade locked into place.

He turned his mind from that thought, watched Leonard skim the metal disk over the broom sedge, Leonard's face intent as he listened and interpreted the messages seeping up from the underworld, moving slow and tentative behind it, like a blind man using a cane. Leonard paused, let the machine comb a small area for a few moments, homing in on something. Travis watched Leonard lay down the machine and get the shovel. Leonard knelt and dug a few moments before raising a bottle cap from the soil.

Travis walked back into the meadow, waited for Leonard to see him and take off the headphones.

"Why are you trying here?" Travis asked.

"Because this is where Keith's soldiers piled them after the killing. The guy I got the detector from knew they were placed here as well, but he may have missed something."

"So I guess he tried it where they killed them too?"

"Yes," Leonard said, pointing near where Travis had stood earlier. "Over by the creek. That's where he found a minié ball, or so he claimed."

"But you've never used it up here?"

"No."

"You swept between here and the creek?" Travis asked. "Maybe something fell out of their pockets while they were being dragged."

"I hadn't thought about that," Leonard said.

"You mind if I try?"

"Go ahead," Leonard said, handing the machine to Travis.

"How does it work?"

"Sort of like tuning in a radio station. Just listen for a humming sound and move the disk to where it increases."

Travis put on the earphones and aimed the metal detector in front of him. He swung the disk back and forth, the machine heavier than he'd imagined. He took a step forward and did the same thing. Leonard motioned for him to take off the earphones.

"Lower," Leonard said. "You want it skimming the ground."

Travis began again, moving slowly toward the creek. He had covered only a few feet when the machine's hum increased.

"I got something," he said, trying not to sound too excited.

"Let me hear," Leonard said.

He placed the headphones on his head.

"Just a rock with a lot of minerals," Leonard said after a few moments.

"How do you know?"

"Experience. There's more sound if it's something worthwhile."

Travis moved across the heart of the meadow tentatively. Twice the machine made noises worth investigating, but both times it was a soft drink can. His arms tired but he kept searching. The machine's hum increased again, the same sound as the cans had made, but Travis laid down the detector and dug.

At first they didn't know what it was, a crust of black dirt barnacling the metal.

"Careful," Leonard said. "Put it in the water to loosen the dirt."

They walked over to the creek and soon scabs of dirt began falling away, what Travis held becoming thinner, lighter, then revealing a straight wire laid across a second straight wire. He rubbed harder, his thumbnail worrying free the dirt under the wires. Soon he saw two perfectly round frames, a coin of glass embedded in one. The silver brightened in his hands as more dirt fell away. Travis was amazed that something so long in the dark could retain such luster. He rinsed the glasses a last time and rubbed them with his handkerchief, then pulled each silver temple slowly from the frames and just as tenderly re-folded them.

"I guess they rightly belong to you," Travis said.

Leonard shook his head.

"I'd have never thought to look there. It's your find so you keep them."

"You sure?" Travis said.

"Yes."

A few yards upstream something rippled the surface. Travis studied the water intently and soon found the fish drifting with the current, a quick shudder of its caudal fin propelling it back to a feeding position. The fish rose again, curving back into the water, a flash of red dots and orange fins. I'll be back for you another time, Travis thought.

He held the glasses carefully as they walked into the meadow, the same way he might a bird egg or tobacco seedling. An idea settled in his mind, quickly became belief.

"These glasses belong to one of them who was murdered," Travis said. "If they belonged to one of Keith's men he'd have picked them back up. The dead don't need to see."

Travis opened his palm, let the sunlight fall full upon the silver.

"I think they belonged to David Shelton," Travis said.

"How can you possibly know that?" Leonard replied.

"It's the size of them. They're a more likely fit for a boy than a man."

"Where did you read that David Shelton even wore glasses?"

"Nowhere," Travis said. "But I ain't read where he didn't wear glasses neither."

"They could have belonged to a small man," Leonard said, "or to someone before or after the war."

Leonard sounded irritated, and Travis supposed there was enough schoolteacher left in him to want the last say-so on things.

"Do you think if we showed them to Dr. Hensley he'd know when they were made?" Travis asked, making it sound like a question instead of an idea.

"Possibly," Leonard said, but his tone was skeptical.

"What about the other lens?" Travis said, voicing what he'd been thinking for minutes now. "Do you think they shot it out?"

"I don't know. How could anyone know?" Leonard said brusquely. "Let's go. It's near noon and I'm getting hungry."

Sweat trickled down the back of Travis's neck. Warm even up here. He felt the glasses in his hand, solid and real like the arrowheads. He would take them by Dr. Hensley's office to-morrow, see if the optometrist knew when they'd been made.

Leonard picked up the metal detector and shovel.

"What ridge they buried on?" Travis asked.

"The one we came down, near where we parked."

"I want to see it before we go back to the trailer."

"Only for a minute," Leonard said, and led Travis up the hill and into a stand of white oaks. It was like entering a darkened theater. Leaves seined out much of the sunlight, the trees themselves pressing close. Travis stepped carefully, holding the glasses behind him in case he tripped over a root or rock. The loamy soil was soft and moist despite it being late summer. He felt his feet settling deeper into the cushiony ground and waited for his eyes to adjust. The names on the oblong block of granite slowly became clearer, as if rising out of a dense fog.

"I'd of thought they'd each have a grave."

"Hard as the ground was that day it's a wonder they got one dug," Leonard said.

"And it was their own people who buried them?"

"Who else would have done it?" Leonard said. "They were trying to get them to the Shelton graveyard, but the oxen gave out. It was bury them right then and there or risk animals getting to the bodies first."

What was left of them lay in this earth, Travis told himself. He wondered if any of their bones remained. Maybe something made of metal like a belt buckle or boot eyelet. Nothing else.

The dying had their lives flash before their eyes, or so folks claimed. Travis wondered what David Shelton had seen. Maybe just happy things like Christmases and birthdays, or a day when he'd caught a big trout or a pretty morning he'd gotten to go outside and play after days of rain. But maybe bad things too, like his daddy getting after him with a strap or fussing with his brothers. Travis rubbed his thumb over one of the wire frames, wondered if whatever David had seen he'd seen through these glasses. Wondered also if David had felt his heart constrict like a slipknot pulled tight in those last moments, as Travis's heart had seemed to when the Toomeys discussed whether or not to kill him.

"Time to go," Leonard said.

As they drove back Travis read each mailbox, SHELTON appearing with the regularity of a last name in a family cemetery. They passed an old man plowing his field, back and head bent toward the steering wheel. Travis was surprised the man wasn't in church. Maybe he'd been sick and gotten behind in his farmwork. Travis slowed. The tractor was an old 8N Ford, what farmers called a *redbelly* because of its colors. He studied the man's face, trying to find something of himself under the wrinkles.

"Why do you reckon people don't talk much about what happened up here?" Travis asked.

"The men who shot them were also from this county. Even after the war some folks got killed because of what happened that morning. People believed it was better not to talk about it."

They passed the white clapboard church. The windows were open and Travis heard a blur of piano, the slow cadence of a familiar hymn. A dim guilt settled over him. No matter how late he'd stayed out Saturday nights, his parents had made him go to church the next morning. I'll go next Sunday with Lori, he told himself. The road plunged downward. Travis looked in the rearview mirror and watched the steeple disappear into the landscape.

"You'd think they wouldn't have done such a thing to their own neighbors," Travis said.

"History argues otherwise. Lots of times people do worse to people they know than to strangers. Hitler and Stalin certainly did."

"Most of the men in Madison County fought Confederate, I guess," Travis said.

"No. That's what a lot of folks think, but it was like most mountain counties, half Confederate, half Union. That caused Jeff Davis a lot of headaches. Bad enough for the South to fight the rest of the United States, then add to that a bunch of homemade Lincolnites. Of course, men like Colonel Allen used the term bushwhackers, which made it easier for something like Shelton Laurel to happen."

"How is that?"

"Because a bushwhacker's a criminal, not a soldier."

The mountains leaned back from the road edge and Travis shifted gears. Sunlight poured through the windshield, but the light seemed softer, less concentrated than in the meadow. The metal detector and shovel shifted in the truck bed, clanged against each other, and resettled. The glasses lay in the glove compartment, wrapped in a handkerchief. They could be worth money because they were old, like the butter churns and kettles tourists bought in Marshall, but Travis knew he wasn't going to sell them. It wouldn't be right somehow.

"You got any books about what Hitler and Stalin done?"

"Yes."

Halfway down the mountain they passed a car parked on the road's shoulder. A fly fisherman stood midstream, his orange line whipping back and forth before it unfurled a final time, settled on the water soft as a dogwood petal. Travis had never fished that way. Something about it had always seemed too fancy, like wearing a suit to hunt rabbits. He wondered if Lori might like to go fishing with him sometime. He wanted her to see him do something he was really good at, better than Shank or Willard or any of the other guys he knew.

"So what kind of student were you in school?" Leonard asked.

"Not too good."

"Why not?"

"What they taught didn't seem important, except for shop class."

The road veered right, the kind of curve that was so sharp you could almost meet yourself coming the other way. Travis spun the wheel hard, leaning his body the way he imagined Richard Petty or Junior Johnson would coming off a banked turn at Rockingham. He had to swerve to stay on the road as the detector and shovel banged against the sides of the truck. He waited for Leonard to get on him about driving too fast, but he didn't.

"But you do like to read," Leonard said.

"Yeah, but just about things I'm interested in."

"Did you ever take any college prep classes?"

"No. I did pretty good on some tests in eighth grade. The teachers told Daddy and Momma I should do college prep in high school, but Daddy said I didn't need college to farm tobacco."

"That happened to me," Leonard said, "except my parents did what the teachers suggested."

Travis couldn't imagine his daddy taking advice about anything, much less on how to raise his own son.

"You glad that happened," Travis asked, "them putting you in college prep classes?"

Leonard paused.

"It enabled me to get a scholarship to college."

His question hadn't really been answered but Travis didn't press. He held his left hand out the window, turning it like a weathervane as air buffeted his palm. He didn't need to check his watch to know it was past noon now, could feel the early-afternoon air clabbering up like butter. Tail end of the dog days, the worst time of year to be working in a field. No breeze, everything dry and dusty. Mornings weren't so bad because the mountains kept the sun at bay awhile, but come midday the sun sizzled directly overhead. The only thing that made it bearable was having someone else out in the fields with you, knowing they were feeling just as frazzled. Travis hoped these last few dog days bristled up good, made the old man so miserable he'd feel like he'd stepped into a whole barrel of yellow jackets.

"You ever thought about getting a GED?" Leonard asked.

Travis glanced over at Leonard, wanting to see how serious he was.

"No. I don't know much about them. Is it sort of equal to graduating high school?"

"Just as equal," Leonard said.

"You have to take classes at night?"

"You don't have to take any classes at all, just pass the test."

For a few moments they rode in silence. They passed a cow pasture where three dead blacksnakes lay draped on the barbed-wire fence. Some farmers believed killing blacksnakes helped bring rain, but his daddy had always sworn that was nonsense. The snakes' bellies were the same milky blue as the old medicine bottles Travis's grandmother used for vases.

"I could find out what you'd need to do," Leonard said, sounding casual, like he was talking about nothing more than looking up a baseball score.

They were silent until the truck bumped up the drive. Beside the trailer Dena lay on a tattered quilt. Her eyes flickered open for a few moments and then closed. All she wore was the bathing suit's bottom. A pale stripe like a lash mark crossed the middle of her back.

"You'd figure she'd have enough sense not to do that after getting boiled the way she did," Travis said.

"You'd think so," Leonard agreed.

The dogs crawled out from under the trailer, their long red tongues unfurled.

"I'll get them some water," Travis said.

"Give those tomato plants a good soaking too."

"You mind if I go in and get a beer first?" Travis asked. "I'll pay for it. I'm near about as hot and thirsty as those dogs."

"There's a Coke in there you can have," Leonard said, "but as long as you're staying here you get no beer or drugs."

"Why?"

"One less charge that can be leveled against me if I get busted."

Travis followed Leonard inside. He got the Coke out of the refrigerator and drank it in three gulps, then went and filled the two hubcaps that served as water bowls. The harsh spray drummed against the metal sides, a full ringing sound he liked.

A small rainbow wavered above as the dogs lapped the water, so thirsty they didn't care when spray hit their faces. Travis slowly raised his eyes, let them pass over the parched grass to where Dena sunbathed.

Dena's eyes remained closed so Travis let his gaze linger until water spilled onto the ground. He unraveled the hose and dragged it over to the tomatoes. Dena got up as he was starting the second row. Travis thought she would cover herself, but she didn't. She walked toward the trailer, seeming not to notice him.

He had seen women's breasts in magazines before but these were different. They drooped more and were starkly pale compared to the rest of her skin. He felt himself grow hard as he watched Dena disappear into the trailer.

When them nipples get hard you know you got them good and ready to give it all to you. That was what Shank always claimed, and Travis had agreed. But that had just been talk on Travis's part. The few girls he'd been out with hadn't let him do more than some kissing. He'd had to make up stuff to tell Shank and the others so they wouldn't be ribbing him about not having his cherry busted.

It didn't look like that was going to change anytime soon if Lori had her way. Friday night she'd told him about her sister getting pregnant at seventeen and how she wasn't going to let that happen to her. Travis hadn't much liked the way she'd said it, like she was lecturing him, but right afterward she'd let him french kiss her for the first time and he'd forgot all about being lectured and most everything else.

Lori would be out of church by now, probably already home helping her mother fix noon dinner. He wished he was with her, helping look after her brother till the food was ready. Maybe afterward him and Lori going for a walk so they could be alone. He'd go over to the café on Monday during his break. Lori would be busy but he'd at least be around her.

Shank and the other fellows would bull-rag him good if they knew he was getting all moony about Lori. You got it bad as a calf bawling for its momma, he could hear Shank saying, and Travis reckoned he sure enough did to be thinking of her all the time.

May 13, 1861

A.M.

Summoned to Allen residence.
Lawrence Allen, age 28.
Complaint: Losing voice.
Diagnosis: Aphonia.
Treatment: Take gargle of honey, vinegar, alum. Slippery elm
  morning and night.
No talking for three days.
Fee: Two dollars. Paid in cash.
Would it be that not just Allen but Zeb Vance and his Raleigh
  firebrands would get aphonia to quite their braying about
  states rights.

P.M.

Summoned to courthouse.
Julius Candler, age 32.
Complaint: Bleeding from nostrils resulting from fisticuffs.
Diagnosis: Fracture of nose.
Treatment: Set nose.
Fee: None.

Summoned to Main Street.
Elish Tweed, age 12.
Complaint: Gunshot through arm and into ribs.
Diagnosis: Same.
Treatment: Sponged both wounds. Probed arm for torn blood
  vessels or broken bone. Removed bullet from rib cage. Shot by
  accident.
Fee: None.

Ransom Merrill, age 48.
Two gunshot wounds. Deceased at time of arrival.

Roland Norris, age 22.
Complaint: Knife wound to arm.
Diagnosis: Same. No severed vein or artery.
Treatment: Sponged wound. Sewed up with cotton thread.
Fee: One dollar. Paid with side of ham.

Abney Shelton, age 19.
Complaint: Bleeding lip from fisticuffs.
Diagnosis: Cut requiring suture.
Treatment: Sponged wound. Sewed up with cotton thread.
Fee: One dollar. Three bushels of oats to be delivered.

Final delegate vote: 28 for Secessionists, 144 Unionists. This folly may yet be prevented.

SIX

"That GED you mentioned a few weeks ago," Travis said. "I'm thinking it wouldn't hurt none for you to look into it."

Leonard's palms pressed his coffee cup to take in its warmth. Leonard wore a sweatshirt, though he would shed it once sunlight settled on the trailer's tin. A raven made its harsh call from the woods. They were hardy birds that would winter out in the mountains, and this one sounded invigorated by the cool late-September morning.

He raised his cup and sipped. The boy wouldn't bring up the GED if he hadn't been thinking about it a lot the last month, maybe had already mentioned the test to Lori. Still skittish though, not yet committing himself. But Leonard had committed *himself*, just blurted out the offer of finding out what needed to be done. Leonard had not brought up the matter again, but now Travis had.

"I guess I could go by the vocational school this morning," Leonard said. "Find out what you'd need to do."

"Thanks," Travis said. He looked down at his cereal. "Would you help me study if I was to make a go of it?"

Leonard didn't answer.

"I reckon that to mean no," Travis said.

"I guess I can help you some," Leonard said.

Soon after Travis left for work, Leonard followed Highway 25 down to Marshall as well. The dogwood trees had begun to turn, stipples of russet now under the green canopy. Dogwoods were always the first to acknowledge that widening between sun and earth. In another week the tulip poplars would yellow, followed by the purpling of the sweet gums. Then all green rubbed off the mountains but for the resolute firs and pines on the high ridges, that and the club moss scabbing the understory's brown skin. The morning shadows transforming as well—deeper, more pronounced. Laying heavier on the ground when cool weather comes, his mother claimed, as though shadows had a corporeal reality.

When he was a child, Leonard's mother had often sat on the steps of their farmhouse, at times half an hour passing as she stared at the mountains rising beyond their pasture. The prettiness of it takes me away from myself, she'd once explained to him, her voice soft as if sharing a secret. She'd told him that sometimes a Bible or church wasn't enough. That's why there's need for a world in the first place, son, she'd said. In the days right after Emily and Kera had left, Leonard had tried to see the world the way his mother had. He'd drive out to the Calumet River, the one place with enough trees to hide a landscape that looked like it had been leveled by a huge rolling pin. He'd sat on the bank and stared at the cottonwoods and birch, the black alders and witch hazel huddled beneath the bigger trees, the slow brown water, trying to find the same inner peace his mother had years earlier on those farmhouse porch steps.

When he arrived at the vocational center, Leonard almost turned around and drove back to the trailer. He didn't owe the boy this. He could tell Travis the person in charge of adult education hadn't been in. Tell the boy if he wanted a GED he could find out about it himself. Minutes passed before Leonard finally walked through the main door.

Even blindfolded he'd have known he was in a high school. Cheap perfume and cologne clogged the air, a smell of linseed oil on the waxed wood floors. The secretary gave him a room number and Leonard walked down the hallway. Students were changing classes, lockers clanging shut amid a muddle of voices. He moved around clots of teenagers, and each time one brushed or bumped against him his stomach tensed as if expecting a blow.

Mrs. Ponder had been his high school's guidance counselor, but now she was the county's GED director. She'd helped Leonard apply to colleges the fall of his senior year, but when he said his name she didn't appear to remember him. He told her why he'd come, mentioned the reading Travis had done during the last month.

"All that's good," Mrs. Ponder said. "This test is more about interpreting what's read than specific subject matter. Of course it will be different with the math. He can probably do the multiplication and division, but he'll need an understanding of fractions and decimals, a few formulas as well."

Mrs. Ponder turned to the bookshelves that flanked her desk. One afternoon after school she had helped Leonard fill out forms for Chapel Hill and NC State. She'd been thinner then, her hair longer and unstreaked by gray, only a few years out of college herself. He was one of many male students with a crush on her. They had sat at a table in the library, the applications and transcripts spread before them. Close enough that he could smell the soap on her skin and see the bared rise of her collarbone, the fine blond hairs on her forearm. I'd bet a month's salary you'll end up teaching at some college, she'd told him that afternoon. A bet he should have taken, Leonard now thought as Mrs. Ponder ran her index finger over a row of books.

She lifted a thick paperback titled *Essentials of Mathematics* from the shelf. "If he can work through all the problems in these first ten chapters, he'll do fine on the math part."

Mrs. Ponder handed the book to Leonard.

"Courtesy of the state of North Carolina," she said.

"How often is the GED given?"

"First Thursday and first Saturday of the month at Asheville-Buncombe Tech. Let me know at least two weeks in advance and I'll reserve him a place."

"I'm thinking April. Math's not my strong suit so I may be learning right along with him."

"I remember," Mrs. Ponder said, meeting Leonard's eyes. "If your math scores had been higher you'd have received scholarships to out-of-state schools as well. Maybe you would have gotten far enough away not to find your way back here. That's what I hoped for you."

Mrs. Ponder looked out her window at the mountains as if to emphasize they were still in Madison County and not some bucolic New England college town.

"I'm glad I'm not at the high school anymore," she said. "There are fewer disappointments here. Be able to read a safety manual. Balance a checkbook. Get a job as a secretary or foreman at a mill. That's all I have to hope for now, Leonard."

He wore what he always wore these days—ragged jeans and a tee-shirt, work boots. His hair long, his beard unkempt. Leonard knew what Mrs. Ponder saw before her, heard it in the bitterness of her voice. Whatever she knew or didn't know of his life since high school, his appearance evidently verified enough.

"Is this for your son?" she asked, and he knew this was a judgment of him as well.

Mrs. Ponder had grown up in Madison County herself, come back after graduating from UNC-Greensboro and married her high school sweetheart, a dairy farmer who'd barely graduated high school. Mrs. Ponder's left hand rested on the desk, and Leonard saw she no longer wore a wedding ring. He thought about telling her it appeared he wasn't the only one whose life hadn't turned out as expected.

"Thank you for your help," he said.

Leonard walked back down the hall, studentless now. He passed classrooms, some doors open, some shut. Chalk tapped a blackboard, a projector whirred, typewriters clattered, then a room where a man near Leonard's age spoke of the past.

Why can't you just let them take a different test on the material? one of the parents had said that afternoon in Illinois. Six people had been in the conference room: the principal, Leonard's department head, himself, and three parents. He'd looked out the window before he spoke at what passed for landscape in southern Illinois—a few scraggly cottonwood and bald cypress poked into an endless unscrolling west toward Missouri and Kansas. At that moment Leonard had realized how truly oppressive the openness was, its wide possibilities he no longer believed in. By then he was no longer living with Kera and Emily. He and Kera passed each other in the school's hallways with little acknowledgment, negotiated evening and weekend exchanges of their daughter with the cold formality of pawnbrokers.

School policy stated cheating was an automatic zero, and Leonard had reminded the parents and principal of that policy, then gotten up and left the room. But school policy had been only part of why he refused. Stacks of unmarked tests and essays cluttered his desk. Lesson plans unwritten. Finding the energy and focus to make a new test had seemed impossible.

On the way back to the trailer, Leonard stopped at the Winn-Dixie and bought two cases of beer to bootleg. He paid with the twenty dollars in rent money Travis had given him last night. Money he shouldn't feel the least bit bad about taking, because Travis couldn't have found any place short of a tree stand where he could have stayed as cheap. Leonard was barely out of the parking lot before he'd downed a beer and pulled another from the opened case. Entering the school had brought back memories he'd tried to keep submerged. The dark glossy sturdiness of the lawyer's desk. An ink pad's plush, mossy dampness as the policeman blacked his fingers and thumb. Emily asleep in his bed while he spent the night on his apartment's ragged couch. The click of metal locking around his wrists.

"YOU CAN'T GIVE UP BEING MR. TEACHER, CAN YOU?" DENA said the following Friday night. "Even after what that little bastard did to you in Illinois."

She sat up in bed, still fully dressed as she manicured her nails. Dena kept them long and pointed, painted bright red like a warning. Sometimes they seemed to be what she cared most about, these hard inflexible parts of herself that could be cut into and feel nothing. She spoke rapidly, and her hands moved restlessly from nail file to cigarette, switching the radio station as well whenever advertisements replaced music. All sure signs she'd been helping herself to the black beauties.

"That's not what I'm doing." Leonard was searching the closet for a book Travis had asked for. Dena reached for the radio on the bed stand, trolled the red dial through static and song snippets before settling on Johnny Cash singing "I Still Miss Someone." Even if he'd never heard the song before, Leonard would have known it was Cash. No one else had a voice like that, smooth and rough at the same time, like water flowing over gravel. A voice capable of transforming sorrow and regret into something beautiful. Surely some consolation in that, Leonard thought, but evidently not enough to keep Cash off pills and out of drunk tanks. For a few moments Dena appeared immersed in the song as well. Then she picked up her nail file.

"Bullshit," she said. "This trailer's turning into a damn schoolhouse. Nobody wants to do nothing but read and talk books. I can't even turn on the TV without one of you complaining."

Leonard found the paperback and marked a chapter.

"Let's go to the Ponderosa," Dena said, unable to keep her mouth any more still than her hands.

So much better when she took quaaludes, Leonard thought. Maybe he should hide the uppers from now on, but she'd bitch about that, remind him she'd doubled his sales. Which was true, for she seemed to know every doper and pill freak in the county.

"Not tonight," Leonard said.

"I'm tired of being cooped up in a tin box in the middle of nowhere."

"Nobody's making you stay."

"I know that." Dena pouted. "I just want to go out once in a while. That boy's seventeen, and he gets out more than I do."

Leonard laid the book on the bureau beside his car keys. He sat back on the bed edge, bent down to untie his boots.

"At least let me borrow your car so I can go myself. I'll take some pills and sell them, make you some money."

"High as you are you'd likely run my car into a ditch."

"Pills make you drive better," Dena said. "That's why truckers take them."

"Truckers usually aren't drunk as well."

"I ain't going to drink nothing. I just want to get out for a couple of hours, do a little dancing."

Leonard pushed his boots under the bed, felt them bump up against Dena's suitcase. The trailer was getting crowded. After he and Kera split up, he'd turned on the TV or radio each evening just to hear a human voice, not only in Illinois but when he'd moved back to Madison County. Often he'd leave the radio on all night, something to mask the emptiness if he couldn't sleep. He had done that until Dena moved in. Now he had all the background chatter he needed. The way it always was, Leonard reckoned—wanting what you no longer had, what you hadn't wanted when you did have it. "Everybody Wants to Go to Heaven, Nobody Wants to Die." He couldn't remember who sang that one. Not Cash, though Cash had the voice for it.

"Please," Dena said. "I'll be back by twelve."

Some peace and quiet at the risk of a wrecked car. Not a great deal but he decided to take it.

She lifted the keys off the bureau and left, but not before putting on lipstick and perfume, a pair of tighter jeans.

Leonard cut off the radio, went to the kitchen, and got a beer. He picked up the paperback and leaned against the bed's headboard. The rain had come hard that afternoon, and the stain was back on the ceiling, hanging over his head like some ominous cloud in a cartoon. More of the past making itself visible, same as the glasses the boy had found. Dr. Hensley had verified Travis's notion that the glasses were fitted more for a child's head than an adult's. The straight temples verified mid-nineteenth century, Dr. Hensley had added, and the lens was made for someone nearsighted, not farsighted. In other words, not some older man's reading glasses, which had made Travis even more certain they belonged to David Shelton.

Leonard sipped the beer and listened to the night. The cross-fire racket of crickets and cicadas sounded more intense, almost frantic, as if warning each other of the coming evenings when their voices would be stilled. Not long till then, Leonard thought. Fewer bird sounds soon as well. The whippoorwills and broad-winged hawks would fly south first, then the catbirds and sparrows. Copperheads would crawl into rock gaps and under cliff hangs to den, a week or so later the timber rattlers some folks called satinbacks doing the same, twining into medusan knots of fang and flesh. Everything getting dark and less, as if the mountains had spread their shoulders and pushed out much of the world as they braced for the coming winter.

Leonard picked up the paperback, opened it to the chapter he'd marked about warfare between the Cherokees and the Creeks. The boy continued to surprise him. Being interested in Shelton Laurel was one thing. That was local history, the boy's own kin involved. But reading about Germany and Russia and now Indians, then asking perceptive questions about what he'd read was impressive. Many people would wonder how that kind of intellectual curiosity could be suppressed. But Leonard knew. Twenty years earlier he'd gone to the same high school. Unlike Travis, he hadn't tried to hide his capabilities. The teachers hadn't either and filled his hands with plaques and certificates at year-end assemblies.

He'd paid a price for that. The students from Marshall, especially those from well-to-do families, resented how his success emphasized their shortcomings. They made jokes about his patched jeans and his family's weathered clapboard farmhouse. The boys who came from backgrounds like his own shunned him, though one might occasionally trip him in the lunchroom, bump books out of his hands in the hall. It was only the poorer girls, the ones mapping out futures other than babies and farm chores, who respected him. Sometimes former classmates came to buy his drugs. Thought you were going to make something of yourself, he'd heard more than once, and knew they were pleased he had not, that his life was no better than their own.

After the fourth beer Leonard took the letter from the bottom drawer. Two pages but not many words because of a child's high wide letters. He went into the front room and dialed the number included in the letter. Static sizzled in his ear, then the Australian-inflected message he'd heard for six months saying, *This exchange is not in service.* No idea on earth—Leonard supposed he was one of the few parents who could say that about his child's whereabouts and mean it.

It was almost one when Dena returned. Travis was back from his date with Lori but still awake, reading the chapter Leonard had marked. When she came in, Dena told the boy there were better ways to have fun at night than read. Leonard heard the couch springs squeak as Dena sat down. She took the book from Travis's hands and laughed when he asked for it back. I can show you some things you won't find in a musty old book, Dena told him.

"You need to leave him alone," Leonard said when she came to the bedroom, her lipstick smeared, reeking of cigarettes and beer as if she'd lain down on the bar floor and rolled in the butts and spills.

"Why?" she asked. "Jealous?"

"No."

Dena raised the back of her hand to show a fresh burn mark.

"Bet Hubert Toomey ten dollars I could do it," Dena said. "I won. Even got to keep the cigarette."

Dena closed the door and undressed, letting the clothes fall to the floor. "Striptease," she said, and flung off her bra. She was removing her panties when she lost her balance and fell giggling onto the bed.

"I told you not to get drunk."

"Maybe I don't like being told what to do," Dena said.

"If you don't want to be told what to do you can get out of my trailer."

"Maybe I'll just do that. There's men that would take me home. The Toomeys offered. Carlton's always been sweet on me. Next time I might take them up on it."

The bedsprings creaked as Dena moved closer to the nightstand, her hand reaching for the radio. She fumbled with the dial until she raised a soft rock station from the static, then got up from the bed and stood before Leonard, her eyes closed as she swayed to the music.

"See anything you like?" she said.

When he didn't answer, Dena sprawled on the bed again. Leonard wore only boxer shorts and she rubbed the flat of her palm over his stomach. She pressed closer and let her head lie on his shoulder.

"Show me you still want me," she said, almost tenderly.

"OK," he said, "but cut out the light."

Dena removed her hand from his chest.

"Why? So you can't see me. So you can pretend I'm some-body else. Probably that ex-wife of yours."

Nothing was said for a few moments.

"You go to hell," Dena said, and turned her back to him. Leonard cut off the radio and light, but sleep wouldn't come. He should have drunk more tonight, he told himself, taken some pills as well and fallen into a spinning, incoherent darkness.

Dena did not stir when he turned on the lamp. The ledgers filled the closet's top shelf, each in chronological order, be-ginning in 1848 and ending in 1863. Leonard took down the 1859 and 1860 volumes. It had the heft of a family Bible. He knew it was the cotton rag paper, so much more substantial than wood-based paper, that and the leather binding, but the words themselves seemed to give the volume much of its weight. The binding creaked like a rusty hinge, pages falling open to the entry Leonard had turned to most often over the years. The words were printed in a careful hand, as if the writer had anticipated a moment like this in the future when the entry would be read by other eyes.

Leonard imagined the good doctor putting on his hat and wool overcoat and placing the CLOSED sign on the office's front door, maybe even a note tacked underneath telling his where-abouts. Taking with him his wooden medical case as he walked the hundred yards down Main Street to his white clapboard house to tell his wife where he was going. Surely picking up his daughter, holding her in his arms, and promising a peppermint or play-pretty when he returned. Then out to the stable, his mare curried, tacked, and watered, the medical case strapped behind the cantle. It was the worst time of year for such a journey, winter solstice making the day the shortest of the year, balancing dark and light. Snow falling as well, cold air getting colder as he rode into the higher mountains. Not just the snow would slow the horse but the land itself as it bowed up, hardened into granite outcrops that allowed only a diagonal ascent of switchbacks and cliff hangs. As the chill seeped under his collar and gloves, he'd have wished he were home with his daughter and wife by the hearth. All the while knowing there was a very good chance he would be too late, find not a patient but a corpse.

Doctor Candler hadn't turned back, perhaps in part because he remembered the first time he'd saved Maggie Shelton's son. Or parental empathy, thinking what if it were his own child. No doubt he continued through that hard country mostly because it was his duty as a physician. That made it easier, Leonard supposed, not really a choice after all. It would have been full dark by the time he got there. He'd have let one of the Shelton men walk the horse out while he went into the cabin to do what he could.

Leonard studied the entries, imagined the raspy sound of the quill pen each time Dr. Candler took the ledger off the fireboard and wrote more words. He imagined the family gathered by the hearth, younger children going to bed first and then the older ones. Dr. Candler would have sent the parents to bed as well. The cabin would have grown quieter, the only sounds the hiss and crackle of the fire, the rustle of corn shucks as the family settled into sleep.

The handwriting on the 3 A.M. entry was not as clear and

precise as the others. Letters blurred into one another, as though the page had been tilted and ink bled beyond the quill pen's dips and slants. Leonard wondered if this reflected the doctor's weariness or a lack of light. He imagined Joshua Candler seated by the bed, squinting to check his pocket watch by candlelight and then writing the entry. Up all night, maybe smoking a briar pipe or drinking chicory coffee to stay awake as the freezing air slashed through gaps in the cabin's chinking. He'd have kept his heavy wool overcoat on, used the poker to coax fire from the hearth's graying log mound. It would be inevitable that he'd think of his own child asleep back in Marshall. Leonard wondered if Doctor Candler talked to the boy through the night, called him by name, bent his head to say his own prayers for David Shelton.

But this was not the entry Leonard was searching for. He opened the 1860 volume, then turned through January and into early February before he found it.

David Shelton, age nine.

Complaint: Blurred vision. Headaches.

Diagnosis: Nearsighted. Eyes possibly afflicted by Scarlet fever.

Treatment: Sent to Asheville to Doctor Vaughn for optometric exam.

Fee: None.

January 2, 1863, Marshall
(Last day of furlough)

Nancy Ponder, age 58.
Complaint: Grievous flow of bowels.
Diagnosis: Flux.
Treatment: Purge of bear oil and peach leaves.
Fee: Promise to check on Emily daily after baby born.

Ellie Winchester, age 8.
Complaint: Chicken pox.
Diagnosis: Same.
Treatment: Hot sassafras tea three times daily. Oatmeal and
*   baking soda bath morning and before bed.*
Fee: None.
Transcribed letter to take to her father.

Nancy Cathey, age 26.
Return visit from Dec. 30.
Much improved. Continue to drink ginger tea twice daily at
*   onset of menses.*
Fee: None.

Marcie Alexander, age 51.
Complaint: Puniness.
Diagnosis: Torpid liver.
Treatment: Mayapple-root tea twice daily.
Fee: None.

Received word today Julius wounded at Corinth in October.

SEVEN

The fishing rod rattled in the truck bed as Travis drove north toward Antioch. Daylight savings time had ended at midnight and Travis felt disoriented when he checked for rain clouds. Twelve o'clock, his watch said, but for six months the sun had not been overhead at noon. The sky seemed to have slid forward, dragging the sun with it.

Lori came out the door in jeans and tennis shoes, a purple sweatshirt with ASHEVILLE-BUNCOMBE TECH printed on the front. The same denim backpack she'd brought to the hospital dangled from her right hand. Probably some sandwiches inside, though he'd told Lori to eat before he picked her up.

"This one's for you," she said, and pulled from the backpack not a sandwich but a sweatshirt. "It's just like mine. Got them Friday when Momma took me to fill out financial aid forms."

"Thanks," he said, and laid the sweatshirt on the seat between them.

"Don't you want to put it on?"

"No," Travis said, trying not to sound irritated. "I'd just get fish slime on it."

Lori took a book from the backpack. "Got some reading for English tomorrow. Thought I'd get a little of it done while we're driving there."

We ain't driving, he thought, I am. Lori read as he drove west a few miles, then turned onto the gravel road that led to Spillcorn Creek. Shank and the other guys Travis knew spoke of the future in vague generalities—joining the military or farming, a mill job in Asheville or Winston-Salem. You'd have thought a girl from Antioch, which was the back of beyond even in Madison County, would have done much the same, especially one who sat on the back row and said near nothing until forced to. Most folks would figure a girl like that wouldn't have the confidence to plan much of a future, but Travis knew better now. Lori believed she could do most anything she put her mind to, and didn't mind letting you know it. She reminded Travis of places on the French Broad where banks tightened and the water flowed quiet and the surface looked smooth, but once you stepped in the current ran so strong you couldn't stand up against it.

Travis wanted to share some of that confidence, and because of his reading he'd begun to. He was learning in a new way, every reading assignment and every discussion linked to a single chain. Except *chain* wasn't the right word to describe it, because chains held things close and what Travis felt was the opposite, a widening like ripples in a pond. Synthesis. That was what Leonard called this kind of connecting, and he claimed a lot of folks at college, including some who taught, couldn't do what came naturally to Travis.

Starting to think you're too good to get dirt under your nails. That's the kind of thing his daddy would say if he heard such talk, finding fault because there was no pleasing him. Wednesday morning Travis had seen the old man's truck parked in front of Pinson's Feed and Seed. He'd finished putting groceries in the customer's backseat but hadn't rolled the buggy back inside, instead taking a few steps closer to the street. Travis now two months on his own when his daddy claimed he'd be back in a week. Travis had waited, his hand half raised to wave. But when the truck passed the parking lot the old man hadn't even glanced his way.

Travis gripped the steering wheel tighter, the memory of how foolish he'd felt making his face burn. Next time he'd have a big rock in his hand. He'd throw it right through the damn windshield and see if the old man would notice him then. He remembered the slap, how it seemed the poison of the yellow jacket stings coursed from all other parts of his body into his left cheek. Somehow still there, like a brand. But he didn't have to worry about not pleasing his father anymore. He could do what *he* wanted, work on a farm or in a grocery store or even behind a desk if he had a mind to. He could read a book and take that book apart the same way you might a car engine to see how it runs.

Yet when Travis glanced down at the purple sweatshirt, he couldn't shake the notion that maybe not much had changed after all, that he was still trying to please someone other than himself and nothing he did was quite enough. When he'd told Lori about the GED, he thought it would finally stop her nagging about his returning to school, which was what she'd done pretty much nonstop since August. Getting the GED was something he wanted to do, but soon as he told Lori she started pecking at him about his going to Tech with her come fall. Leonard too kept bringing it up, not just A-B Tech but schools like Western Carolina and Chapel Hill. Wants you to have what he had and screwed up, Dena had claimed.

They parked beside the bridge. Spillcorn was low, surfacing enough sand and rocks so they wouldn't get much more than their feet wet. First frost had withered the trillium and jewel-weed. On the stream's banks sumac had blistered to a deep velvety red. But it was warm for late October, in the high sixties, the leaves of the trees thinned out enough that the sun laid a scattered brightness on the water. A sagging barbed-wire fence bordered the creek, and they eased through the strands, careful not to let the rusty thorns snatch shirt or jeans. A dead walnut tree rose on the other side, leafless, dry branches beneath. Travis saw a hole in the trunk, reached inside, and brought out a single butternut-colored feather.

He held it up for Lori to see.

"A yellowhammer feather," he explained. "A man in Marshall makes trout flies out of them."

He unzipped his vest's side pocket and placed the feather inside. Having good luck already, Travis told himself as they stepped onto the creek bank. He tied on a Panther Martin, its treble hook wrapped in crimson thread, then bit off the excess line. He tested the knot and checked the drag.

"When I told Momma we were going fishing she said to bring some back to eat." Lori smiled. "I think she wants proof we weren't just looking for an excuse to get off by ourselves to do some sparking."

"I'll do my best," Travis said.

They moved upstream, Lori hopscotching between sand and rock while Travis took a straighter path. The water seeping into his shoes was cold enough to have him do some hopscotching of his own, but he didn't want Lori thinking he couldn't stand a little cold water. Nearing the first pool Travis moved slower, hunched over to be less visible. He paused in the tailwaters. In the pool's eddies red and yellow leaves laid a thin quilt on the stream's surface. The more sodden leaves blackened the bottom, made hang-ups harder to see.

He aimed for the white foam at the pool's head, but the cast was too long and snagged rhododendron. As Travis moved forward to free the lure, water rippled on the pool's far side as a trout shot under the bank.

"I'm rusty," he said.

He unhooked the spinner and they walked up the creek. His next casts were better, but it was only where the stream bowed and made a deep undercut that a strike made the rod flex and shudder. A flash of red and silver darted downstream, then threw itself against the air, the spinner dangling from its mouth. It was a big fish for a creek, fifteen, maybe sixteen inches. The trout turned back upstream and the reel's drag made a zipping sound as the fish veered under the bank. A brown would have stayed there, trying to tangle the line up in a snag, but rainbows liked their fight in open water. The trout came out and jumped once more before giving up.

Travis knelt on the shore, pinning the fish so it couldn't flop back into the water. The trout beat its black-spotted caudal fin against the sand, its body struggling under Travis's palm like one long slippery muscle. He gripped a fist-sized rock and struck the fish's head. It shuddered and went limp. His hands trembled as he laid the trout in the shallows and rinsed the sand off. For a few moments he just stared at it, the gold-ringed eyes and small head, the long red slash on the flank. He'd only caught a couple of trout this big, and it didn't yet seem fully real.

Lori came up behind him. Travis hooked his index finger through a gill and lifted the fish so she could see it.

"This one ought to keep me on the good side of your mom."

"I think so," Lori said. "That one could probably feed near the whole family."

Travis dipped the trout in water one last time and placed it in the deep pouch of his fishing vest. He pulled the vest back on, felt the trout's damp weight between his shoulder blades. His hands were sticky with scales that glistened like slivers of silver. He washed his hands in the creek, keeping them in the cold water as long as he could stand.

Lori smiled at him.

"You worried I won't hold your hand if it smells like trout?" she asked, which was exactly what he'd been thinking. He blushed and that just caused Lori to smile wider, like she'd got him good.

Travis had three more trout in the vest when they came to where the creek split. One smaller branch went into a meadow while the main stream disappeared into a stand of poplars. Travis took the meadow fork, the rivulet no more than two feet wide, in most places the water thin and clear. He and Lori walked thirty yards before Travis made his first cast into a pool no bigger than a truck tire.

"There can't be a fish in there," Lori said, but the spinner barely touched the surface when a six-inch trout shot out from under the bank and struck. Travis raised his rod and lifted the fish, set it down in the broom sedge. He dipped his right hand into the water before cradling the fish in his palm so Lori could see the gray-black back, the red and olive spots on the flanks and deep-orange dorsal fins.

"It's prettier than the others," Lori said. She pushed her hair back and leaned closer. "What kind is it?"

"A speckled trout."

"I've never seen one before. Are they rare?"

"Didn't used to be."

Travis gently freed the hook and eased the trout in the water. It surged from his hand and disappeared under the bank.

"What happened?"

"Browns and rainbows got stocked in streams. Speckleds don't compete well. Plus they need purer water than other trout."

"How'd you learn all this?"

"Read about it."

"Probably in the school library when you should have been doing classwork," Lori said, though not in a chiding way.

"The stuff we did in class was boring. Or at least the teachers made it boring."

"But Leonard doesn't?"

"No, he makes it interesting, even the science and math."

A gray squirrel chattered in a big hickory across the meadow. Enough leaves had fallen to expose its nest wedged in the tree's highest fork. Another squirrel answered deeper in the woods. Squirrel season was just days off, and Travis figured these two wouldn't last very long.

"Does he have any idea when you'll take the GED?" Lori asked.

"Maybe soon as April. He said it depends on how quick I get through the math."

"That means we can start A-B Tech in the summer."

Lori spoke matter-of-factly, as if it were already decided, and Travis knew how Shank and his other buddies would react if they were there. They'd wink at one another, talk later about how Travis didn't have to make up his mind anymore because he had someone to do it for him.

Lori moved closer, leaned her head into his shoulder.

"I bought some new perfume." She raised her hand and let it rest on his cheek. "Smell," she said, pressing the back of her wrist to his nose.

Travis breathed in the perfume's sweetness, and it gave him the same easy downshift into mellowness as a second beer. His aggravation seemed to settle on the rivulet's surface and drift away.

The sun fell full upon them, a soft warming that made the whole meadow drowsy, the jorees silent, a big yellow and black writing spider motionless in its web. No hint of a breeze, as if even the wind had lain down for a nap. The cloudless sky like a painting too, its color a light but also denser blue. Cerulean, he thought, remembering the word he'd read last week, one he'd asked Leonard to pronounce for him.

"The sky's cerulean," Travis said.

"What does that mean?"

"Cerulean," Travis said again, enjoying the way the word's sounds moved from the closed front teeth, then up and down in his mouth and ending in the throat as though the word had to be bitten off, chewed, and swallowed. "It means a clear blue."

It also means you don't know everything, which maybe you ought to remember when you try to decide everything I need to do, Travis could have said, but he didn't say those words because Lori had brought her lips to his and at that moment nothing else much mattered. So this is what all those songs are about, he thought, remembering nights he lay in the dark listening to radio stations, songs coming from faraway places like Chicago and New Orleans and Memphis, and pretty much every song saying the same thing—that love was near the only thing worth singing about. He wished he'd brought his transistor radio, because it would be like all those singers were singing just for him and Lori.

They sat down in the broom sedge, and the cooler ground reminded Travis that despite the warm sun it was October. Soon enough there'd be cold days after snow when the low sky turned a blue so dark that come dusk it would seep like ink, stain the white ground deep blue as well. Not long before such nights would be here. He thought about how good it would be to hold Lori once it turned cold, let the press of their bodies warm them as they kissed, maybe did more than kiss.

"Even when I was little I loved to find a place like this on a cold day," Lori said, as if she too thought of the coming winter. "I'd close my eyes and it was like being inside a cocoon. That Christmas after Daddy left was a bad time. Not just Daddy being gone but Momma so upset. I went out and found a warm place in the pasture. I had me a couple of oranges, and feeling that sun and eating those oranges made things not so bad."

"Were those the oranges Slick Abernathy gave you?"

"You remember that?"

"You held on to that bag like you didn't want anyone to know what was in it, but I saw bulges so I knew it was fruit."

"Did I hold it like I was ashamed?"

Travis was unsure how to answer.

"I don't know, maybe a little."

"I was, but not too ashamed to take them. About all any of us got that Christmas was those oranges." Lori looked up at him, her hand shielding her eyes from the sun. "Which is why I'm going to Tech. That way I won't ever have to do something like that again. Or ever be in the fix Momma was in."

"You don't want a good man to look after you?" Travis meant it as a joke but Lori did not smile.

"Momma and Sabrina taught me better than that. Momma says men are like cats. Don't count much on them because they come and go as they please."

"Not all men," Travis said.

"That's pretty much what I've seen until now."

"I can show you different," Travis said, trying to sound confident.

"If I didn't think you could I wouldn't be here right now." Lori paused. "I remember something about you in school, what I remembered that first day I saw you in the hospital."

Travis grimaced.

"I hope whatever it is ain't too bad."

"Mrs. Rodgers was checking out my library books when Mr. Abernathy came in and saw you in the magazine section. He asked Mrs. Rodgers if you were causing any trouble, and she said you were never trouble. She told him you were smart."

"I guess Slick had something to say to that," Travis said.

"He said he knew you were smart from your test scores but you'd never use your intelligence for anything except getting into trouble. Mrs. Rodgers said she didn't believe that."

Travis remembered how Mrs. Rodgers let him keep books he'd checked out longer than she was supposed to, let him read magazines before school when the library wasn't officially open. She'd picked out books for him, taken them off the shelves herself and put them in his hands. Try this one, she'd say, and give him Jesse Stuart's *The Thread That Runs So True* or Hemingway's *Nick Adams Stories*. Books he'd never have picked up on his own but always enjoyed.

"She's a nice lady," Travis said.

"I told her last week about you getting a GED and she said one day you'd prove a lot of people wrong. I believe that too. I wouldn't be here with you if I thought otherwise."

Travis slipped off his vest. Lori lay on her back now, eyes closed as she let the sun settle on her face. He lay beside her, the sun like a warm dry rain, the broom sedge cushioning the backs of their heads.

"When you went to live with Leonard I almost decided not to see you anymore," Lori said. "I thought he'd change you for the worse, have you doing what he does. But he's never tried to do that, has he?"

"No," Travis said.

"He's doing bad things but he's not a bad person. I've never known anybody like that."

"Maybe he doesn't see what he's doing as wrong," Travis said. "If they don't get drugs and beer from him they'll get them from somebody else."

"Then how come he never gives you any or lets you buy them? You know it's not the reason he says."

"So what's the reason?" Travis asked.

"Because Leonard's like me. He cares about you."

The broom sedge made a raspy whisper as Lori settled her head deeper. For a few minutes they lay still. The sun's light rose slowly up Sugarloaf Mountain, leaving a widening shadow beneath. Travis guessed one o'clock, then remembered to adjust for the end of daylight savings time. He knew he'd gained an hour but it didn't seem that way. He felt he'd lost time, much more than just an hour, and he could never get it back.

Travis turned to Lori so they could kiss again. He felt her tongue on his, her arms against his back. They held the kiss a long time, Lori's breasts flattening against his chest, her thighs and his pressed close. Travis slipped his hand under the sweat-shirt, rubbed the small of her back with his palm. He let his hand slide upward and settle on her bra strap.

"Enough of that, boy," Lori said, sitting up, brushing twigs and straw from her hair.

"Why?" Travis said. "It feels good, doesn't it?" He tried to match her lighthearted tone but couldn't. Three months and nothing but some kisses. It was another thing that Shank and the other guys would laugh at. He reached for her arm to pull her back down but she slipped his grasp.

"That's the problem," Lori said. "It does feel good. It felt good to Sabrina too."

So I have to have the blue balls because your sister was stu-pid enough not to make some guy use a rubber. That was what he was thinking, but saying such words to Lori didn't seem possible, anymore than showing her the rubber in his billfold. Travis felt ashamed just thinking about sex around her, which only made it more frustrating.

"We best be getting home," Lori said. "I got to cover for Mandy and her shift starts at four-thirty." She kissed him on the cheek, the same sort of kiss his aunt or grandma might give him. He put his fishing vest back on and picked up the rod.

"Don't go getting sulky on me," Lori said, telling him one more thing not to do.

WHEN TRAVIS GOT BACK TO THE TRAILER, LEONARD'S CAR WAS gone. Dena sat on the couch, an ashtray and near-empty bottle of Boone's Farm strawberry wine balanced on the armrest. On the coffee table an array of pills filled a plastic baggie. The television was going, some show about doctors.

"Where's Leonard?"

"Went to the county library," Dena said. "Gone to get more books for you. Evidently a trailerful ain't enough."

Travis picked up the science book he and Leonard were using and sat in the recliner. Dena watched him read, a smirk on her face. Her eyes were glassy, their blue opaque like the color in cat-eye marbles.

"What?" he finally said.

"You and him are quite a pair," Dena said. "You quit school and he gets fired from one, so you all set up your own school in this shit hole of a trailer. It's one of the most screwed-up things I ever seen in my life."

A cigarette smoldered in the ashtray. Travis felt a need strong as thirst or hunger. A month now since Lori had nagged him into quitting but it didn't seem to be getting any easier.

"He got fired because of pissants like you," Dena said.

"What do you mean?"

"He caught some students cheating. One of them put some pot in his car and then called the cops. He can't teach anymore because of that, leastways in a school. What's worse is that conviction got his wife full custody of their kid."

"He has a kid?"

"Oh, yeah, only he don't never see her. His wife took her off to Australia."

Travis tried to envision some physical feature of the child but nothing came. There was no photo on Leonard's wall or night table, no letter ever in the mailbox from or to her. No phone call. Her existence seemed something Leonard should have mentioned to him. Travis felt betrayed, though he could not say exactly why.

"How come he never talks about any of this?"

"Because he has to be bad drunk first. He ain't been that way for a while."

Dena drank the last of the wine and set the empty bottle on the floor.

"Where's your little honey?"

"She's covering for another waitress tonight."

"Too bad. I bet you were hoping to get something sweet from her."

Dena's words reminded Travis of what had happened in the meadow. They were like a taunt, and he wanted to be out of the trailer.

"How long ago did Leonard leave?" he asked.

"Not long. He won't be back for at least an hour."

Dena cut off the TV.

"Nothing but boring shit on," she said, and let her hand brush his knee as she went to the back room.

Travis finished the chapter in the science book, then walked into the narrow hallway to put it on the shelf.

"Come here," she said, calling him to the back room.

He stood at the doorway but did not go in. Dena lay on the bed naked. She faced him and he could see the heavy breasts, the dark patch of hair between her legs. He lowered his eyes.

"You want to lay with me?" she said. "You can if you want to."

Her voice wasn't gentle, but it wasn't mocking either.

"Come here," she said, patting a spot on the bed beside her.

"I can't," Travis said.

"Why not, big boy?" she said, mocking him now. "Afraid?"

Maybe he was a little afraid, but it was more than that. He didn't look at her but at the window Leonard had painted black. Travis had once asked Leonard why he'd done this and Leonard said he'd been drinking, as if that were explanation enough.

"Because it wouldn't be right," Travis said, his eyes still on the window as if he could see through the black paint.

He expected Dena to jeer at him more but she didn't. She lifted the bedsheet and covered herself. He looked at her now.

"I guess not," she said. She stared at him intently, as though trying to memorize his features. "Last summer you wouldn't have said that. You about got me believing people can change."

He didn't know how to answer her, or even if he was expected to. He wanted not just out of the trailer but to be miles away. He'd go and find Shank. Dena tugged the sheet until it covered most of her head as well. She looked like a creature peeking out of its lair.

"I'm going down to Marshall," he said.

"You know where I'm going?" Dena asked.

She didn't give him a chance to respond.

"I'm going to hell. I've known that since I was seven years old."

She said it the same way she might look out a window and say it was raining.

"You can't know something like that," Travis said. He knew

there were Bible verses to support him, but he couldn't think of one. He stepped back from the door, wanting to leave.

"Yes, you can," she said. "You learn it early and you ain't allowed to forget. You even get to spend time there when you're still alive. Just to give you a little taste of what's waiting."

She turned, facing the wall when she spoke.

"Go on now," she said.

Travis saw the purple scar on her back shoulder and knew that, as with him, someone had taken a knife to her flesh. He also believed that she'd deserved that blade less than he had. His jeans were almost dry now but the tennis shoes and socks were soggy, so he sat on the couch and changed socks and put on his boots. Dena had left the pills on the coffee table. At least fifty in the bag, enough that a few wouldn't be missed. He picked three of the shiny black ones that looked like licorice, the ones he'd heard Dena call black beauties. He wasn't sure what they'd do but that didn't matter as long as they made him feel different from the way he felt right now. He washed them down with a glass of water and went out to the truck.

Travis headed south toward Marshall and in a few minutes drove past the Harbin Road turnoff that led to his parents' farmhouse. He passed a harvested tobacco field that was nothing now but stubble. There were people who could drive by this field and have no idea how much work had been done here, Travis knew, recalling how he and his father had planted seeds in February before laying down sheets of black plastic anchored by creek rocks. Come April they'd removed those rocks and lifted the plastic sheets careful as they'd pull a bandage from a wound. He and his daddy had knelt in front of the plants and gently freed the stem and roots from the soil, then laid the plants on a burlap sack before putting them back in the ground with tobacco setters. That had been just the beginning, watering and worming and topping and suckering still to come. Finally the cutting, which was the sweatiest fieldwork of all. Now those plants hung from the barn's rafters, muted to a brittle dusty gold, a smell like old leather musking the air. The barn would be shadowy, except for early mornings and late afternoons when sunlight slipped through the slats and the tobacco leaves brightened and shimmered as if tinged with fire.

By the time he crossed the river into Marshall, the pills had taken hold. It was like a lamp had been turned on inside his head. Everything was brighter, more defined. His heart raced and he imagined blood rushing through his veins like whitewater. He wished he had a tape player so he could hear some fast hard music like Skynyrd or Black Oak Arkansas.

He found Shank and a few of the other guys at the Gulf station, their cars and trucks facing the passing traffic. Travis pulled beside Shank and cut the engine. The good feeling he'd had just minutes before was gone. His heart pounded even faster and thoughts came almost too quick for his mind to organize them. Like a truck in the wrong gear, everything felt out of sync. In the rearview mirror Travis saw the same glassy stare he'd seen in Dena's eyes. He put on his sunglasses.

"Damn, boy," Shank said loudly. "Lori loosened the leash on you a few minutes?"

"She's working."

"Lucky us," Shank said, and winked at the others.

Travis got out of the cab and set himself on the Ford's hood, all of them perched on car and truck hoods. Travis knew each face and name and they nodded back at him familiarly. He and Shank were close enough that Shank leaned toward Travis, punched him in the shoulder. Not a hard punch, but he'd had enough of people hitting on him the last few months. He hit Shank back hard, ready to trade a few more punches if that was what Shank wanted. Shank rubbed his shoulder where the blow had landed.

"Miss you at school," Shank said. "I got no one to sit with in detention." Shank waved his hand at the other guys. "These boys ain't outlaws like we used to be. You remember when Slick Abernathy called us that in his office, said we'd end up in prison if we didn't change?"

Irritable as he felt, Travis still had to smile.

"We did raise some hell, didn't we? I bet Slick won't ever forget me."

"No way," Shank said. A souped-up Mustang drove by, the driver revving his engine as he passed. A couple of the guys cheered when the driver flattened the accelerator pedal, left two wavy smears of rubber in his wake.

"I reckon you really are a outlaw now," Shank said, "what with you and Leonard in cahoots. We're liable to see your ugly mug in the post office before long. I figure to turn you in and get a big reward."

"Maybe it's already up there," Wesley said. "That's how come he's got those shades on."

"Come on, son," Shank said, "tell us some stories of the

cutthroats and desperadoes you've been riding herd on, what kind of big dope deals you got going down."

He liked Shank calling him an outlaw, liked the respectful way the other boys looked at him as they waited for him to tell what it was like to live with a drug pusher and bootlegger. Travis thought about saying he and Leonard were like Butch Cassidy and the Sundance Kid, partners in crime and good buddies. Fast as his mind was working he could've come up with all sorts of bullshit. Instead he just gave a little smile, like there was stuff going on but he wasn't saying.

"So what you got stashed in that truck?" Wesley asked. "I wouldn't mind getting high."

"Nothing but fishing equipment."

"Not even a nickel bag?" Shank asked.

"No."

"Maybe you ain't quite the outlaw we were thinking," Shank said.

"I don't give a damn what you think," Travis said. Shank's words were like gnats swarming around his head. He wondered if you were supposed to take just one of the pills.

For a few moments they watched the vehicles pass before them.

"Leonard been practicing to defend his title?" asked a younger boy nicknamed June Bug.

"He shoots a few cans every once in a while," Travis said, glad to have the subject changed. "Good as he is he don't need much practice."

"I don't know why those other fellows even try," Shank said. "They might as well hand Leonard their entry fee when they show up. Not even shoot so they don't waste their bullets."

A Dodge filled with girls passed. The windows were down and the girls waved and shouted. Shank lifted his arm in a beckoning wave, but they kept going.

"That girl driving," Shank said. "I saw her tubing in the river last summer and she didn't have enough clothes on to wad a shotgun."

"If I had been there I'd of asked her to go skinny-dipping," June Bug said.

"I bet that's what you'd have done," Shank said, rolling his eyes.

"June Bug, even if she'd got naked you wouldn't have known what to do next," Wesley said. "You'd have froze up like a deer caught in headlights."

"That ain't so," Shank said. "June Bug would have got in the water and told her he hoped she didn't mind that he'd kept his clothes on."

While the other boys were laughing Travis slid off the hood. He acted like he was going to piss, but once behind the building he just walked around the back lot, kicking empty motor-oil cans, throwing a few rocks. Doing something for a few minutes besides sitting and listening to a bunch of stupid talk. Travis paused and placed his hand on his chest, was surprised he could not feel a wild battering against his ribs. He was worried about his heart, afraid it could only take so much before exploding. Shank met him on the way back, motioned for Travis to sit with him beside the gas pumps so they could talk alone.

"So Lori giving you what you need?"

Travis stared at the black smears the Mustang had made. He wished it was his truck that had made those marks and he was now someplace else. But where? He seemed to have run out of places he could go. Some of the other guys shouted as the girls in the Dodge drove back by.

"I bet you hadn't even rubbed her titties yet," Shank added.

"I'm getting what I want," Travis lied.

Shank grinned at him.

"In your dreams maybe. Boy, the rate you're going you'll be laid up in the old folks' home before she puts out."

"I've got to go," Travis said, standing up.

"I'm just trying to help you out," Shank said. "Anyway, little as you come around these days I'd think you'd want to stay awhile and visit." Shank no longer smiled. "If you ain't careful I may get to thinking you don't have time for your best buddy anymore."

Travis wanted to tell Shank it wasn't that way at all. But he was afraid to say a single word, because once he started he didn't think he'd be able to stop. He'd tell Shank how hard living away from home could be, how scared he was sometimes because it was like there'd been a net beneath him that was now gone. He'd probably start bawling like a baby before he got through. Besides, for all the talking he'd already done today little good had come of it. He thought how much better the day would have been without words, catching the trout, laying with Lori in the meadow, even sitting on a truck hood with his friends. All those were good, until Lori and Shank opened their mouths and ruined them. Even Dena. It was her words that had brought him to the back bedroom. Words seemed to ruin everything.

Travis got in his truck and cranked the engine. *What can be spoken is already dead in the heart.* That was something Leonard had said last week, quoting some philosopher. At the time he'd had no notion of what that philosopher was getting at, but now those words went barb deep.

The sun had finally begun to nestle into the folds of the mountains. He was only supposed to have gained an hour but this day seemed like forever. A flock of redbirds flew across a cornfield, bright against the gloaming. The birds compressed and expanded, lifted a few feet higher and compressed again as if trying to mirror his own racing heart. Travis rolled down the window, hoping the brisk air would make his body feel something beside the pills.

The road began a long climb that ended where Harbin Road intersected with Highway 25. He could go home. It was as easy as making a left turn. That's what his mother wanted, said as much during her weekly shopping trips, trips Travis knew she arranged to coincide with his work schedule. They always talked a few minutes, about his sister and her husband, his grandmother's health, even his studying for a GED, which had done a lot to change his mother's mind about him living with Leonard. Almost every time he saw her, her eyes teared up and she told him she wished he'd come back home. She told him his room was just as he left it. Travis had clothes and a bed there. His fishing equipment and rifle were in the truck. He wouldn't even have to go back to Leonard's trailer.

But not once had she brought a single word from his father.

It was like the old man refused to acknowledge that Travis existed anymore, the same as when he'd driven by the grocery store's parking lot. Travis remembered all the work they'd done together in the fields, his father never noticing how straight he made his rows or how good Travis was at spotting cutworms and hornworms, just noticing things done wrong like stepping on a plant or leaving a hoe in a furrow. Then the work inside the barn come harvest time, Travis hanging thirty-pound sticks of tobacco while balancing on a crossbeam no wider than a railroad tie. That was the hardest work of all, not just hanging the plants but the resin sticking to you like tar, flecks of tobacco burning your eyes. Dangerous work, because it was easy enough to slip off a beam and end up in a wheelchair like William Revis. Travis had done good work up there in the rafters. Others had said so, men who'd spent time on those crossbeams. But it was the same as in the fields, his daddy only noticing what didn't suit him—Travis taking a break when he could hardly raise his arms anymore, or a plant with barn burn because it had been hung too close to another.

Travis figured a couple of beers might help mellow him out, so at the next crossroads he turned right and drove until he came to Dink's. The bootlegger met him at the door, took what money Travis had with him and brought back three beers.

"I figured five dollars would get me a six-pack," Travis said.

"You figured wrong," Dink said. "That price is just for my regulars, and you ain't been around in months."

Once on the main road Travis drove north before turning onto an old skid trail lined with second-growth hardwoods. He parked and pulled the tab on one of the cans, poured its contents down his throat like vital medicine. He drank the second almost as fast. Soon the alcohol began taking the edge off the pills, or maybe the pills were wearing off now on their own. Whichever, he no longer felt as agitated. He opened the last beer and watched darkness seal up the last gaps in the branches. When the can was empty he did not leave. Dena wouldn't miss just three pills, he was sure of that, but if he went back now Leonard would realize he was buzzed, might look closer and notice how dilated his pupils were. Nothing good could come of that. He'd wait another hour or two.

Travis leaned back farther in the seat and closed his eyes. Think about something good, he told himself, and settled his mind on the fish he'd caught, not the big rainbow but the speckled trout. Large enough to eat but Travis was glad he'd let it go. He thought of the orange pectoral fins spread open like small bright fans as the trout hid under the bank, safe from otters and kingfishers, anything else that might snatch it from the water. The speckled trout would be sore-mouthed and wary from the hook, but soon enough it would move out from the undercut and feed again on a crawfish or nymph, maybe a grasshopper that survived first frost. Then as winter came on it would feed less, stay near the pool's bottom where the water wasn't as cold. The water a still, dark place becoming darker and even more still as a caul of ice settled over the pool, shutting the trout off from the rest of the world. A dark, silent place, Travis knew, and the trout down there, its metabolism slowed, as close to hibernation as a fish could get. Dogs dreamed. He'd seen them make soft woofs and kick their back legs, eyes closed as they chased a rabbit or coon through the dark woods of their sleep. Travis imagined the speckled trout under the ice, rising in its dreams to sip bright-yellow mayflies from the surface, dreaming of spring as it waited out winter.

PART TWO

PART TWO

EIGHT

That morning when his principal, Dennis Anderson, and the sheriff's deputy came to the classroom door, Leonard believed something terrible had happened to Emily. He was so exhausted and depressed that his mind could summon forth no other reason. A month had passed since the separation. Each afternoon he drove across town to a run-down apartment complex that rented by the week. His landlord was a laconic Cambodian immigrant who demanded payment in cash, the neighbors grizzled drunks whose lives Leonard suspected were fast-forwards of his own. Sleep came only if he drank enough to spiral into darkness, and he always woke an hour or two before daylight. What dreams he had were garish and violent, more like fevered hallucinations.

When the principal motioned him to come into the hallway, Leonard had been unable to move from behind his desk. An image from the worst of his nightmares—Emily prostrate in a hospital bed, a sinister array of tubes embedded in her flesh—seized his mind with the certainty of prophecy.

Dennis Anderson motioned again, spoke his name aloud as students shifted in their seats and began whispering. Finally the sheriff's deputy came into the classroom and took him by the arm. As the deputy led him out, Leonard looked at his class and saw curiosity and concern. Except for Robert Tidwell, one of the students he'd given a zero to for cheating. Robert slouched in his seat, legs sprawled before him, smirking.

"They found marijuana in your car," the principal said.

"So nothing is wrong with Emily?" Leonard asked.

"No," Anderson replied. "This is about you."

"I have to handcuff him," the deputy said.

"I know," the principal replied, "but let's wait until we're outside."

For a few moments all he felt was relief, even as they walked to the patrol car. The officer recited Leonard's rights, then removed handcuffs from his belt and motioned for him to hold his hands out. The steel made an audible click as it secured his wrists.

"I'll let Kera know what's happened as soon as the class period ends," Anderson said. "Do you want her to come to the station now?"

"No. Tell her to come after school and not to bring Emily."

The deputy took his arm and opened the rear door.

"Watch your head," he said, and guided Leonard into the backseat. Leonard looked up at Anderson.

"Robert Tidwell did this. He's getting me back for giving him a zero."

"How can you know that?"

"The way he was acting in class just now."

"I'll check into it," the principal said. "But that's not much to go on."

As they pulled out of the lot, Leonard watched Anderson walk rapidly toward the school's main entrance. He wondered if the principal would confront Tidwell directly or wait until the boy's father had been informed.

After they searched and fingerprinted him, took his belt, and confiscated the contents of his pockets, the deputy led Leonard to a vacant holding cell, its one piece of furniture a sagging urine-soaked cot. On the wall outside, a clock's hands moved beneath wire mesh, even time imprisoned here. It was fourth period, his European history class. If he were at school, he'd be talking about the French Revolution. Trying to sound coherent, make it to the last bell so he could go back to the apartment and drink. Leonard lay down on the cot and closed his eyes and did not open them again until he heard footsteps approaching his cell. Following the deputy were his principal and Dr. Trevor, superintendent of the DeKalb County schools.

"We need to talk to you," Dr. Trevor said as the deputy unlocked the cell door. As Leonard stepped out, the clock showed he'd slept two hours. They took him into a room in the building's basement where four metal chairs surrounded a battered oak table. The deputy did not sit down but stood by the door.

"I talked to Robert and his father," Anderson said. "Robert says it's you who have it out for him. Mr. Tidwell believes his son, and he's talking about bringing in a lawyer."

"It's your word against his," Dr. Trevor added, "and that's a bad situation for all involved."

"What makes it bad is that Tidwell's father is on county council. Right?" Leonard said.

"I'd be careful making an accusation like that," Dr. Trevor said.

"Look," Anderson interjected. "This is a hard time for you because of your and Kera's separation. I understand that. Which is why I've cut you some slack lately. I've seen you come in late and leave early, and I've not written you up. Students have complained that your teaching's not what it was before the separation. Mrs. Robertson smelled alcohol on your breath last week."

"That doesn't have anything to do with that marijuana being in my car," Leonard said. "And I've never come to school drunk."

"We didn't say you had," Dr. Trevor replied, "but there is a track record that you haven't been very professional lately. If I were on a jury, I'd see a pattern of behavior that would make me believe it was your marijuana. To be quite honest, I'd find that more feasible than Robert Tidwell putting it there."

Trevor and Anderson playing good cop/bad cop was almost amusing. Leonard looked down at the table as he yawned. Initials and profanity scarred the surface, the letters childlike in their rigid lines and angles. Leonard wondered what a prisoner could have used to etch into the wood. Or were the notchings made by bored policemen? He wanted to fold his arms on the desk and lay his head down. The two hours in the cell had been his first sober sleep in a month, but it seemed only to have made him more tired, as if reminding his body of what he'd lacked for so long.

"We've talked to Sheriff Petrie and Judge Stoneman and believe we've got a solution that will work best for everyone," Anderson said. When Leonard said nothing the principal continued. "He's agreed that if you plead guilty to a charge of simple possession, you will get a small fine and probation. No trial. Nothing dragged out. We can do it this afternoon. The paperwork is already done."

"What about my job?"

"You'll lose it," Dr. Trevor said. "That's state law. But if you go to trial and lose you could do jail time."

"If there's a trial the publicity is going to make it harder for Kera as well," Anderson said, and nodded for the deputy to bring in the paperwork. "Believe me, Leonard, this is best for everyone."

Leonard had just gotten his car keys and wallet back from the deputy when Kera met him in the courthouse foyer.

"I saw Anderson and Dr. Trevor in the parking lot. Did they bail you out?"

"No, I don't need bail," Leonard said. The keys and wallet were in his pocket but the belt looped around his fist like a rein. He thought about putting the belt on but doing so felt somehow inappropriate.

"So they got the charges dropped," Kera said, her words more confirmation than question. Kera looked so relieved it appeared she might actually hug him. Leonard looked around the large room, which was silent except for their voices. Several benches lined the walls but only one had an occupant, a man in a dark suit who did not bother to hide his interest in their conversation.

"Let's go outside," Leonard said, their footsteps echoing hollowly as they crossed the foyer and passed through the heavy main doors. They stood between the entrance's two marble pillars. Though it was almost April, a crusty gray snow lingered on curbs and in corners. The cold whitened their breath. Kera wore a heavy wool overcoat and she pulled the flaps up, hands tucked in her pockets. She stood close to him, closer than she'd been in a month. For a few moments Leonard did not speak. He wanted her to stay this close. He smelled the lotion she'd rubbed on her skin that morning, smelled traces of her shampoo.

"I took a plea bargain," he finally said.

"Having it in your car," Kera said, shaking her head slowly, exasperation in her voice. "How could you have been that stupid, Leonard?"

"I've never smoked pot in my life. You know that."

"Then how did it get there? How could that have possibly happened?"

"Robert Tidwell. Paying me back for the zero I gave him."

"Then why in God's name did you plead guilty?" Kera said. "This doesn't make any sense."

"Anderson said it would be best for everyone if I did."

Kera took two short steps backward, pressed her back against a marble pillar. Her knees bent slightly, as if she wanted to push the pillar to create more space between them.

"How could you do this? Did Anderson and Trevor tell you this will cost you your job? Did they tell you you'll never get another teaching position with a drug charge?"

"I'll find other work." Leonard paused, was about to step closer but her eyes warned him not to. "If it had gone to trial it could have been a lot worse."

"No, this is worse," Kera said. "Even if you were convicted you'd have at least fought it. You wouldn't have just let it happen."

The man who'd been sitting on the bench came out the door. He looked at Leonard's face circumspectly as he passed between them. Kera watched the man as he walked across the greenway, past the monument on which the names of the county's war dead were chiseled. "You know, I thought we might try again. Start this weekend with dinner at the farmhouse. Try because of Emily."

She turned her head and met his eyes. "Convicted drug offenders lose more than their jobs. But you didn't think about that. Or did you?" she added after a moment, her words slow, deliberate, spoken as much to herself as to Leonard.

"I was so tired. I couldn't think straight."

Kera did not appear to hear him.

"God, you had to know what could be lost. You knew, and you did it anyway."

"I love Emily more than I've ever loved anyone," Leonard said. "You know that."

"I do know," Kera said. "And that's why I can't comprehend your letting this happen."

For a few moments neither of them spoke.

"I suppose I should be grateful," Kera finally said, "because everything I do is easy now. All I have to think about are Emily and me. But one thing I'd really like to know, Leonard.

It doesn't matter, not anymore, but I'd just like to know. Why are you unable to do anything you might be held accountable for? Are you that weak, that afraid? Which is what I've wanted to believe, because I can forgive that. Is it that you like being able to blame other people when things go wrong because it somehow makes you feel better about yourself?"

Kera grasped the coat's lapels and pinched them tight against her neck. A small woman, her straight dark hair cut short, she looked waiflike in the thick coat.

"Or is it just selfishness," she continued, "that you want to be left alone and never have to worry about anyone but yourself. If that's what it is, you've gotten your wish, because as soon as the school term is over I'm resigning and going back to Charlotte. Emily and I will live with Mom and Dad until I find a place. The lease on the farmhouse is for a year, so you can move in when we move out. Just think, Leonard. For three months you don't have to decide where to live. I've taken care of it for you."

LEONARD RAISED THE CUP TO HIS MOUTH AND SIPPED. A FUSS came from the woods, not a gray squirrel's saucy bark but the more insistent chirruping of a smaller red squirrel, what his mother called a boomer. Enough leaves had fallen to see the Smokies, their dark peaks jagging into the blue sky. Crisp weather always made the mountains appear more defined, as if created with scissors and construction paper. *Landscape as destiny*. Leonard had carried that phrase in his head for years, though he could not remember the context or where it came from. But he knew what it meant here, the sense of being closed in, of human limitation. So different from the Midwest, where the possible sprawled bright and endless in every direction. He wondered if people in the Himalayas and Andes were affected similarly. Did they live in the passive voice, as if their lives were not really happening but instead were memories, fixed and immutable? Even die that way, as his Grandfather Shuler had, refusing to go to the doctor when his arm burned with pain and his face grayed to the color of cold ashes. The old man kept working in his tobacco field until the afternoon Leonard's grandmother found him face down between two rows, hoe resolutely clutched in his hand.

A certain comfort in living like that, Leonard believed, the universe's machinery set up to run oblivious to any human tinkering. You could lose your career, your marriage, and your child and accept that it couldn't have been otherwise. You could sell beer to underage kids at an Illinois convenience store to pay child support checks and a farmhouse's yearlong lease. You could return to Madison County and sell pills and pot as well as alcohol. Keep doing it even when the child support checks you sent weren't being cashed. If a kid you'd sold to slammed into a tree or telephone pole, it wasn't your fault. The kid would have gotten the beer or drugs from someone else.

Inside the trailer, Travis stirred. In a few moments Leonard heard the boy's feet pad toward the bathroom, then the sound of the shower. It was Saturday, and Travis didn't have to work until afternoon. Leonard calculated the time in Australia. Emily would probably be in bed by now, maybe listening to the radio or reading, maybe already asleep. His last three letters had come back with NO FORWARDING ADDRESS stamped across them. Sent into a void, same as the phone calls he couldn't stop making on nights he drank too much.

The sun continued its slow haul over the eastern mountains. For a few minutes Leonard watched light slide across the pasture, a wide bright wave that sparked the frosted grass. He'd always liked this time of year, the world seeming to shed its old skin the way a snake did, everything original and vivid, stronger pulsed. Not only what your eyes saw but also the clang of a cowbell, the smell of wood smoke, the cold-iron feel of a cattle gate. Landscape as destiny, but beauty in that landscape as well.

When Leonard's father died, his mother had sold the farm and gone to live with Leonard's sister in south Florida. She'd never gotten used to the heat and congestion in a place where nothing but concrete and brick rose around her, the only foliage palmettos his mother claimed were more like stunted telephone poles than real trees. She'd quit eating, become listless, and died after six months. Died of homesickness, Leonard believed, though he knew that could be mere sentimentality on his part. Even in the mountains, his mother had endured what she called "dark spells." She'd stayed in bed for days at a time, left the bedroom only to whip Leonard and his sister for playing too loudly. She'd given him more than a sense of wonder. Those dark spells had been her legacy as well.

He went inside and lifted Handel's *Messiah* from his record crate and pulled the first disk from its cardboard sleeve. He set it on the turntable and poured himself a second cup of coffee.

"Damn, Leonard," Travis said when he came into the front room. "You need to get some albums by someone who's still alive."

Travis poured his cereal and sat down with Leonard at the kitchen table.

"How'd you start listening to that stuff anyway?" Travis asked. "You sure didn't hear it on a radio or jukebox."

"My Music Appreciation professor in college," Leonard said, pausing to sip his coffee. "He'd lost a leg and half a hand during D-Day. I figured if a man who'd been through World War Two found classical music important I should at least give it a chance."

"Did he talk in class about what happened during the war?"

"No," Leonard said, "at least not directly."

Travis ate his cereal as Leonard listened to "For Unto Us a Child Is Born," the choral voices tentative as though afraid to speak this truth—God come to the world as child. These uncertain voices were the direct opposite of the bombast at the symphony's conclusion. That was the wonder of it, Leonard knew, the balance of the thing, everything countered, not just balanced but *reconciled* as the tenor voices resonated below the ethereal sopranos. Even the words proclaimed an order, *the crookedness of the world made straight*. It was, Leonard recognized, such a magnificent order as to demand devotion, the same kind of devotion his mother had shown as she embraced the world from her porch steps.

In the last class meeting they had listened to the overture of the *Messiah*. Professor Heddon sat in the corner and raised his mangled right hand as the music began. Three fingers and half a palm slowly waved back and forth, a calm stroking motion, as if the music were something to be coaxed from the vinyl. When the record ended Professor Heddon stood before the class and said his final words, holding his right hand up, what remained of his palm open as though to absolve them. There is beauty in this world, he told them, more beauty than any of us can fathom, and we must not ever forget this.

"Got something to show you," Travis said when he'd finished eating. He handed Leonard a black book thick as a family Bible. "Found it in the library."

The book smelled of decades steeped on a library's back shelf, an odor that always reminded Leonard of the fishy smell of a pond or slow-moving river. The title on the spine had been rubbed away, so Leonard turned to the cover page: *The Civil War in North Carolina* printed in stark black letters.

"It's got five pages just on Shelton Laurel," Travis said. "I sat down in the library and read it then and there, but I figured you'd want to see it."

The pastoral symphony's last notes ended and the needle lifted and set down on its armrest with a dull click. Travis seemed to be waiting for him to turn the pages, begin reading, but Leonard left the book open to the title page.

"There's things in there that ain't, I mean aren't, on the marker or in that book you have," Travis said, his voice thickening. "When they first got into the Laurel they rounded up the women and whipped them with hickory sticks. Tied some of them to trees in the middle of winter. Those bastards whipped an eighty-five-year-old woman."

"I know," Leonard said, closing the book. He looked not at Travis but at the worn cover. "I've read this book. It's got one big flaw as history, though. It fails to show the other side."

"What other side?" Travis asked.

"How the Sixty-fourth had been shot at for days. How miserable the weather was, how rough the terrain. They figured those women could tell where the snipers were and save them a lot of time and work. Save some of their own lives as well."

"It was still wrong," Travis said. "I wouldn't have shot a twelve-year-old boy."

"Saying that here and now is different than if you'd been there," Leonard said, handing the book back to Travis. "Some soldiers didn't want to shoot at first, but Keith told them if they didn't they'd be killed as well. What if you had a wife and a child? It's 1863 and they're about starved to death as it is. The man giving the orders knows where your family lives. It's no longer about just you. You've already seen an eighty-five-year-old woman being beaten, so you know he'd as likely do the same to your wife or daughter."

"I still wouldn't have shot a twelve-year-old boy," Travis said, his face reddening. "If they'd made me shoot I'd have missed on purpose. Either that or I'd have untied them the night before so they could get away."

"The soldiers didn't know the prisoners were going to be killed," Leonard said. "Allen had left Lieutenant Keith in charge and Keith told his men the same thing he'd told the prisoners, that they were going to the stockade in Knoxville. Nobody knew Allen had decided otherwise until Keith gave the order to halt and told the prisoners to line up."

"Maybe if I'd been at Shelton Laurel I'd have shot Keith," Travis said. "Maybe if someone had done that one person would have been killed instead of thirteen."

"But what if you had to kill more than one?" Leonard

asked. He stepped over to the bookshelf, thumbed through a thin paperback to an underlined passage. "Listen to this," Leonard said. "Force is as pitiless to the man who possesses it, or thinks he does, as it is to its victims; the second it crushes, the first it intoxicates. Those who use it and those who endure it are turned to stone . . . a soul which has entered the province of force will not escape this except by a miracle."

Leonard closed the book.

"That was written by a woman named Simone Weil in 1940, in Paris. She wasn't theorizing. She was witnessing."

"If you believe that how come you shot that fellow up in Illinois?"

Leonard laughed.

"Which version have you heard, the one where I shot the guy in both shoulders or shot off two of his fingers?"

"Both shoulders," Travis said.

"I've never shot anybody in my life. That's a story concocted by someone who heard I was arrested up there. But I haven't spent a lot of time setting the record straight. It's not a bad thing for the people I deal with to think I shot somebody. Most of the bastards know they deserve to be shot, but they aren't especially wanting to hurry it along."

"Anybody who's seen you with that Colt would know you could shoot a man's fingers off."

"All the better," Leonard said. "Like I said, some of the folks I deal with need to know that if I ever did decide to take aim at their sorry asses I wouldn't miss."

"That why you're doing the contest Friday?"

"That's reason enough, isn't it?"

Travis nodded. "You going to practice this morning?"

"I thought I'd shoot a round or two," Leonard said.

"Mind if I shoot some with you?"

"No. Get your rifle and set us up some targets. I'll be out there in a minute."

Leonard went to the back room and took the Colt .45 and a box of wadcutters from the top drawer. Dena still slept and Leonard doubted even the shooting would rouse her. When she'd come in at 4 A.M. she hadn't bothered to undress, just dropped the car keys on the bureau and lay down, bringing to his bed the smell of aftershave and cigarettes. Probably used the backseat of his car as her boudoir. Three crumpled ten-dollar bills lay beside the car keys, so at least she'd sold the dime bags of pot. Keeping her end of the bargain, as she put it.

"You mind if Lori goes with us Thursday night?" Travis asked when Leonard came outside.

"Fine by me," Leonard said. He aimed the Colt at one of the cans Travis had set on the row of stumps and fired. A can lifted into the air and landed beside the stump upright as if placed there, a hole in its center. Leonard shifted the Colt to his left and hit another can. He shot four more times, the cans leaping and spinning into the grass.

"Your turn," Leonard said.

Travis raised the rifle, slowed his breath, then laid his index finger on the trigger. The bullet hit low, a solid thump as it burrowed into the stump. He shot and missed again.

"You're jerking the trigger," Leonard said. "Slow and gentle. It has to be a surprise when the gun goes off."

"It could be the iron sights are off plumb," the boy said defensively. "If I had that Colt I could hit them easy."

"I doubt it's the iron sights," Leonard said. "Let me try."

Leonard raised the .22 and shot the can off the stump. He handed the rifle to Travis.

"Try it again. Look at the target and squeeze the trigger slow. Don't think about anything else. Just those two things."

Travis raised the rifle, let his finger rest on the trigger half a minute before the shot. A can leaped like something alive before falling onto the grass.

"That's better," Leonard said.

After Travis left for work, Leonard sat down in the recliner, a cotton cloth and bottles of Hoppe's bore cleaner and oil in his hand. He took the pistol apart and cleaned and lubricated it thoroughly. As he worked Leonard remembered how during his first week at Chapel Hill he'd gone into Wilson Library and asked the research librarian about a Civil War massacre in Shelton Laurel, North Carolina. Thirty minutes passed before the librarian handed Leonard a roll of microfilm labeled *The New York Times, July 1863*. He'd threaded the microfilm onto the reels and moved through time until he came to the July 24 headline BARBAROUS OUTRAGES PERPETRATED UPON UNION MEN BY THE REBELS. Leonard remembered how he'd slowly scrolled down the page, learning not just boys but grandfathers had been killed. Learning the killing had not been done just with guns.

The gun cleaned and lubricated, Leonard pushed in the recoil spring and the plug and barrel bushing. The empty magazine locked into place with a satisfying click.

January 11, 1863, Bald Mountain, Tennessee–North Carolina line

Boyce Alexander. Shot by sniper in upper left arm. Minié ball so bone shattered. Amputation. Whiskey. Chloroform—ten drops. Used capital saw. Arteries tied off with horsehair. Cauterized with flat blade of Lieutenant Keith's Bowie knife. Mortification possible. Two drams of laudanum for pain when awakened.

Emmit Johnson. Frostbite, left foot.
Billy Revis. Frostbite, both feet.
Thomas Rigsbee. Frostbite, left foot.
Bryce Ross. Frostbite, right big toe.
Immersed limbs in cold water before intense movement of affected skin. Tincture of iodine applied. Removed black tissue from Revis's left foot. Refused chloroform but imbibed draught of whiskey. Even in peacetime Billy never averse to spirits.

Dewy Morton. Still dangerous with fever. Fifth day. Continue to drink tea made of boneset and feverweed.

Claude Frizzell. Dyspepsia. Calamus tea. Epsom salts and mayapple purge to remove morbific matter.

Isaac Ponder. Bloody flux. Tea made with dogwood bark (no blackberry root obtainable). Mustard plaster on stomach. Only real cure better victuals.

Recommended Ponder, Revis, Alexander relieved of duty.
Note: Address Allen of need for more iodine, chloroform, laudanum.

Jeremiah Cantrell. Gutted with knife or bayonet. Found at sentry post. Two drams of laudanum to dim his final suffering. When brought back to camp the poor man's intestines dragged the dirt like an umbilical cord. A more dismaying sight no man could ever find words for.

NINE

"Looks like most of the county decided to come," Dena complained as they followed a long line of cars and trucks into the fairground's dirt parking lot. "I thought it wouldn't get crowded till the weekend."

Leonard glanced over at Dena. Her irises had narrowed to pinpricks, like the quickness of her words evidence she'd found the black beauties he'd hidden last week behind the ledgers. Probably sniffed them out, he thought, the same way a drunk sniffs out whiskey in a dry town.

"The men have come to see Leonard show everyone else up," Travis said from the backseat.

Dena scoffed as Leonard pulled into an empty space.

"More likely to watch some hootchie-cootchie dancer shake her ass."

Leonard opened the trunk and took out the .45 and a box of wadcutters.

"They let you tote guns around the fairgrounds?" Travis asked.

"No," Leonard said. "Sheriff Crockett isn't the most diligent upholder of the law, but he won't allow that. I have to check it in at the main gate. A worker takes the pistols and ammunition to the arena."

They moved through the tight maze of vehicles toward the entrance. The fairgrounds looked like a desert mirage of some bright but far-off city. The pulsating lights of the sky rides radiated deep into the dark. As they got closer, a kaleidoscope of sounds became more individualized—bells and shrieks, the clatter of a roller coaster. From the livestock barns, calls of haw haw echoed as cattlemen finished the team penning for the night.

"I'm buying the tickets," Leonard said at the entrance as he handed over his pistol and ammunition, took out his billfold.

"Look at the big spender," Dena said as he paid. "Twelve whole dollars."

As he pocketed his billfold Leonard wondered if the man at the ticket booth assumed he and Dena were husband and wife, Travis and Lori their children. Maybe thought the four of them just another farm family come to spend harvest money on what passed for exotic in these hardscrabble mountains. *Mirage*. It seemed he could hear the word's soft syllables whispered beneath the fairground's louder sounds.

"We'll need to decide where to meet later," Leonard said as he handed out tickets.

"What time's the pistol shoot?" Travis asked.

"It's the last event, so not until nine-thirty."

"Let's just meet there," Travis said, and took Lori's hand.

Leonard watched them walk up the midway, knowing they would linger before every game and ride and tent because they were too young to know how tawdry and fleeting the midway's exotica were, how in a week you would come back here and find only sawdust and trash.

"I'll go with you if you'll win me a teddy bear," Dena said, placing her elbow in the crook of Leonard's arm.

"The games are all rigged," Leonard replied.

"You can at least try," Dena said, leaning into him. "I'm worth a few quarters, ain't I?"

They walked toward the midway, passing shadowy sideshows, their imploring barkers in front of lurid paintings promising giant reptiles, freaks, and scantily clad women. Leonard felt the sift and give of sawdust under his feet, the crisp fresh smell of powdered wood mingling with candy apples and french fries. They were soon on the midway, passing a cart selling corn dogs, another where a woman swirled feathers of cotton candy onto paper cones as if performing a magic feat. They passed a dunking booth, then bumper cars whose metal rods sparked like lit fuses. Dena stopped where horses on a merry-go-round paused mid-gallop while a carny dismounted children.

"Give me fifty cents," she said. Leonard fished two quarters from his pocket and watched Dena join the line of waiting children. She paid and mounted a horse whose eye had been chipped away, its teeth bared like a grimace. The last children were hoisted up and the platform began turning, the horses slowly rising and falling as a discordant lullabye crackled from the speakers. Dena sat erect, hands on the knobs sprouting from her horse's ears, eyes straight ahead as though looking for some obstacle she might have to leap.

Leonard turned and watched the red and white ride called the Octopus fling riders into the sky. Beneath its flailing arms, in the nexus of thick black cables, grease-caked gears, and pulleys, crouched a man in a grimy tee-shirt and jeans. He was old, brow and biceps wrinkled, long hair falling to his shoulders in a gray tangle. But he moved with the dexterity of a spider monkey as he hunched and scurried between the supports and electrical systems to keep the machine going, its wide arms appearing to hurtle forward but in reality returning again and again to where they had always been. Like God at the center of his universe, Leonard thought, watching the scabbed, grizzled hands at the controls.

Never a sparrow falls from the sky but God knows it.

Leonard remembered how the Fairlane had faltered that last half mile before crossing over the Eastern Continental Divide, the mountains ensuring his return to Bloody Madison, to a run-down trailer where he sheltered a boy whose last name was Shelton. Then the glasses literally rising up out of the past. And now the yellowhammer feather. He had come in last week, and there it was on the coffee table. When Leonard mentioned that during the Civil War Alabama soldiers called themselves yellowhammers and wore such feathers in their hats, Travis had said all he knew was they made good trout flies.

The merry-go-round's music began to wind down and

Leonard turned to see the bolder children already sliding off their mounts. Dena stayed on her horse until the next group of riders stepped onto the platform.

"I always wanted to ride one," she said as they walked on up the midway.

"Disappointed?" Leonard asked.

"No," Dena said. "It's a real good feeling. Kind of like floating just above the earth but never quite touching."

They walked on to the far end of the midway and entered a makeshift arcade. Dena spent two dollars maneuvering toy cranes that rooted sand for prizes, cursing when a watch slipped repeatedly from the dull steel teeth. Leonard threw rings and won a fake-silver bracelet. The booth operator engraved Dena's name on the bracelet's plate.

"Keep you from forgetting who you are," the carny said, a comment that struck Leonard as sinister. The man laughed harshly, exposing yellow teeth crooked and gapped. The teeth reminded Leonard of gravestones in a derelict cemetery.

"All the magazines say giving her jewelry means a man's got serious intentions about a woman," Dena said. She clasped the bracelet on her wrist, the bright metal clicking as it locked. "So I reckon long as I'm wearing this we're honest to God sweethearts." She held out her arm so he could see the bracelet better. "This means you'll have to take care of me," she said, "for better or for worse."

Out on the shadowy grass beyond the midway, a guitarist, bass player and drummer crowded a wooden stage so small and rickety it swayed each time the musicians moved. From where Leonard stood, the three men appeared to be performing on a waterborne raft. They were older men, probably in their sixties, and played the staples, "Your Cheating Heart," "Long Black Veil," "Wolverton Mountain." Leonard checked a passerby's watch.

"Let's go over and listen," Leonard said. "We still have half an hour."

"Not me," Dena said. "If I want to listen to that hillbilly yowling I can turn on the radio."

"Meet me at the arena then."

"You got a couple dollars I can borrow?"

Leonard gave her two ones. She clinched the bills in her hand and walked back into the arcade.

Leonard sat down near the front of the stage. A good-sized audience filled the aluminum bleachers but no one Travis and Lori's age. That didn't surprise him. When Leonard was growing up, his family's radio was on dawn till bedtime, always tuned to a country station. But he rarely listened. Country music had seemed too depressing, most lyrics a litany of yearning and regret. He'd preferred the energy of Jerry Lee Lewis and Chuck Berry, later the bliss and magnificence of classical music. But country music had a rough-hewn honesty Leonard had come to appreciate. He remembered something a Nashville songwriter had once said, that a great country song was nothing but three chords and the truth.

As the musicians played the last verse of "Long Black Veil," the bass player turned to the guitarist and nodded at the far bleacher. Leonard leaned to get a better look and saw the person being gestured toward was Carlton Toomey.

As a child, Leonard had heard the stories about Toomey

and seen him often enough on the streets of Marshall. He remembered a big man who wore short-sleeve tee-shirts even in winter, displaying meaty upper arms that appeared ready to split the cloth, his thick black hair swept back in a pompadour. That hair was gray now, the face more furrowed. One morning last March Leonard had sold out quicker than anticipated and driven over to the Toomeys' farmhouse. Carlton sat at the kitchen table with a sharp-dressed dealer from Atlanta. Leonard joined them at the table, waited for the two men to finish their transaction.

It had been like watching an actor give a flawless performance. Toomey's accent was thick, his grammar mangled. He'd slouched in the chair, head tilted back and slack-jawed. The one thing Carlton could not conceal was the quickness in his eyes, studying the dealer as if an opponent in a poker game who might reveal his hand with some small gesture. The Atlantan had been abrasive, downright insulting, but Carlton had ignored the slights, calmly restated what he'd pay, and gotten the price he wanted. As Leonard watched that morning, he came to believe much of what he'd heard about Toomey was hyperbole, like Leonard's own criminal acts in Illinois.

But what Carlton had done to Travis changed that belief, not just the act itself but its cool deliberateness. If killing the boy was in Toomey's own best interest, he would have raked his knife across Travis's windpipe with no more regret than slicing an apple.

Carlton's forearms rested on his knees, hands clasped, back and head leaning forward, listening so intently he didn't notice the men's gestures. He appeared mesmerized by the music.

The song ended and the bass player stepped to the edge of the stage and spoke. The big man shook his head. The guitarist leaned toward the microphone.

"Help me get him up here," the guitarist said, "and you'll hear a voice so pretty you'll wish you could put a bow around it and give it to your sweetheart." People clapped and cheered until Carlton left his seat, the boards sagging perilously as he stepped onto the stage and positioned himself behind the microphone. He did not speak to the musicians or the crowd, just leaned closer to the mic and began singing "Poor Wayfaring Stranger." The musicians did not join in. They kept their hands at their sides, deferring to the power of Carlton Toomey's voice.

It was his delicacy that Leonard found most disconcerting. The big man sang softly, the words easing from his mouth with the gentlest of phrasing. Toomey's eyes were closed, hands clasped to his stomach like a man concealing some private wound. The midway's rambunctiousness became more distant as the people on the front row leaned slightly forward. Leonard wondered what Professor Heddon would make of this performance, especially if he knew what had been done to Travis. Tears streamed down the face of the woman who sat next to Leonard as Carlton Toomey sang of crossing Jordan.

Leonard got up and walked back to the midway, Toomey's voice soon lost amid other sounds. He found Dena at the arcade, maneuvering the same toy crane toward the same watch. Leonard watched the crane's jaws hover, then fall, dull steel teeth dribbling colored pebbles as the crane raised up. She put in another quarter. The crane dropped, grazed the watch, and rose.

"We need to get to the arena," he told her.

"I had it one time," Dena said. "I really did. But it slipped out at the last moment."

Since he'd won the last three years, Leonard went last. He had shot against all the men before and knew his only serious competition was Harold Watkins, a former Green Beret from Spillcorn Creek. Watkins shot fifth and his Ruger placed three rounds in the bull's-eye. As the next-to-last shooter stepped to the line, Leonard took the clip out of the Colt and six wadcutters from the cardboard box. He held the bullets in his fist a few moments. Despite being metal they had a waxy feel as they rolled in his palm. He loaded the clip and pushed it into the magazine.

"Your turn," the man in charge of the contest said.

Leonard stepped to the line and set his feet, drew in a breath and closed his left eye. He squeezed the trigger and didn't hear the shot.

"Bull's-eye!" Travis shouted from the stands.

Leonard did the same four more times.

They walked back down the midway afterward, the hundred dollars stashed in Leonard's billfold. Travis carried the trophy, and Leonard knew the boy wanted the people they passed to think he'd won it. Many of the booths and tents had shut down for the night, and the wind blew steady as though summoned to fill the void left by the now-absent crowd. Loose tent flaps made a dense slapping sound. Tension ropes creaked. Like walking through a ghost town, Leonard thought, and wondered, as he had in a Midwest farmhouse years earlier, if a place could feel truly lonely only if humans had once been present.

—

TWO NIGHTS LATER THE TOOMEYS SHOWED UP AT THE TRAILER. Dena drove back from the Ponderosa and a pickup followed, its high beams aimed at the front window as the vehicle idled. The Plotts made a few perfunctory barks before returning to the trailer's warmer underbelly. As Dena climbed the steps, Leonard heard a deeper male voice behind her. She came in laughing harshly, her pink blouse unbuttoned. A few moments later Carlton Toomey filled the doorway. The big man smiled when he saw Travis.

"Didn't know you and Leonard had a guest tonight," he said to Dena.

"He ain't no guest," Dena said. "He lives here."

"Lives here, does he. That kind of explains a few things," Carlton said, then nodded toward the back room. "Go get what you come for and don't be all night about it."

Dena walked unsteadily down the hallway, knocking a book off the shelf as she passed. Carlton Toomey resettled his eyes on Travis. There was something disturbing in how he stared at the boy, the absolute blankness of the gaze, the way Leonard imagined a shark's eyes would be.

"How's that leg of yours?" Carlton asked.

"It's OK," Travis muttered, looking at the floor as he answered.

"I reckon you learned your lesson about climbing waterfalls."

The truck revved outside, followed by three quick blasts of the horn.

"Young people," Toomey said, speaking to Leonard now. "They got no patience. They want something never a second later than right now. Most times the sooner a body gets something the sooner it's gone."

Carlton stayed in the doorway, as if unsure the trailer's floor would support him. Leonard wondered exactly how big the man was, at least six-two and three hundred pounds. If Carlton Toomey wished, he could keep everyone in the trailer the rest of the night. There was no way Leonard and Travis could have moved him from the doorway.

"It's sort of like this young coon dog I had," Carlton Toomey continued. "Ran him with a couple of older dogs but paid no mind to them. That whelp was always out ahead, like as not rushing right past where the coon was. One night them dogs got after an old sow coon, ran it all the way into the river. The old dogs knew what that was about, but that young one went in after her. That coon got out midriver and let the pup get good and tired. Then she just swum over and tapped his head with her paw, that head going down for a second and then popping back up like a fish cork. Just kept doing it till one time that head didn't come back up."

Carlton Toomey looked at Travis and smiled.

"If that dog had got away he'd have known better than to do it again, don't you reckon? I bet he'd have paid more mind to them older dogs."

Dena rejoined them in the front room. She'd smeared more lipstick on, more paint dabbed on her nails as well, but her blouse remained unbuttoned. Surrendering, Leonard thought, the same way an animal losing a fight bares its belly. In her hand she carried a battered yellow suitcase, its cloth covering torn in the upper right corner. The suitcase had been lived out of, opened and closed enough that now only one of the snaps shut.

She walked past Leonard to the door. Her high heels clacked on the linoleum, each drunken step careful as though maintaining her balance on a foot log. Carlton stepped inside the doorway so she could slip by.

"Don't worry," Carlton said. "We just want her for the weekend."

He lingered in the doorway a few moments longer, his eyes on Leonard.

"This boy and me are square, provided he keeps his mouth shut to the law. You know what I'm talking about, right?"

"Yes," Leonard said.

"Figured you'd know."

Carlton Toomey opened his massive right hand and revealed the car keys. "She won't need your car no more tonight," he said, and tossed the keys to Leonard. The truck horn blew again but Toomey ignored it. He looked the room over, let his gaze settle on the stereo.

"I saw you at the fair, professor. From the look on your face you hadn't reckoned I could sing that good." Carlton settled his eyes on Leonard. "There's some who said I should have tried to make a go of it in Nashville, but it seemed too doubtful a way to make a living. I never was much for taking risks." Carlton paused. His voice became more contemplative. "I'd not do it for money anyway. A few things in life ought to be done just to lighten folks' loads, and there ain't nothing that'll do that better than a good gospel song."

Leonard couldn't tell if Carlton was being ironic. Toomey half turned, put his foot on the first step.

"I sung once at a big tent revival in Hot Springs. Sang 'Just as I Am' and had them that was never saved and them that was backsliders all crying and getting right with the Lord. Even the preacherman claimed it was my singing more than his sermon brought them up front. The way I figure it I've done enough good for the Lord that he will cut me some slack in other areas. Just like he done Old King David."

Carlton turned and walked out to the truck. The high beams scouring the window veered away and were gone. Their appearance and departure had been so sudden Leonard could almost believe it had been a hallucination.

The trailer seemed to expand in the big man's absence. Travis sat down on the couch but didn't pick up a book or turn on the TV. He merely stared out the window where darkness had regathered. The only sound in the trailer was the heat pump's steady hum.

"What's bothering you?" Leonard finally asked.

Travis looked up but said nothing.

"She's thirty-four years old," Leonard said. "She has to look after herself."

"I don't think she knows how," Travis said.

Leonard walked over and locked the door.

"If that's true it's too late to teach her," Leonard said.

DENA DID NOT RETURN UNTIL MONDAY MORNING. LEONARD was in the kitchen when the truck came quickly out of the woods and swerved to a stop in front of the trailer. Dena gingerly got out of the cab. Hubert Toomey was already turning around as Dena lifted her suitcase from the truck bed. The handle slipped free from her hand and the suitcase flung open when it hit the ground. The truck did not pause as it bumped down the drive. Dena stood there a few moments, arms at her sides, shoulders hunched, the gaping suitcase and its contents littering the ground around her. Leonard was reminded of jerky black-and-white newsreels in which European war refugees stared blankly at the camera. Dena stooped to gather up her cosmetics, the hairbrush and toothbrush. She picked up her nightgown last, brushing off the dirt before folding it delicately in a precise rectangle. This gesture, more than the blank stare, made Leonard leave the window and go outside to help her.

Dena looked worse up close, bloodshot eyes, lower lip split and swollen. She smelled, a dank cloying smell, like newspapers rotted by water. Leonard was glad the boy had already left for work. Dena walked stiffly and winced when she sat down on the bed's edge.

"I'll run you a bath," Leonard said.

When the water reached the right temperature, he went back to the bedroom. Dena lay on the bed, her eyes open but glazed. He helped her to the bathroom and got her clothes off. Dena let the warm water cover her body, almost to her chin, the back of her head pillowed by the bathtub's porcelain rim. Leonard rubbed some soap on a wet washcloth and handed it to her.

"You really are my sweetheart," she said, her voice slurred, "taking care of a bad girl like me."

She lifted the washcloth and tentatively dabbed her lip.

"I'd have stayed with them if they'd let me," Dena mumbled. "They're rough but at least they think I'm sexy. They don't have to pretend I'm somebody else."

She let the cloth slide from her hand, closed her eyes.

"Call if you need help getting out," Leonard said, and went into the front room. If she passed out, her head might slide underwater. Probably would be a blessing, he thought, but soon he checked on her. Dena's eyes were closed but she smiled faintly.

"I'm just resting," she said. "I'll get out in a minute."

Leonard sat down in the armchair. On the coffee table was a book he'd checked out from the library, but he did not pick it up. The volume was a study of conflicts between the Cherokee and rival tribes, conflicts not always settled by negotiation. Like Keith's Confederate troops at Shelton Laurel, the Cherokee sometimes killed their prisoners, larding captives with fat before burning them at the stake.

Others.

That was the word at the bottom of the January 17 ledger entry, placed after the names of the regiment's sick and injured. A word far enough down the page it could be easily missed. Leonard believed he knew who those others were. He imagined Doctor Candler applying salves and plasters to the streaked backs of the women, maybe ministering to some of the men taken prisoner as well. Perhaps one of those he treated had been David Shelton. Leonard imagined the doctor tending to the boy, noting how much he had grown since that long winter evening four years earlier and telling David Shelton's father as much, for the father would be locked in the cabin as well. The two men reminiscing about the night David almost died. One father talking to another, forgetting for a few minutes the two sentries posted outside, the war itself beyond the cabin door as they recalled other shared moments—a hunting party they'd both been part of, a horse auction or lazy hour passed one Saturday outside Tom Whitley's General Store. The other men huddled in the cabin's one room would surely join the conversation. Dr. Candler had probably ministered to every man there at one time or another. They would have their own memories of arms set, stitches sewn, fevers cooled, memories not of just when Doctor Candler had ministered to them but to their families as well.

Perhaps they had talked into the night, late enough that David Shelton would grow sleepy and lie down on a tick mattress in the corner, his glasses folded and placed on the fireboard. Perhaps the boy's father placed a quilt or coat over him as he lay there, and all the other men, including Doctor Candler, thought of the beds and homes their own children slept in and then not just thinking but speaking aloud of them, their number and ages, speaking their children's names like incantations. Each recollection bringing more of the old world back inside those hand-hewn logs as if that world might yet be recovered. It could have occurred that way, Leonard believed. Only Lieutenant Keith knew the men would be executed in the morning. Doctor Candler, like the prisoners, believed they would be marched to the stockade in Knoxville.

But two days of being shot at from outcrops and ridges might have caused the doctor to be less amiable. The prisoners would have known what had happened to their women. The two gold stars on his coat collar marked Doctor Candler as a healer, but the butternut uniform itself was the same as those worn by the torturers of their mothers and wives and daughters. Perhaps all that passed between the doctor and each of the men was a tense, cloaking silence, glances that never met the other's eyes.

Nevertheless, whatever else had or had not occurred, Doctor Candler had ministered to them. The obliqueness of *Others* implied he'd done so at the displeasure of Keith and Allen and probably other men of the 64th. He had noted again, in an entry only two weeks earlier, his low supply of chloroform and laudanum. Medicine used on the enemy might not be available when needed for men in the 64th. But Doctor Candler had followed an oath he'd made before the one given to Jefferson Davis and the Confederacy.

January 17, 1863, Shelton Laurel

*Dewy Morton. Dead at roll call. At least laid to rest in his home
county. Many in this war will not have even that.*

*Boyce Alexander. Left arm amputation due to minié ball.
Improved. Laudable pus. Gangrene unlikely since no black
spotting on wound. Gave one-half dram of laudanum.*

*Isaac Ponder. Flux lessened. Continue to drink tea of dogwood
bark every four hours.*

*James Jackson. frostbite. Immersed limbs in cold water before
intense movement of affected region. Tincture of iodine
applied. No blackened skin.*

*Billy Revis. Amputated two toes left foot.
Chloroform—five drops. Capital saw. Cauterized with flat blade
of Keith's Bowie knife.*

*Note: Address Allen about need for more chloroform and
laudanum.
Recommended Revis, Ponder, Alexander relieved of duty.
Recommended Ross, Johnson returned to duty.*

Others

TEN

Dena returned late New Year's Day in a white pickup driven by a man who'd introduced himself as Gerald the night before. He'd actually knocked on the trailer door and made small talk with Leonard as Dena dried her hair. Well mannered, Leonard thought, at least compared to her other two recent suitors, who'd merely blown their car horns until Dena appeared. Nevertheless, when Leonard heard the pickup turn off the blacktop, it occurred to him that the truck might belong not to Gerald but to Carlton Toomey. Not coming for Dena—one weekend had evidently been enough for her and the Toomeys both—but to find out why Leonard hadn't picked up his January quota of pills. Tomorrow morning I'll go see him, Leonard told himself, get it over with.

"You need to get rid of that thing," Dena said as she came in. "It's bad luck to keep it up past New Year's."

The scraggly fir beside the stereo balanced precariously on a stand made of crossed planks and ten-penny nails. The colored lights Leonard had strung around the trailer for the potheads' amusement draped its branches, the fir so puny and thin-needled it sagged under their weight. Red and white fishing bobbers served as ornaments, strips of tinfoil covering the tree's slumping shoulders like a ragged, gaudy coat. The tree had been Travis's doing, cut and set up early Christmas morning. Gifts for Leonard and Dena had been set under it as well, some Hoppe's gun oil for Leonard and a Whitman's Sampler for Dena. When Leonard had taken a five-dollar bill from his pocket, Travis had refused the attempt at a return gift. I wasn't expecting presents from you all, he'd said.

"I'll take it out soon as we finish studying," Travis said now. "I don't need any bad luck with the GED coming up."

Dena sat down on the couch and picked up a *Redbook* from the pile of out-of-date magazines Travis had brought from the grocery store. Travis turned back to the math workbook on the coffee table. The dogs began barking and Leonard peered out the window, thinking it might be another of Dena's boyfriends, come to have his turn. A battered silver Mustang pulled up to the trailer, a carload of teenagers inside. Leonard went outside and saw one of them was Shank.

"What you boys want?" Leonard asked. He wore a sweat-shirt but the cold went straight through it. If he'd had a ther-mometer nailed to the trailer, he knew the mercury would be stalled near zero.

"What we want is some pills and a couple of six-packs," Shank said, "but since you won't sell them to us anymore we just come to wish our buddy a happy new year." He nodded toward the trailer. "I don't reckon you'd let Travis come out and play, would you?"

"He's studying for his GED."

"Damn," Shank said. "Between you and Lori he never gets out."

Shank followed Leonard into the trailer, the other boys staying in the car. Leonard sat back down in the recliner.

"Why don't you come with us," Shank said to Travis. "We'll get higher than the moon."

Travis nodded at the book.

"Can't tonight."

"Just for a hour," Shank said.

"Can't," Travis repeated.

Shank raised open palms in front of his chest as if to ward Travis off, stepped back. "Fine. Sorry to bother you."

"We'll get together soon," Travis said.

"Sure," Shank muttered, let his eyes settle on the textbook in Travis's hands.

"Lori's been telling it around town that you're going to A-B Tech come fall."

"What if he does go," Dena said, closing her magazine. "What problem you got with that?"

"Who says I got a problem with it?" Shank said. "I'd just like to know what's going on with my best buddy since first grade."

"Real friends support each other," Dena said, mouthing some advice-column wisdom Leonard knew she'd read in a magazine.

"How can I support him unless I know what he's doing?"

"I'll tell you when I decide," Travis said, frustration in his voice. "But I ain't decided nothing yet. Nobody else will decide for me neither."

"Why don't you finish the math tomorrow?" Leonard said after Shank and his friends had headed back to Marshall.

"No," Travis said. "I want to do it now."

Travis sat down and spread the workbook open on the coffee table. He hunched forward and peered at the page as he would a pool he was about to cast into. The boy's eyes did not shift as he reached for the pencil and wrote an answer in the workbook. Dena came out from the back room, a clear plastic baggie in her hand.

"This all we got left?" she asked, nodding at the half-dozen pills in the bag.

"Yes," Leonard said.

"And you're not getting more from Carlton?"

"I've been telling you that for weeks now."

"Is this some kind of stupid New Year's resolution?"

"No, just a matter of staying out of jail. The SBI is starting to show up around here and Crockett's having to make some busts."

"And you're really going back to work at that Seven-Eleven?"

"It'll do for now," Leonard said.

"You could make as much money picking up drink bottles on the side of the road," Dena said, and laughed derisively.

"Maybe you could pick up bottles to pay for your pills then," Leonard replied.

Dena shook her head.

"You're not keeping up your end of our bargain. I didn't come here for this crap."

Travis rose from the couch and stepped between them. He spoke to Dena, his voice soft.

"Maybe you could just quit using those pills."

Dena stared at Travis a moment.

"I'm the only one who hasn't told you how to live your life," Dena said. "I'd think you'd do the same for me." Dena clutched the bag tighter, enough to where her knuckles whitened. "The hell with both of you."

Dena went into the back room and slammed the door, the sound reverberating through the trailer. For a few moments neither Travis nor Leonard moved. Then Travis sat down and began working again. He wrote an answer but immediately erased it.

"I don't get this one."

"Give me your pencil," Leonard said, and wrote the solution's first three steps in the margin. "Here's where you messed up."

"How?"

"You tell me."

Travis peered at the problem intently.

"I still don't see what I did wrong. The formula says the area of the triangle is equal to half the base multiplied by the height."

"Except that's not what you've done," Leonard said.

Travis leaned his head closer, squinted his eyes as if farsighted.

"Don't look at the problem," Leonard said. "Just go through the formula."

Then Leonard saw it happen, as he had numerous times, something not just mental but physical, the boy's shoulders loosening, eyes coming on in understanding like a pilot light.

"I multiplied by the hypotenuse, not by the height," Travis said, writing down the correct answer.

Dena had turned off the light in the back room by the time they'd finished. Travis marked his place in the workbook as Leonard lifted himself from the recliner and went over to turn down the thermostat. The furnace rattled a last time, became silent as Travis unraveled lights from the Christmas tree.

"I went to the library during my lunch break yesterday," Travis said. "I looked up the rolls for the Sixty-fourth."

"Why'd you do that?" Leonard asked.

"I was hoping to find a Toomey on the list. Their folks seemed the type that would have done such meanness. It would give me another reason to hate them."

"But Toomey wasn't on there, was it?"

"No, but lots of names you'd recognize as being from around here. Names like Revis and Candler and Evans. And Allen and Keith. Those sons-of-bitches' names were on there of course."

"People long dead," Leonard said. "Whatever they did, they did it themselves, not their descendants."

Travis lifted the tree but paused.

"So you're saying it shouldn't matter to anyone anymore whether your family did the killing or was killed?"

"No more philosophical arguments tonight," Leonard said,

and went to the bedroom and undressed. The heat had been lowered only five minutes earlier but it was already noticeably colder. Leonard lay down and listened, as quiet a night as any he could remember. No barred owl or phoebe voicing the trees, no dog or fox claiming the dark. Even the wind appeared to succumb to the cold, stalled in the air like garments stiffened on a clothesline.

That August afternoon when he'd called, Kera had told him not to come. She'd remarried by then, her husband in the Economics department at UNC-Charlotte, a visiting professor from Australia. That was the key word, visiting. Leonard coming would make leaving harder for Emily, Kera had told him. If he'd believed that was true, Leonard wouldn't have done what he did, decide at 3 A.M. to drive the hundred and thirty miles to where his daughter slept. Sleeping for the last time on the same continent as her father—that was what he told himself as he drove.

He'd parked down the street, keeping close to forsythia and hedges because first light already seeped into the eastern sky. The morning bustle of the suburbs gearing up for jobs and carpools had yet to begin, and the neighborhood was momentarily so tranquil Leonard believed he heard his own heart as he approached his daughter like a thief. He'd found her room and tapped the glass. Emily woke slow and must have thought herself still dreaming when she saw her father's face peering through the window's mullions. He motioned for her to open the window and she had, but only enough that they could speak.

I don't think you're supposed to be here, Emily had said, her face inches from his but separated by glass. He thought Emily might not let him come inside and they'd communicate as if in a prison visitation room. But after a few moments she'd opened the window. They'd sat on her bed, side by side in the attitude of travelers, but all that moved was time, its seconds ticking away on Emily's bureau as she told about the goodbye party at her elementary school, the beach they'd live near in Australia. *Soon,* he said when Emily asked when he'd come to see her.

It was only when he heard an alarm clock ringing that Leonard said anything approaching what he'd come to say, telling Emily that he knew she might be a little scared moving to a new place but that was how everybody felt. He told her she'd make new friends in Australia, maybe see a real live koala bear. Leonard told her he loved her and always would and then tucked her back in bed. He had not seen her since.

LEONARD DROVE TO THE TOOMEYS' FARMHOUSE THE NEXT morning. He could have called Carlton, but Leonard knew it was better this way. A matter of respect. When he got out of the car, he paused to look at the empty pasture, beyond it the rich bottomland that had once been planted in tobacco. Nothing grew there now but weeds and wire grass, some kudzu in the upper portion casting out its first tendrils from the field edge. More and more farmland was like this, either abandoned or razed to build vacation and retirement homes.

The green pickup was nowhere in sight, and Leonard wondered if just one or both of the Toomeys were gone. He climbed up the steps and was about to knock when Carlton opened the door, a pencil in his massive right hand. The black reading glasses the older man wore made him look almost scholarly despite the overalls and gray bristle on his chin.

"About to figure you to have got another partner, professor," Carlton said as they sat down at the kitchen table. A newspaper lay on the table, folded to the crossword puzzle's page. Only two lines remained blank. Carlton took off his glasses and placed them beside the paper.

"Don't tell nobody you caught me with a newspaper," Carlton said. "It's an amazing thing. You get a fellow convinced he's smarter than you and he'll pretty much open up his billfold and give you whatever you ask for. Especially them from Charlotte and Atlanta."

He pushed back his chair to get up.

"You wanting the usual?"

"No," Leonard said, trying to keep his voice matter-of-fact. "I'm not going to deal anymore."

A flicker of irritation, maybe anger, creased Carlton's face, gone so quickly Leonard wondered if he'd imagined it. The big man eased back into his chair, saying nothing for a few moments.

"Well, if that's what you want to do," Toomey said. His tone revealed neither pleasure nor displeasure, but his eyelids sagged, as if he were suddenly sleepy.

"Yes," Leonard said. "That's what I want."

"OK, then," Carlton said. "Mind if I ask you why? I'm kind of curious."

"Just getting out while I'm ahead. Crockett's starting to make some busts."

"You might notice none of them folks worked with me, professor. That ain't no coincidence." Carlton shifted his body, leaned back in the chair. "So be it. You done good work for me, for yourself too. I figure you to have quite a good nest egg, probably over ten thousand. That'll tide you over for a while."

"More like half that," Leonard said, pushing back the chair. "I guess I better be going."

Ribs that had felt pulled taut as a child's shoelaces loosened as he stood. More air filled Leonard's lungs and the oppressive sense of confinement lifted. Toomey put his glasses back on and peered at the crossword puzzle. He didn't look up as he spoke.

"You know a seven-letter word for error?"

The answer should have been obvious, but almost a minute passed before it came to Leonard.

"Mistake," he said.

Toomey pointed at the word penciled into the squares.

"I figured it out too," Toomey said, "and a whole lot quicker than you did."

ELEVEN

It was Travis's idea to visit Shelton Laurel on the massacre's anniversary. Snow had fallen all night, half a foot by noon, but that made the boy only more determined. It will be just like the day it happened, he told Leonard. Travis didn't have chains so they strapped Leonard's on the Buick's tires and drove north, first to Antioch to pick up Lori.

"That's it," Travis said, and Leonard stopped where a rusty mailbox squatted on a cedar post. There was no driveway, just a bare spot by the house where a decade-old Mercury Comet was parked, no hubcaps and no radio antenna, a wadded rag in place of a gas cap. Leonard had known Lori's family was poor, but he was still surprised. If smoke had not been rising from the chimney, someone driving by could easily believe the place had long been ceded to whatever crawled or slithered through the cracks. The rust-rotted gutter had separated from the roof soffit, and blue plastic tarp replaced glass in a window. Out in the yard, a doll without arms, a tricycle with a missing back wheel. Nothing seemed whole.

The door opened and Lori came out, cautiously traversing the snowy steps. She wore a worsted wool coat short in the sleeves, the top button missing. A hand-me-down from her mother or an aunt, Leonard knew, the scuffed barn boots and mustard-colored scarf as well. All purchased by someone too worn down by life to take much stock in her appearance. The jeans alone looked to be something Lori picked out herself.

She closed the door and squeezed in beside Travis, took off her mittens, and pressed both palms against the heater's vent.

"Momma says we haven't any more sense than shirttail young'uns to be out in weather like this," Lori said. "She about didn't let me come."

"Well, I'd agree with her," Leonard said, "but your boyfriend insisted."

They recrossed the French Broad and followed its tributary westward. Leonard drove slow, keeping to the side of his lane farthest from the drop-offs. There were few guardrails, for the most part nothing but loose gravel between road edge and gorge. White covered the rocks sprouting up in the stream, skimmed the pools and slow runs. The road narrowed where a granite outcrop loomed above, its jutting chin lengthened with pale beards of ice. Snowflakes settled on the windshield like miller moths, the gray sky so low it seemed to be resting its belly on the ridgetops.

"How long has your family been in Antioch?" Leonard asked.

"Daddy's people came over from Tennessee after the Civil War. Momma's family didn't get up here till the nineteen thirties."

"Where's your momma's family from?"

"Down near Shelby. Momma says her daddy got tired of hot weather, said if he and his family were going to starve they might as well not be miserable hot while doing it."

Leonard laughed. "I guess he had a point."

"What about your people, Leonard?" Travis asked. "They been up here long?"

It was a question Leonard had anticipated for months, but he still stammered slightly as he replied.

"The Shulers came from Swain County in the 1890s," he said.

"Probably a good thing for both your families," Travis said. "If they'd been on the Union side there's no telling what kind of terrible things would have been done to them."

"It happened to Confederate sympathizers as well," Leonard reminded Travis. "Nance Franklin had three of her sons killed right in front of her by Union troops. They made her watch them die."

Lori shook her head.

"It must have been awful up here."

"I can't believe there was a worse place to be for either side," Leonard said. "If you lived near Bull Run or Shiloh at least the armies moved on after the battles. Here it settled in for four years."

"They were still fighting even after Lee surrendered," Travis told Lori. "A fellow bragging about some meanness he'd done in Shelton Laurel got shot dead over a year after the war ended. That happened down at Mars Hill, right Leonard?"

"Right," Leonard said, and glanced over at Lori. "Bet you didn't know your boyfriend was one of the world's leading experts on the Civil War in Madison County."

"I'm beginning to believe it," Lori said. "We just have to make sure he knows enough math so he won't have to do remedial courses at Tech."

Lori looked out the window and didn't see Travis's face redden or hear the muttered obscenity. The boy didn't understand. Travis thought Lori was just being bossy, but Leonard knew it was more than that because he'd gone to high school with girls who came from similar homes and wore similar hand-me-downs. Like Lori they'd learned early on that any hope for a good life lay in a series of carefully planned steps, with no margin for error. They always did their homework and kept themselves out of backseats on dates, knowing if they didn't they'd end up with lives as tough and hopeless as their mothers, old women by age forty. A-B Tech hadn't existed then, so they'd worked especially hard in typing and shorthand classes to get clerical jobs in Marshall and Asheville. Over the years Leonard had run into several of these former classmates. They were always friendly enough but there was a certain hardness in their eyes, as if believing what they'd worked so hard to have could be snatched away in an instant.

They met only one vehicle after they entered Shelton Laurel, a pickup whose bed was loaded with pewter milk canisters. A few final flurries lit on the windshield as they made the last turn, passing the white clapboard church and the mailboxes with *Shelton* printed on them. Some of the mailboxes had red flags up, expectant. Leonard turned off the road and parked. He glanced over at Travis and saw the anger had dissipated. The boy's moods changed so quickly they seemed to never quite stabilize. Mercurial, that was the word for Travis's temperament.

"I guess you want to go to the meadow first," Leonard said.

"Yes," Travis said. "You want me to carry the machine?"

"No, I'll get it. I don't know how it'll work in the snow, but we can try."

Travis and Lori went on ahead, holding hands as they made their way down to the meadow. The boy's leg appeared to be almost healed, only the slightest limp discernible now. Travis slipped and pulled Lori down with him and they got up laughing. Leonard followed, the metal detector in his right hand.

His Grandfather Candler had brought him here two weeks before Leonard left for his freshman year at Chapel Hill. A Sunday afternoon, his grandfather was still dressed in his church clothes. They had not come down a ridge or on the blacktop two-lane but followed a rhododendron-flanked skid trail that ended on the creek's far side. They parked the truck and crossed a foot log where the creek ran slow and deep. His grandfather stood in the meadow's center and waited as Leonard walked over to the roadside and read the marker. Leonard had known some killing had occurred up here during the Civil War, something people didn't like to talk about much, but only when he read the marker's inscription did he know exactly what.

"I wanted you to know about this from your own people

before you learned some other way," his grandfather told him. "My father's father, your great-great-grandfather, was Joshua Candler. He was in the Sixty-fourth."

"So he helped kill them?" Leonard asked.

"I don't know that, if you mean did he actually shoot any of them, but he was here when it happened, and he knew every man and boy who did get killed that morning." His grandfather had paused, then spoke, his voice softer. "Before the war, he was their doctor."

They didn't speak for a few minutes, just stood in the meadow as a breeze moved through, brushing the broom sedge as if it were the mane of some huge golden animal. Surely there were sounds of insects and birds, but all Leonard remembered was how the wind seemed to be saying *hush, hush, hush,* calming the meadow.

It was Leonard's grandfather who broke the silence.

"You know a place is haunted when it feels more real than you are," the old man said, and began walking back toward the creek.

Leonard followed.

"I've got his journals and I'm giving them to you soon as we get back to the house," his grandfather said as they walked. "You'll learn things in them related to what happened here, but there's another reason I want you to have them. Your smarts didn't just spring up like a daisy in a bunch of hogweed. There's been smart folk in this family before. You read those entries and you'll see what I mean. Knowing that ought to confidence you some when you're down there at the university."

When they'd left the meadow his grandfather did a curious

thing. They didn't cross on the foot log but walked through the creek, a place thirty yards downstream where the water ran fast and thin. Leonard asked why. Because a ghost can't cross quick-moving water, his grandfather had answered matter-of-factly.

Lori shrieked as Travis aimed a snowball at her. She turned and the snowball hit the back of her coat. They were near the marker and Lori chased after Travis, both of them falling and laughing, Travis finally stopping and raising his hands in surrender. Leonard set down the metal detector, wondering why he'd bothered to bring it. The machine sank into the snow, only part of the disk above the white leveling.

The Sunday afternoon his grandfather gave him the ledgers, Leonard had laid the sixteen volumes on his bed. The mattress's middle sagged under the weight and there was barely room to prop himself against the headboard. The bed seemed precarious as an overloaded barge. Leonard had read the volumes in chronological order. At first there had been no observations other than what was relevant to Doctor Candler's duties, but that changed as the months passed. The ledgers began to include more than just his patients' complaints: tonics learned from a Cherokee midwife, a description of a bear hunt, a poignant note about an infant whose mother had died. Other comments confirmed that Joshua Candler's book learning had not stopped when he'd left Chapel Hill, including a note about the purchase in Asheville of *The Collected Plays of William Shakespeare*. An intelligent man. You saw that in the way he began questioning treatments learned in his two terms at the Louisville Medical Institute. He was, in the parlance of the day, a botanic physician, a small group of healers best known for their use of plant remedies and their refusal to bleed patients.

It had been after midnight when Leonard opened the 1863 ledger, soon coming to the January 17 entry, at the bottom of the page the word *Others*. Even now, two decades later, Leonard remembered the moment he'd turned the page—the dusty closed-closet odor of the paper and the leather binding, the way the lamp's soft light nestled on the bed. Most of all how quiet it had been, everyone else asleep, the only sound the grandfather clock in the hall dripping its seconds as he lay there among more time, days and months and years of it. On the next page was only whiteness. At first Leonard thought the page had been accidentally skipped and turned to the next and found the January 19 entry noting the continuing treatment of several men for frostbite. But no mention of the prisoners or of Shelton Laurel. He'd examined the ledger's concertina fold carefully. No January 18 entry had been torn or cut out.

"I'll be up there in a minute," Travis said, his words shouted to Lori but breaking Leonard out of his reverie. Leonard turned around and watched Lori trudge up the ridge.

"She was cold," Travis explained when he joined Leonard. "I told her to go get warm in the truck." The boy took a hard plastic case from his coat pocket, removed the silver-framed glasses. Travis lifted each wire temple slowly before walking to the creek edge where the men had been massacred. He turned and faced Leonard before rubbing the lens with his handkerchief, setting the temples on his ears and pushing the bridge higher on his nose. The boy stuffed his hands back in his coat pockets for warmth.

"They're too tight to be a good fit for my head," Travis said. "But they could fit David Shelton."

A snowflake stuck to the one lens and the boy delicately brushed it away. He squinted his left eye. "It's kind of blurry, like looking through water, but I can see you well enough." Travis opened his left eye. "David Shelton could have been looking through these glasses when they shot him. Standing right where I'm standing."

For a few moments the boy appeared transfixed, not wiping away the snow that thatched his hair and lay on his shoulders like epaulets. Leonard gazed across the creek at a white oak, an old tree a good fifty feet high, its branches gray and skeletal. Leonard imagined the rings inside the oak, the darker whorls for the winter when growth slowed, the lighter wider ones of summer's expansion, all spiraling back into the past, maybe as far as 1863. The flurries increased, flakes big as the lens Travis peered through. Snow spread clean and level over the meadow. Maybe a blank page was all history could be in the end, he thought, something beyond what could be written down, articulated.

Travis took off the glasses.

"I'm going on up. We'll be in the truck or at the grave."

"I'll be there in a few minutes," Leonard said.

"You going to sweep some?"

"No."

Travis came over and handed the glasses and case to Leonard.

"What am I supposed to do with them?"

"Put them on. It's kind of hard to explain, but it makes you feel different being here. Closer to it somehow."

The boy moved on up the ridge as Leonard stepped across the meadow and stood by the creek. White drifts and ice narrowed its banks, the water quiet and dark. Snowflakes fluttered into the creek, lit the creek's surface a moment and dissolved. Ephemeral.

Lieutenant Keith's fourteen-year-old nephew had been shot and killed shortly after joining the 64th. The Shelton Laurel killings, especially the killing of David Shelton, could have been nothing more than a belief in Old Testament justice. But the treatment of the dead implied something more than mere retribution. A sergeant had danced on the bodies when they'd been dumped in a ditch, vowing to push them into hell. By the time kin had gotten to the meadow, wild hogs had eaten one man's head off. *The true object of war is the warrior's soul,* Simone Weil had claimed. Easy enough to believe here, Leonard thought.

Leonard turned from the creek. Snow filled footprints quickly now. What gray light the sky gave made the ground appear unmarked, no footprints, no squirrel or rabbit tracks. He stepped into the meadow, the snow shushing under his boots.

Lieutenant Keith and Colonel Allen had chosen this open area deliberately, for they knew eyes watched from nearby cliffs and ridges. The killings were a performance for the men who hadn't been captured, a warning acted out like a play. And what role for a man who'd been against secession yet had not fled to Tennessee with his first cousin to join the Union forces? A man who had not volunteered for the Confederate army but had been conscripted, evidently letting his allegiance be decided by which side first chose to place its claim on him. Several of the prisoners begged for time to pray, but Keith had only raised his sword in response, then let it slice the air to loose the first volley.

Leonard suddenly felt lighter, less substantial, as though the meadow were absorbing his very being. He looked down at his hand, making sure the glasses hadn't slipped free. They were still there, held loosely as if he'd captured some small fragile creature. His hand tightened so fingers as well as palm could feel the glasses' solidity. Leonard no longer knew if his eyes were open or closed. For a few moments the glasses seemed the one thing keeping him in the world. Then gravity resettled on his shoulders, replanted his feet firmly on the ground. He felt the snowflakes brushing his face, the cold working its way under his coat collar.

According to the *New York Times* article, David Shelton had been killed after his father and three brothers. The boy had seen his father shot in the face and begged the soldiers not to do the same to him. At first they hadn't, by accident or design shooting him in both arms. He continued to plead for his life until a bullet hit something vital. Then they dragged him over to lie with the others, probably by the feet, not noticing or caring when the glasses slipped from his face.

Leonard opened his palm, held the glasses a few moments as if measuring their weight. He did not raise them to his face so he might see this place through their silver frames. Instead, he walked up the ridge, pausing once to look back at his footprints fading behind him. Footprints that morning in 1863 as well, veering off Knoxville Road and into this meadow. Afterward thirteen fewer sets of prints walking out than had walked in.

Travis and Lori waited at the grave site. He handed the glasses to Travis, who placed them back in the case. The wind blew harder on the ridge and Leonard tugged his lapels tighter around his neck. Travis or Lori had brushed snow off the grave marker, but the names quickly disappeared again.

"We better go," Leonard said, turning away from the grave. "I don't want us on these roads in the dark."

The snow had quit by the time he and Travis dropped Lori off. On the western ridges, a band of intense pink-orange light singed trees stark and black. The light seemed to flatten out beyond the horizon, as if its source were more earth than sky. They drove south, talking little. When they got to the trailer, Travis's truck was there but Dena wasn't. Leonard went to the bedroom and found the bottom drawers open and empty, all her clothes and toiletries taken from the bathroom.

"It was wrong for her not to let us know she was leaving," Travis said, visibly upset. The boy went to see what kind of vehicle had taken her away, but snow had erased the tire tracks. He came back inside and searched for a note. But there was no note.

Leonard's only surprise was that Dena had stayed long as she had.

March 23, 1863, Clinton, Tennessee

*Robert Winchester dead of scarlet fever. The wonder is he hath
endured so long.*

Jesse Harmon. Flux. Treated with tea made of blackberry root.

Tyler Matheson. Flux. Same treatment.

*Thomas Jenkins. Coriza. Fever abated. Pallor much more
sanguine.*

Lamar Davis. No fever. Laudable pus.

*Recommended Harmon and Matheson relieved of duty.
Recommended Davis returned to duty.*

*Hard snow after midnight brought a sight this morning that
shall never dim in my memory. Waked by a vexing dream at first
light, I arose and perused our campsite. In the clearing where
men had bedded down, there was to be seen only unmoving,
white mounds. I could not allay the sensation that I stood before
fresh, unsettled graves and for a few moments it seemed everyone
on earth save I alone was dead. Then the officers stirred from
their tents at the clearing's edge. Isaac Ponder blew his bugle,
and I watched the land tremble alive as men rose in the whiteness
as though arrayed in the fine linen of the righteous on the world's
last day.*

TWELVE

On the first Thursday in April, Travis waited in a windowless basement classroom to begin the GED exam. His stomach felt queasy. Despite six months of studying, he feared everything learned might slip from his grasp quick as a trout returned to water. Two women who looked to be sisters sat in the back. Another woman, much older, was on the front row, her long gray hair pulled tight into a bun. A heavyset man sat closest to Travis. It wasn't just the overalls and black-rimmed fingernails that made clear the man's livelihood. The odor of turned-up earth and spring onions clung to him, reminding Travis it was planting time. The room was warm and the farmer used a balled-up handkerchief to dab perspiration off his forehead. Then he opened the bib pocket on his overalls and set a pair of glasses and a pocket watch on the desk. The watch made a soft click as it sprang open.

In a few minutes a man came in carrying a cardboard box. He introduced himself as Mr. Atwell and passed out pencils and the first test before going over the instructions so meticulously Travis felt like an idling engine about to overheat. Finally Mr. Atwell set a stopwatch on the Formica desk. "Open your booklets and begin," he said.

Travis did what Leonard told him to do—read each question slow and not guess unless he'd narrowed the answer to two possibilities, focus on each question the same way he'd focus before casting a lure or squeezing a trigger. Most of the questions were so easy Travis wondered if some were trick questions that merely seemed obvious. He finished every test but the math, three problems to go when Mr. Atwell called time.

"How'd you do?" Leonard asked as they walked outside to Travis's truck.

Travis rolled his head in a slow circle and heard a soft crackling in his neck. The sun was so bright he lowered his gaze. It felt like he'd spent the morning chained up in a dungeon.

"The math was pretty tough, but I tried to do what you said, narrow to two and guess. I was pretty nervous at first."

"That's natural."

"At least I got the one right about two points being equidistant from a central axis."

"I'm glad we went back over that one last night," Leonard said.

They got in the truck. Three pages stapled together lay on the passenger seat, *State Employment Application* at the top of the page, beside it a brown paper bag.

THE WORLD MADE STRAIGHT

"That the application for the library job?" Travis asked.

"Yes, I filled it out while I waited."

Leonard opened the bag.

"I went and got you some lunch," he said, and handed Travis a hamburger and Coke. "Go ahead and eat. You have to be hungry after four hours in there."

He ate the hamburger while Leonard perused the application. The farmer came out of the building and sat on a bench, took out a pack of rolling papers and a tobacco tin. He tapped out his tobacco and expertly rolled a cigarette.

Travis finished the Coke and drove out of the parking lot. Travis thought about a question he hadn't been able to answer. It was the one formula he and Leonard had not gone over, one that dealt with consecutive positive integers. Too late to fret over it now, he told himself.

"How long before you get the results?" Leonard asked.

"Mr. Atwell said since there were just five of us he'd have them graded by the end of the afternoon, but the results wouldn't be mailed till next week. That big farmer was about to bust a gut to know how he did. He fussed so much about having to wait a week that Mr. Atwell finally said we could call him at home." Travis pulled the piece of paper from his pocket with the number written on it. "We can call after six."

The temperature was only in the mid-sixties, but as they drove out of the lot Travis rolled down the window. He smelled the plowed earth and wondered if he would ever stand in a tobacco field again or spend minutes with his hands under a spigot rubbing off tobacco resin. His daddy was one of the few growers who still wove his plants into thirteen-leaf bunches, what the old-timers called hands. Near any jackleg can grow corn and the like, his daddy often said, but there's got to be pride in you to grow tobacco right. Spread on the market floor, those knit bundles had been irrefutable testimony to their devotion and hard work, *their* pride, his as well as his father's. The buyers from Winston-Salem and Durham who gathered in the auction barn acknowledged as much, always paying a little more for his daddy's crop. Some of the older buyers claimed they could pick out Harvey Shelton's burley blindfolded, that it had a richer smell.

If he'd passed the test, Travis could have pride in something else, not just for graduating high school but how he'd done it living on his own and holding down a full-time job. The old man might not care about the degree, had never cared much for what he'd called book learning, but he'd have to admire the effort it took.

"You mind if we stop by the library?" Leonard asked when they came to the Mars Hill turnoff. "I got to drop off this application."

"Fine by me," Travis said.

The librarian nodded at them familiarly when they came inside. The main library in Marshall contained a lot more books, but Travis liked this library better because it was less crowded. He could wander the stacks without bumping into other people, find a corner and not hear so much as a whisper while he read. It made him feel like every book had been placed on the shelves just for him.

"Did you bring your paperwork?" the librarian asked Leonard.

Travis was in the stacks, but he peered through an empty shelf as Leonard laid the papers on the desk.

"It's not a great job, mainly shelving books and haggling over fines," the librarian warned, "but like I said last week, if you're willing to take some library science classes over at Western Carolina it could lead to a good position, one with full benefits."

"Anything else I need to do?"

"No, just be ready to start May fifteen."

The librarian placed the papers in a drawer.

"Have you talked to the folks at Western?"

"Yes," Leonard said. "They offer a class this summer which meets once a week, in the fall a night class that does the same."

"Good. That will make it easy to work them around your library schedule."

"I appreciate all your help," Leonard said, "not just getting this job but the other things."

"Did the phone numbers I got you help any?" the librarian asked.

"Yes," Leonard said. "They were very helpful."

"Well, if you're going for a visit down under, make sure you're back by the fifteenth."

"I'll do that," Leonard said.

"I'd think a plane ticket to Australia would be awfully expensive," Travis said when they were back in the truck.

"I've got enough money saved up," Leonard said. "Now that I have the library job I can put in my week's notice at the store."

"How long you plan to be gone?"

"I don't know for sure but I'll be back by May fifteenth. I figured you could take care of the dogs while I'm gone."

"I guess I can," Travis said. He wondered if Leonard was going to bring his daughter back for the summer and, if so, whether he'd still be welcome at the trailer. Leonard's daughter coming didn't seem real likely—after all, who'd look after the girl while Leonard worked—but he couldn't be certain, especially close-mouthed as Leonard got whenever Travis asked about her.

Leonard was changing, changing in good ways, but somehow it still bothered Travis. He glanced out the window, the trees a green blur. The winter had been slow, as if cold weather could clog up time, but now everything was speeding up. Not just Leonard but everything was changing. In two months Lori would be out of high school, and she was talking more and more about starting Tech not in the fall but this summer. His passing the GED, if he'd passed it, was another good thing, maybe the best thing he'd ever done in his life. But the sheer unfamiliarity of all that was happening felt like more than he could get hold of.

When they pulled up to the trailer, Travis did not get out. It was a cool day for spring, the kind of day older folks called red-bud winter. The sun was out though, and inside the cab the sun soaked him like a warm bath. He'd taken the whole day off from work and thought he might drive up to Spillcorn Creek. He hadn't fished since fall, and it would be good to feel the water pulsing against his legs, even better to feel that moment a trout hit, that jolt running from his wrist up his arm and all the way to his brain, as if the current was not water but electricity. At that instant, before you could measure the heft by how much the rod bent or the whir of the drag, you didn't know if that trout was no longer than your hand or the biggest of your life.

But this felt good too, just being in a truck that wasn't going anywhere. Not having to do a thing but sit and feel the sun. Travis closed his eyes and soon heard water. He stood before a creek, one he'd seen before but never fished. Speckled trout swam in the stream, some over a foot long, the red spots on their flanks big as buttons. Travis knew this somehow, but when he peered into the water he couldn't see them. *Where are they?* he asked aloud, because he knew there was someone with him, someone who could see the trout. *You need these,* the boy beside him said, and handed him the glasses. *Put them on and close your left eye, like as if you was a-sighting something to shoot.* Travis saw them then, the speckled trout curving their bodies with the current as though they had been woven into the water the same way a bright design was woven into a wool bedspread. The boy spoke softly. *You'd have not likened them to be that pretty, would you?*

When Travis awoke the sun had disappeared behind Brushy Mountain. For a few moments he thought he still heard the creek, but it was only wind whispering through the trees. His neck ached from slumping against the driver-side window. He checked his watch and went inside. Leonard was reading but closed the book when Travis came in.

"I came out there, but you looked so sacked out I didn't want to wake you," Leonard said. "A test that long would exhaust anyone."

"I guess so," Travis said.

"You plan to call right at six?" Leonard asked.

"Yes."

"Good, because I have to be at the store by seven. I'd like to know before I leave." Leonard checked the alarm clock beside the couch. "I guess I'll have to buy one of those since I'll soon be working mornings."

"Wouldn't hurt to have a calendar either," Travis said. He sat down on the couch and untied his tennis shoes. "I'm going to take a shower. I was sweating like a stuck pig in that classroom."

He took his time, let the warm spray massage his stiff neck. For a few moments Travis was able to close his eyes, let his mind drift as if on a slow, easeful current. He remembered the speckled trout in his dream, how it seemed it wasn't water that made the stream flow but the trout themselves, the water merely a larger fluid skin the fish carried with them.

After getting dressed, Travis came back into the front room and picked up a magazine, but his mind strayed from the words. His earlier fears that some of the questions had only appeared to be easy returned. The fifth time he checked his watch it was finally six o'clock. He dialed the number and got a busy signal. Bet that farmer is on the line, he told himself. The second time he got through.

"I passed," Travis said when he'd put down the phone.

"Congratulations," Leonard said. "This is something you should be real proud of."

They exchanged an awkward handshake.

"I'm going to drive down to the café and tell Lori," Travis said, already getting up from the table.

Leonard smiled.

"You could call her as easily."

Travis blushed.

"I guess so. I kind of wanted to tell her in person."

"I'm just teasing you," Leonard said. "You should tell her in person."

Travis took the truck keys from his pocket.

"We'll need to celebrate," Leonard said, his smile widening. "Lori too. You know you wouldn't have done this without her whipping you into shape. Right?"

"I guess," Travis said.

"We'll go eat at Jackson's tomorrow night," Leonard continued. "Lori could get off, couldn't she?"

"Probably. Amy owes her a night."

"Good," Leonard said, looking out the window. "By the way, when I went over to Western Carolina last week I didn't just talk to the people in library science. I talked to an admissions counselor about you. You can get in with a GED, even get financial aid and work-study money. That and a Pell grant and you could go to Western next fall. Lori could do the same."

"That's supposing I'd want to go, ain't it," Travis said. He gripped the keys tighter. Not even one night to celebrate the GED without somebody expecting more. Travis wondered if there'd ever be one time in his life when someone would just say "great job" and leave it at that.

"Of course," Leonard said, sounding like the decision made no difference to him one way or another.

The casual tone made Travis angrier, as if the older man didn't think him smart enough to catch on, wouldn't remember that Leonard had brought it up in the first place. Travis realized that it might well be the same if he went to see Lori, her talking about A-B Tech. Or maybe Western Carolina. For all Travis knew Leonard and Lori had already been talking together about Western. He thought of how Leonard had made plans to take classes come summer, Lori talking about going to summer school at Tech as well. It was like he'd just crossed the finish line in one race, a long hard race, and Leonard and Lori were already in a new race, expecting him to catch up.

"You're right," Travis said, putting the keys back in his pocket. "No sense driving all the way down there when I can call. Anyway, it ain't no big deal." Travis waited for Leonard to correct his grammar, but Leonard didn't. Instead, he turned from the window and looked directly at Travis.

"Look," Leonard said, "I'm not trying to push you into something, but you need to know some things are possible you might not have realized. If you decide you don't want those possibilities, that's fine. I just want you to be aware they're out there."

"OK," Travis muttered. The math workbook lay on the coffee table. He had only needed to do the problems in the first third of the workbook. Those had been hard enough. One night he'd tried to solve some of the problems in the last chapter. A bait-cast reel's backlash would have been easier to untangle.

"Regardless, not many people could have passed the GED without classes, and not that quickly either." Leonard smiled. "Western Carolina isn't something you have to think about tonight. Tonight just enjoy what you've accomplished."

That's what I was trying to do, Travis wanted to say. You're the one bringing up other stuff. Travis glanced over at the cardboard boxes that served as his chest of drawers. He wondered if there might be a pack of cigarettes in the bottom of one. He hadn't smoked a cigarette in months, but his mouth and lungs ached for one now.

June 17, 1863, Clinch River, Tennessee

William Pendley. Emesis. Eat goldenseal root every four hours.

Hubert McClure. Phthisic. Continue to smoke jimsonweed twice daily.

Percival Flowers. En route to Alabama for furlough. Applied fresh dressing to amputated arm. Poultice of peach leaves for stone bruise.
Insisted I take his yellowhammer feather for my hat as act of gratitude.

Ezra Blankenship. Bloody flux. Tea of blackberry leaves and roots. Tincture of valerian.

Robert Caldwell. Shot in forehead. Deceased.

Joshua Candler. Shot in lower bowel.
Much pain as God is just. Refuse anodynes. Want mind clear to pray for my soul, ask forgiveness for what cannot be hidden from my Maker. In Articule Mortis.

THIRTEEN

On Friday night when he went to pick up Lori, Mrs. Triplett hugged Travis and said how proud she was of him, though all the while making clear she believed it was Lori's doing as much as his. Travis supposed she couldn't help doing that, Lori being her daughter, but he'd been the one who'd sat all Saturday morning in the classroom and figured out the answers. Whenever he'd screwed up in his life, no one had ever stepped forward to share the blame, but now that he'd done something good, folks lined up to take credit.

"Lori's dressing up special pretty for you," Mrs. Triplett told him. "You might mistake her for one of them catalog models."

When Lori came out from the back room, Travis saw Mrs. Triplett wasn't exaggerating. Lori turned around slowly so he could see the emerald-green dress that matched her eyes, brightened her red hair. Lori's hairstyle was different too, bundled up but not in an old-lady way like his mother's, more like how Miss Davis, the prettiest teacher at the high school, wore hers. The lifted hair revealed her neck's whiteness. Lori's bare neck aroused him like seeing a partially exposed breast or thigh.

"Momma and I finished this dress last week," Lori said. "I wasn't going to wear it till the prom, but I decided tonight was too special not to."

As they were leaving, Mrs. Triplett handed him a five-dollar bill. "A graduation present," she said. "You buy you some fishing line and such so you can catch me another mess of trout."

When they got in the truck Lori slid close and kissed him, her tongue finding his. She shifted slightly, her left hand reaching up to press the back of his head so she could kiss him harder.

"There will be more of that later," she promised.

They drove down Highway 25 toward Marshall. The sun hid behind Brushy Mountain now, but enough light lingered to see redbuds and dogwoods blooming in the understory. The older fishermen swore trout didn't bite good until the dogwood petals fell off. Not too long, he thought. The five dollars would buy him new line and a couple of Panther Martins. Or maybe instead something to fish with for the big browns, like a Rapala or Johnson Silver Minnow.

When they pulled into the restaurant's parking lot, Travis saw his father's Dodge pickup parked beside Leonard's Buick.

"I invited your momma and daddy and sister, as a kind of surprise," Lori said. "Leonard said he thought that would be OK."

When Travis didn't respond Lori touched his shoulder.

"It is, isn't it?"

"Did you talk to Daddy or Momma?" he asked.

"Your momma. She was real nice on the phone, said she'd been wanting to meet me."

"And she said Daddy was coming too?"

"Yes. She said her and your sister and your daddy. Said they'd all come together."

Travis wondered if the old man would finally give him some credit, perhaps say he was proud of Travis or even apologize for slapping him. Not likely, Travis reckoned, for that wasn't his father's way. He'd no more admit being wrong about Travis than he'd admit being wrong about some particular of tobacco curing. But he'd come tonight, and that in itself said almost as much as any words. Maybe that was all the old man would ever give him.

It was full dark now, and stars winked above. For a few moments Travis did not move but studied the sky. The science book he'd read had a section on astronomy, and some of what he'd learned came to him now as he found Orion and the red dot below that was Mars. Lori took his hand and urged him toward the entrance.

Inside the light was muted, his eyes adjusting slowly. It took him a few moments to find the large table near the rear, brightly wrapped packages heaped at the table's center.

Leonard sat across from his mother and older sister. The chair at the head of the table was vacant and Travis wanted to laugh out loud at himself for thinking his father would come.

"There they are," Lori said, leading him to the table.

His mother and sister hugged him and told him how proud they were.

"Your daddy wanted to be here," his mother added soon as they sat down, "but you know how much farmwork there is this time of year."

The lie was so transparent Travis wondered why she even bothered to tell it.

"How come you-all drove his truck?" he asked.

It was Connie who answered.

"My car's in the shop."

"I'd of figured with all that farmwork he would have needed it," Travis said.

"He's mending fence," his mother said, not meeting his eyes.

"Must be hard to mend fence in the dark," Travis said.

No one spoke again until the waiter came to take their orders. Jackson's was the nicest restaurant he'd ever been in, candles on the tables and waiters dressed in white shirts and black vests. His mother and sister wore dresses and Leonard wore khakis and a maroon dress shirt. But he had on jeans and a flannel shirt. Travis figured everybody in the restaurant thought him some ignorant hick who didn't know any better.

"Why don't you open your presents," Lori said, and handed him two brightly wrapped gifts. He unwrapped the packages, found inside a blue dress shirt and a pair of brown slacks. He thought briefly of going into the bathroom and changing into the new clothes, but that seemed a stupid idea. People would notice he'd changed. He'd have no belt on either. The food finally came and his steak had no more flavor than a wad of kleenex. He wanted to ask for some ketchup, but that would be just one more way to make himself look backward.

"Let's go," Travis said, though Leonard and his mother still ate. "There's something I got to do."

His mother lowered her fork. "Long as it's been since me and you and your sister has set down together, I'd think you'd want to stay awhile."

"Your momma's right," Lori said, her face flushed red.

"Got to go now," Travis said, and gripped Lori's upper arm. He thought she might resist but she rose, telling his mother and sister how good it was to see them, about to say more except he pulled her away.

"That's a rude way of acting," Lori said as they got in the truck. "They did a special thing for you."

He shoved the truck into gear and headed up Highway 25.

"Where are we going?" Lori asked.

"To see my father, the one that has to work all day and all night. There's something I need to tell him."

"I know he hurt your feelings, but I don't think that's a good thing to do," Lori said.

"Well, I'm damn well doing it anyway," Travis said, not bothering to soften his voice.

They did not speak again until Travis drove onto the grass in the front yard, the truck's high beams aimed at the front door.

"Please don't do this," Lori said. She held her hands in her lap and her voice trembled.

The light was off in the living room but Travis could see the television's blue glow. He blew the horn and the front door opened. His father stepped onto the porch in his socks and a tee-shirt, suspenders hanging from the sides of his pants like lariats. Travis cut the engine but kept the lights on. The old man squinted to see better, craning his neck forward like an old tom turkey. Even got those saggy neck wrinkles, Travis thought. Just an old tom turkey strutting around trying to act big and important.

"I came to tell you something," Travis shouted, leaning his head out the window.

"Have you now," his daddy said, straightening up, stuffing hands in his back pockets. "Well ream it out then. I'm listening."

Lori touched his arm. "Please, Travis, let's go. I've got a gift I want you to open."

"I've done something you couldn't do," Travis shouted. "Did it on my own too."

"I expect you're ever so right about that," his daddy replied. "But I've got more pride than to hang my hat with some half-ass drug dealer." The old man paused. "I was of a mind to come haul you out of that trailer, but it wouldn't have done no good. Trash always settles back to the same place."

"I'm not trash. I never have been," Travis shouted back.

"I knowed you'd amount to nothing when you started getting into trouble in junior high, boy. If it hadn't of been for your momma I'd of kicked you out when you was sixteen. As for Leonard Shuler, he carries no more man inside him than a dog-turd butterfly."

"He's a better man than you," Travis said. "He's treated me better than my blood kin have."

"Please, Travis," Lori said, tugging his arm more insistently. "Let's go. You've said what you came to say."

A smile creased his father's face, the same look the old man might give a county agent offering advice on how to better grow his tobacco. "That's kindly ironic, ain't it," his daddy said, "him being a Candler and all. Educated as you are now, I'd figure you to know all about what happened up in the Laurel during the Confederate War. His momma's great-granddaddy helped kill off near every member of your family, but I don't guess he mentioned that to you, did he?"

For a few moments Travis's mind rejected his father's words. Then he remembered the name Candler on the 64th regiment's roll and how Leonard had never mentioned his mother's last name. Other things quickly surfaced as well— how Leonard had reacted when he'd first found out Travis was a Shelton and the fact that he knew so much about the massacre in the first place. It suddenly seemed obvious and Travis wondered if on some level he had suspected all along. It doesn't matter, he told himself, because it wasn't Leonard who'd done the killing. But if it didn't matter, why had Leonard not told him? Travis remembered the first time they'd discussed what had happened in Shelton Laurel, Leonard talking about the cold and snow and other hardships the killers had endured, like he was defending what they'd done.

"I don't understand," Lori said. "What's he talking about?"

The old man stepped closer to the porch edge.

"I didn't figure you to have no back sass to that," his father said. "I reckon the cat's got your tongue and run clear out of the county with it."

"He's still a better man than you and I am too," Travis shouted. "I'm a better man than you'll ever be and I've proved it by getting a GED. There's nothing you can say or do to change that either."

For a few moments Travis felt good, because unlike every other time in his life, he hadn't just taken what his father had dished out. He revved the engine so any reply the old man made would be drowned out. This time he'd have the last word.

They drove back toward Lori's but a mile from her house Travis turned off at the overlook where they had first kissed. He parked facing where the land broke off, opening to a deep far fall. A mile below, house lights flickered like stars reflected in the bottom of a well. For a few minutes he didn't say anything and for once Lori just let him be. He looked down at the lights in the valley. Fifteen miles by road but just one mile if you were a bird. Travis imagined how good it would feel to be a hawk and make a long circling drift down to those lights, leave behind everything tonight had laid on him.

Lori opened her pocketbook.

"Here's your present," she said. "The way you've been acting tonight I've a mind not to give it to you."

Travis didn't much care for her upbraiding him like that, but he accepted the small box wrapped in red and green Christmas paper.

"Sorry about the paper," Lori said. "It's all we had at the house."

Travis tore off the paper and opened the cardboard box. A silver cross and chain lay inside.

"It's to protect you when I'm not around," Lori said, clasping the chain to Travis's neck.

"You got anything else for me?" he asked, his arms keeping her close.

She kissed him, letting her tongue find his.

"More than that," Travis said, and cupped his hand on her breast. Lori didn't move his hand this time. She made a soft sound deep in her throat as he kissed her harder. It was only when he placed his hand on her inner thigh that she tensed and pushed him away.

"Now don't get rowdy and ruin a good night for us, boy," Lori said, her hands straightening her dress.

"It's been ruined already," Travis replied, "and it's more your fault than mine. You're the one invited him to the restaurant. You're the one who gave him another chance to show me up."

"I thought your daddy would be proud," Lori said. "He should have been."

"If you'd asked me I'd have told you better," Travis replied. "You think you always know what's best, don't you?"

"Why are you so mad at me?" Lori asked. "I was just trying to make tonight special for you."

Travis cranked the engine and pulled back onto the hardtop. He drove fast and when Lori told him to slow down he ignored her. He went off the road and onto the shoulder, gravel spraying behind them like shrapnel. Lori began crying, and he drove even faster. When they got to her house he kept the motor running as she got out and ran inside. He jerked the chain off his neck and threw it out the window.

Travis drove toward Marshall, taking the curves fast, the truck window all the way down now. He wanted to feel his speed, try to outrun every bad thing that had happened that night. As the tires squalled coming out of another curve, a raccoon appeared, eyes peaking through its black robber's mask at the loud rush of light bearing down upon it. The raccoon paused a moment, then scampered off the blacktop. A damn good thing too, Travis thought, because he wasn't slowing. Soon he passed the city limits sign. A yellow caution light flashed but he went on through without braking. Travis headed toward his friends, guys who'd been satisfied with the way he'd been and didn't hide things from him, and he couldn't get there quick enough.

He spotted Shank's Plymouth at the Gulf station and pulled beside it. Shank and Wesley sat on the Plymouth's front hood. For a few moments he sat in the cab, arms locked and hands on the steering wheel as if it were a divining rod that had yet to disclose what he searched for.

"I didn't figure a high-school graduate would want to mess around with us delinquents," Shank said when Travis got out.

"Go to hell," Travis said irritably.

"What's got your feathers all ruffled?" Shank asked.

Travis ignored the question.

"You got any beer?" he asked. "I got money to pay for it."

"Lord help us," Shank said. "Six months ago I was buying

from your roommate Leonard and now you're coming to me. Bad enough you two turned that trailer into a schoolhouse. I expect revival services next the way you two are headed."

Shank nudged Wesley.

"What you reckon, Wesley?"

"I figure as much," Wesley said. "Soon you all will be speaking in tongues, maybe catch some big old satinbacks and handle them like those folks up in Wolf Laurel." Wesley slid off the hood. "But I won't be joining you. The only snake I'm handling is this one I'm getting ready to piss out of."

As Wesley disappeared behind the station, Shank turned to Travis.

"So you still ain't answered what's bothering you, though I expect Lori has something to do with it." Shank lowered his voice. "You ain't knocked her up, have you?"

A bitter laugh welled up in Travis's chest and stomach. He choked it back down.

"No," Travis said.

"Well, that's a relief. Just keep that rubber on and you'll be fine."

"I don't need to worry about a rubber," Travis said, the whole evening's frustration in his voice. "Lori says she won't do it till we're married."

Shank whistled softly.

"Son, you're going to have the biggest set of blue balls in history."

Travis took Mrs. Triplett's five dollars from his pocket. "So you got anything or not? If you ain't got beer I'll take some pills, long as it ain't those damn black beauties."

"We got two six-packs on ice in the trunk. Got a pint of Rebel Yell too. Me and Wesley don't mind sharing with our old buddy." Shank nodded at the bill. "But we'll need more than old Abe there to get us some serious medicating."

"I got a whole paycheck in my billfold."

"That'll buy us some good pills," Shank said.

"But not black beauties," Travis reiterated.

"No, we're getting you some quaaludes. You're strung tight enough already."

Shank grinned, punched Travis in the shoulder as Wesley rejoined them.

"Travis is acting like himself again, Wesley. He's ready to raise some Cain."

"I ain't just going to raise some Cain," Travis said, trying to put some of the old strut back in his voice. "I'm going to raise a whole bumper crop. I got catching up to do."

"Listen at him," Shank said, his hand smacking the hood. "We best get a rope and hang on if we're to stay with him to-night."

"Damn right," Travis said.

"Well, let's go get it," Shank said. "Wesley knows a place that will take care of everything we're needing."

"Only if you got some real money," Wesley replied.

"Our boy here's got so much he can't hold it all in his wallet," Shank said, nodding at the bill in Travis's hand. "He just pulled five dollars from his front pocket like it was nothing more than a gum wrapper."

"Want me to drive?" Travis asked.

"No, we can take the Beast," Shank said, walking around to the trunk.

"Shotgun," Wesley said, and slid in the front seat while Travis crawled into the back. Shank got in, the six-packs clutched in his hands. As soon as he sat down, he began pulling cans from the plastic rings.

"Here," Shank said, handing Travis two cold cans of beer. "Those ought to mellow you out some."

Shank gave two to Wesley and kept two for himself, then set the other six-pack on the floorboard. The metal was slick and cold from being iced. Travis jerked the tab and heard the satisfying pop. He drank the beer in two long gulps and threw the can out the window.

Shank turned right at the next stop sign, and soon they crossed over the French Broad. Wesley shoved an Allman Brothers tape into the player and turned up the volume, the speakers on the panel behind Travis's head. All four windows were down. The Plymouth's headlights swept the trees on each curve, darkness regathering, closing behind them as though where they'd once been was forever gone. Maybe it is, Travis thought. And if that's so the hell with it.

He drank the second beer slower, felt the alcohol start to glow inside him. The music that had hurt his ears now seemed not loud enough and he shouted as much to Shank, who turned the volume up until the speakers shook. Travis leaned his head against the speakers. The opening bass lines of "Whipping Post" surged through his body. He thought about his father and how he hoped the bastard really was behind in his farmwork, because then the old man would realize how much Travis had done during spring planting. He imagined his father begging him to come back to the farm and help get the planting done, Travis telling the old man to kiss his ass.

He'd tell Lori the same thing if she called, tell her there were other girls he could date. One of the cashiers had been flirting with him for weeks and he knew for a fact she'd put out. Knew as well she wouldn't be telling him how to live every moment of his life.

Travis threw the second can out the window.

"Need me another one," he yelled.

Wesley turned.

"We ain't got but twelve beers for the three of us."

"Give me another beer or I'll crawl up there and get it my-self," Travis said.

He liked the way he sounded, tough and loud enough that Shank and Wesley couldn't ignore him.

"Give him a beer, Wesley," Shank said. "Travis gets every-thing he wants tonight. We still got that pint if we need it."

Wesley handed him another can. Shank took a curve hard and Travis slid against the door and spilled beer on himself. Shank and Wesley laughed.

"Damn it," Travis shouted. "I look like I pissed myself."

Travis finished the third beer, throwing the empty can into the front seat. Everything that had happened only a couple of hours earlier seemed years in the past now. He closed his eyes and let the music and the alcohol completely envelop him. It was like being inside a watery cocoon. When the Allman Brothers tape ended, Travis leaned forward.

"Put in that Skynyrd tape and forward it to 'Free Bird,'" Travis said. "And get me another beer."

Shank laughed.

"You heard the man, Wesley."

Travis opened the can and took a long drink, then leaned back and listened to Gary Rossington's slide guitar. He knew musicians called their guitars axes, and now Travis thought he understood why, because the guitar's hard sharp notes seemed to split open his skull so the music could pour in and wash everything else out of his head. When Ronnie Van Zant began singing, Travis sang along. It was like the lyrics had been written just for how he felt this night.

HE'D DRUNK FIVE BEERS BY THE TIME SHANK SLOWED AND they bumped up a dirt road. Travis had no idea where they were and didn't much care. Just riding around was good enough, the way the cool air blasted against his face, the music charging through him. He wanted to tell Shank and Wesley they were the best buddies a fellow could ever hope for and they should make a pact to be best friends the rest of their lives.

The Wildebeast jerked to a stop and Travis tumbled out of the backseat and onto the ground. He got up laughing and aimed himself toward the porch. Enough light shone from the farmhouse's front room to see the steps, the shadowy features of a car and a truck off to the left. The place was vaguely familiar and Travis wished he could see better. They stepped up on the porch.

"Who lives here?" he asked as Wesley knocked once and opened the door.

"Your rescuers," Shank said. "You're getting a chance to thank them by supporting their place of business."

Travis stepped back from the door.

"Whoa," Shank said, grabbing him by the arm.

Travis tried to rip free but lost his balance and fell.

"Help me, Wesley," Shank said, and grabbed Travis by the upper arm.

They led Travis into the front room and didn't let go of his arms until he was wedged between them on a sagging red-velvet couch. Carlton Toomey sat opposite them in a recliner, a bottle of Jack Daniels clutched in his massive hand. Hubert sat in a ladderback chair in the corner, attentively trimming his fingernails with a match end. A sixteen-ounce can of Schlitz Malt Liquor rested on the chair's arm. The way Travis's legs felt heavy and wobbly at the same time told him his body was drunk, but his mind felt clear as spring water.

"Him and his girl had a lover's spat," Shank said to the elder Toomey. "It's got him all out of sorts."

Carlton eased back in the recliner a little more.

"I can see that."

Shank pulled the last three beers from the plastic rings, handed Travis one.

"Maybe this will put some color back in you."

Travis pulled the tab and took a sip, then let the can rest on his upper leg. He could feel its condensation dampen the denim. He glanced at the door, mapped his way past the woodshed to the creek. If he could get that far, they'd never find him in the dark.

Carlton Toomey stared intently at Travis, shook his head. "I can't get over how you don't look nothing like your daddy."

"Maybe it was Leonard knocked his momma up," Hubert said. "And that's why he's living with him now."

Travis wished he had his rifle. He imagined how if he did they'd stop ragging him real quick. He lifted the can and drank deeply. His stomach lurched and he felt a sour rising in his throat but choked it back.

"I think we got him riled a bit," Hubert said.

"I got to piss," Travis said, and got up slowly so the room wouldn't spin.

"I'm going with you," Shank said when Travis headed to the front door instead of the bathroom. "You ain't about to sneak off on us."

They went out on the front porch and unzipped. Travis looked up at the stars as he made water. There'd been a hymn called "Will There Be Any Stars in My Crown?" he'd sung at church. He tried to remember the words, something about waking with the blessed in a mansion.

The alcohol was taking hold again, in a good, calming way. He could hear inside his head its faint mellow thrumming. A soothing yellow light beveled the edges of his vision. Making a run for the creek made less sense. If the Toomeys were going to do something besides make sport of him, they'd have already done it. Travis realized that maybe they were a little afraid of him. After all, he could still tell what really happened up here last summer to someone besides Leonard, could tell it to men who wore badges.

He and Shank zipped up and went inside. He lifted the beer and took a long swallow. Wesley had five one dollar bills in his hand.

"Give me ten dollars," Wesley said, and Travis did so. Wesley handed the money to Carlton.

"I always like it when a person pays up front for his drugs," Carlton said, stuffing the bills in his pocket.

"What are we getting?" Shank asked.

"Quaaludes," Wesley said.

"Get these boys their pills, and get that chicken out too," Carlton Toomey told his son. "All this socializing is making me hungry."

Hubert went into the middle bedroom, came back, and handed his father a crumpled brown paper bag. Carlton counted out the pills as Hubert lifted a cardboard bucket from the refrigerator. He laid the bucket of chicken on the coffee table, some paper plates and napkins as well. Carlton placed the pills on the coffee table, then put two pieces of chicken on a paper plate.

"Go take this to her," he said to Hubert.

"You all got a girl back there?" Shank asked.

Carlton nodded.

"Let him take it," Hubert said, motioning toward Travis. "I bet she'd like that. Might even want him to visit with her awhile."

Shank grinned at Travis. "Damn, boy. You might get all your problems solved tonight."

Shank and Wesley pulled Travis up from the couch and Hubert handed him the plate.

"Go get her, stud," Shank said.

Travis walked slowly down the hallway. Something bothered him. He thought it had to do with Lori but there was something else as well, something that wouldn't quite show itself. At the doorway he stopped and saw the single bare yellow bulb on the ceiling, the Venetian blinds covering the window, the same ladderback chair Carlton Toomey had sat in that afternoon last August. He stepped into the room and when he saw her on the bed he was surprised only for a moment.

Dena lay on a bedsheet pocked with yellow stains. All she had on was a pair of soiled panties and a bra. She was on her back, legs slightly open, one arm at her side and one raised like a swimmer. She seemed posed, like a mannequin in a store window. A green-yellow bruise spread over her left cheek. Her eyes were closed and he was grateful for that.

An odor like soured milk filled the room. Travis laid the plate on the bed. There was a trash can in the corner and he was just able to raise it to his mouth in time. Travis set it back down and wiped his mouth with his shirtsleeve. He looked over at the bed and saw Dena's eyelids had partially lifted, the eyes themselves dull, unfocused.

"What do you want," Dena said, the gap between her incisors adding a slight whistle to her slurred words.

Dena's right arm stretched behind her and he saw the baling twine that bound her wrist to the bedpost. A headache settled between his temples solid as an anvil. His stomach lurched again but there was nothing left to throw up.

"This is wrong," Travis said. It was the only thing he could think to say.

"Why?" Dena asked.

For a couple of minutes he could not answer. Too much had happened tonight to keep it all straight. Everything was out of kilter, the world off plumb. It was like being on a ride at the fair, everything loud and bright and swirling around him. And in that swirling the faces of Lori and his daddy and Leonard, glimpsed for a moment and then gone like wisps of smoke. He sat down on the bed and closed his eyes, but that just made the dizziness worse. For a terrifying instant Travis believed he might somehow still be in the bear trap, everything that had happened since that August afternoon an illusion. He thought he heard the sound of the creek. No, I'm not there, I'm here, he told himself, and opened his eyes. He stared at the floor until it again settled solid beneath his feet. He turned to Dena.

"Because you don't deserve it," Travis said. "Nobody does."

Travis walked back into the front room. Hubert had pulled his chair close to the coffee table. He and Wesley played poker while Shank leaned back on the couch and sipped his beer. Hubert had a drumstick in his hand and Carlton was eating as well. For a few moments Travis watched them eat, amazed that the two men could feel anything, even if it was only hunger. Carlton raised a paper napkin to his mouth, then spread it out on his upper knee. It was a strangely dainty gesture.

Travis tried to meet Carlton Toomey's eyes.

"You doing that to her is wrong."

"She done it to herself, son," Carlton said. "She called us.

Said she wanted to live up here, that she wanted to sell pills for us. Turns out she was swallowing more than she was selling."

Hubert laid his cards face up on the coffee table, raked four quarters to his end. The pills were still on the table.

"Sixteen hundred dollars' worth," Hubert said. "That bitch kept saying it was the customers who owed the money, then tried to run out on us when we found out the truth."

"Had to do her like I done you," Carlton said to Travis. "Treat her a little rough just so she'd know I wasn't to be trifled with. But she's learning. Sold two hundred dollars' worth this week and made sure them two hundred dollars got back to me. I even let her have some pills tonight for a little reward."

"That's not such a big thing," Hubert said, "especially when she still owes us fourteen hundred dollars."

"She's whittling it down," Carlton said. "By the end of summer we'll be square."

"I can put the law on you," Travis said. He was trembling and there didn't seem any way he could stop. It was like so much welled up inside him that it shook his whole body trying to get out.

Carlton Toomey smiled.

"Why not talk to him in person? Sheriff Crockett comes by most every Sunday afternoon to get his cut."

"There's other law I could call besides Crockett," Travis said.

"What are you-all talking about?" Shank asked.

Toomey laid his paper plate on the coffee table, leaned back in his chair. He knit his thick fingers together and rested them on his belly, let out a long slow breath, and shook his head.

"You're like a little fyce dog. Barking big but not doing a damn thing."

Hubert looked at his father. "We should have taken care of him last summer, the way I told you."

"What are you all talking about?" Shank asked again.

"None of your damn concerning," Hubert said.

Carlton Toomey stood up, and when he did it seemed to Travis as though a huge black wave had risen up to crest. Travis put his hand in his pocket, ready to pull out the pocket-knife, but Toomey did not move toward him. He stretched his arms and yawned.

"You boys have done worn out your welcome," Carlton said.

Hubert looked at his father.

"Not yet," Hubert said. "Just a few more hands and I'll have all his quarters."

Travis was already up. He walked out to the car and sat in the Plymouth's front passenger seat. A few seconds later Shank stepped onto the porch and lit a cigarette. Travis tried to remember when this day had been going well, and it seemed years in the past, hardly his life at all. He shifted his gaze higher, half expecting the stars he'd seen in the restaurant's parking lot to be realigned into strange new constellations, but they were the same as before.

Shank walked out to the car and got behind the steering wheel. He flicked the glowing cigarette butt out the window. It lay on the ground and slowly dimmed.

"Don't you reckon it's about time you told your best buddy what's going on?"

"Give me one of your cigarettes," Travis said.

Shank lit a cigarette and handed it to Travis, who took a deep draw, pursed his lips around the cigarette, and exhaled through his nose. He closed his eyes and took several more deep draws, savored what he'd known before memory, a smell so omnipresent on the farm that he'd been in grade school before realizing the pungent odor of tobacco was not the smell of the air itself. The smoke began to warm his lungs. Soon he felt a light buzz off the nicotine because it had been so long.

"You going to tell me?" Shank asked.

"Yeah," Travis said.

And he did, not just all of what had happened last August but what was going to happen as soon as the Toomeys went to sleep.

"You're crazy," Shank said. "What if she starts yelling or something? Maybe she *wants* to be up here."

Travis pulled the truck keys from his pocket and set them on the dashboard.

"You just make sure my truck's down at the river bridge come dawn."

Shank pressed his forehead against the top of the steering wheel.

"Is there any way I can talk you out of doing this?"

"No," Travis said. "You going to help me or not?"

Shank lifted his head and looked at Travis.

"You'll do it regardless, whether I help or not?"

"Yes."

"OK," Shank said. "What else besides getting the truck to the bridge?"

"You got a flashlight?"

"In the dash."

Travis got out of the car and quietly shut the car door before moving into the darkness. When he got to the shed he sat down and pressed his back and head against the rough splintery wood. There was comfort in that resting, wood the one solid thing he'd encountered the whole day. In a few minutes Wesley came out of the house and he and Shank drove off. Travis watched the red taillights grow smaller, fighting the impulse to run after them.

The light in the front room remained on. Travis checked his watch. Almost twelve-thirty. He wondered why it should matter to him what happened to Dena when she hardly cared herself. He set an open hand on the grass and felt his palm dampen with dew the night had summoned forth. Something moved near the creek, probably a raccoon, maybe an otter. A breeze came from the west, strong enough that the woodshed's door hinge gave a rusty squeak. Travis smelled coming rain, looked up and saw clouds now concealed most of the stars. He remembered something Leonard had told him, that you weren't seeing the stars but their light, the stars themselves no longer existing.

He pressed his hand firmer against the ground to feel the earth's solidity. The taste of the cigarette lingered in his mouth. Travis wished he'd gotten a couple more and some matches from Shank, given himself something to do besides think bothersome things such as whether Lori would ever see him again. Probably not, he figured, probably not even talk to him if he went to her house to apologize. It wasn't all my fault, he said softly, but he knew much of it was.

The watch hands had swept past 2 A.M. before the last light

went out. Travis studied the house's outline, a denser shadow among shadows. He hadn't seen any guns, but he knew they were there, within easy reach and no doubt loaded. He almost hoped they were. If things went wrong, he'd rather be shot than have Carlton Toomey's hawkbill slice his windpipe. Nothing could be worse than that. He got up to piss and realized the alcohol no longer hummed in his head. Which was unfortunate. What he'd planned didn't seem near so easy sober.

Thirty more minutes passed before he made his way to the back of the house, the flashlight's beam bobbing on the grass in front of him. He peered inside the bedroom window, let the beam crawl slowly across the covers to the foot of the bed, crossing only one pair of legs. He placed the flashlight in his jeans pocket and straddled the sill.

The half-raised blinds rattled as he brushed against them. Travis waited a few moments, half in and half out. When no one stirred, he set both feet on the floor and crossed the room, cupping the flashlight's front with his hand to mute its glow.

Dena woke slowly, reluctantly, and when he told her why he'd come she at first seemed not to understand. He tried to unknot the twine, quickly gave up, and cut it with his pocketknife.

"My knight in shining armor," Dena said, and when he told her to speak softer she laughed.

"They're so drunk you couldn't wake them with a two-byfour."

"Come on," he said, helping her to a sitting position. Travis swept the light across the room and found a blouse and a pair of jeans thrown on a chair, her shoes in the corner. Dena's eyes kept closing as he helped her dress.

"You got to wake up," he said.

"Quaaludes," she said.

One of the Toomeys coughed and Travis froze. The house became still again and Travis finished buttoning her blouse, put her shoes on.

"Where's your bridge?" Travis asked.

"I don't know," Dena said. "Hubert took it from me." Her head drooped from the effort of putting together two complete sentences.

Getting her out the window took another five minutes, and the mile trek down the creek to the bridge seemed more daunting now than it had an hour earlier, likely impossible. Cold water was his one hope of waking her so he half-led and half-dragged Dena past the shed to the creek. He splashed water on her face and then put her whole head in the water but it made no difference. He dragged her onto the bank and sat down beside her. She was drenched, water matting her hair, yet within moments she snored softly. His watch said four-fifty. Even if he went alone, it would take an hour to get down the creek.

The hell with it, with everything and everybody, he thought. Travis began crying, his index finger's bent knuckle digging into his cheek so hard it seemed he was not so much wiping tears away as grinding them deeper into his skin. Everything in the world was slipping away, and he had the feeling all of it, even parts of himself, might soon become so remote he'd never be able to bring them back, that he would be like those stars—nothing but light moving farther and farther away from what they had once been.

He decided to put her on the front porch and be done with it. Dena muttered that she was cold as he dragged her back up the bank. When the land leveled out Travis paused to catch his breath. He raised his flashlight and saw the flayed animal hides on the shed's back wall. Then he saw the marijuana. The plants were no more than six inches high, nothing like last August's tall thick greening, but they grew in the same place, the same configuration of rows.

Travis kept his upper body still as he checked the earth around his feet. But no steel spring tensed under him. He searched the ground with the flashlight before each step, staying on grass and walking wide of the tilled soil. Not hurrying despite his legs trembling from supporting two bodies. He finally got to the porch and laid Dena on the steps.

She opened her eyes.

"You're leaving me, aren't you?"

He would have if she had not spoken.

"I don't know yet," Travis said, and walked over to the pickup. No key was in the ignition so he checked the car. The key was in it and Travis immediately wished it hadn't been because now he had a choice. The breeze had a damp feel to it, and Travis looked up and saw the last stars had been rinsed from the sky. Out near the creek a barn owl hooted. Nothing but the dark answered. He walked around to the passenger door, the hinge emitting a whine as it slowly opened. He helped Dena into the car and closed the passenger door just enough to hear a click.

Tears still wet his cheeks but he no longer wiped them away. It seemed more had happened in the last twelve hours than the whole rest of his life and none of it was good. Travis tried to imagine a way things could be straightened out. Maybe he was too tired or too hung over but he couldn't even imagine such a scenario. Nothing left to lose, just like that song on the radio said. Travis whispered the words again and again as he walked back to the shed and searched inside until he found a hoe. He went around back, using the hoe to poke the tilled ground around the plants. No steel leaped from the soil to snatch the wood handle. Travis aimed the blade and chopped at the marijuana like it was a nest of copperheads. Not one plant remained rooted when he threw down the hoe.

He went back and knelt beside the pickup, cutting into the rubber with his pocketknife until the tire hissed and slowly sagged. Not much more meanness I can do to them, Travis thought as he closed the knife, knowing it was a good thing for the Toomeys that Shank's matches weren't in his pocket.

When he got in the car, Dena moaned softly and leaned her head against his shoulder. His hand was on the key but he didn't turn it. For all he knew the car might not start at all. Two tries, he told himself, then I make a run for the creek.

But the engine started. He turned the car around and headed down the drive, a gray sunless dawn already seeping in through the trees. He looked in the rearview mirror and did not see the front door fling open and he reckoned the Toomeys drunk as Dena had said. He drove toward the river, glancing nervously in the rearview mirror.

His truck was at the bridge, keys on the right front tire

where Shank said they'd be. Travis got Dena inside, then stepped up to the bridge railing. He smelled the creosote on the thick pine beams that held him above the water, the same smell as railroad cross ties. He threw Carlton Toomey's key into the creek. For a few moments he stared at where the key had splashed, then let his eyes follow the stream to where it disappeared into a stand of white oak and poplar. In the oaks mistletoe floated among the limbs like green snagged balloons. A gust of wind shook a flock of sparrows from the tallest poplar like an instantaneous unleafing, the birds quickly regathering in midair and flying away. Travis wondered if they were lucky enough to know where they were headed or if it was just something decided by what weather or field or big tree they encountered.

"Where we going?" Dena asked when he got in, her eyes closed as she spoke.

He turned the ignition and pressed the gas so the engine might stammer and catch hold, but he did not reach for the gearshift.

"I don't know," Travis said. "I didn't figure us to get this far."

For a few moments he thought he might not go anywhere, just wait for the Toomeys to come, go ahead and get whatever they would do to him over and done with.

"Go to Leonard's," Dena said.

"OK," he said, because he could think of no alternative.

My frend Joshua Candler passed this evening neer suppertime. I witnessed his final mortal breaths. His aggitation was lessoned neer the end, a good death. Burried here at Big Creek Gap with all Cristian writes. If it be the Lord's faver to have me die I pray you who find this leger get it to his wife Mrs. Emily Candler in Marshall North Carlina.

FOURTEEN

When Travis had not come back by 6 A.M., Leonard was unsure what he should do, being neither parent nor guardian. He called the hospital but there had been no overnight casualties from car wrecks. There seemed nothing else to do after that but stay put in case Travis, or someone calling about Travis, telephoned.

When the pickup finally appeared, Leonard chided himself for getting so worried. Then Travis and Dena got out and stood before him. Both reeked of vomit and alcohol. Travis's face was chalk white, his usually clear eyes webbed with red veins as if all the blood had drained from the rest of his face to pool there. Dena looked worse, hair greasy and matted, face bruised. A full minute passed as Leonard waited for Dena or Travis to speak, to begin to explain. The surrounding woods seemed to listen as well, no raucous crows or chattering squirrels, even the spring peepers silent.

"What happened?" Leonard finally asked, and Travis told him, including what he'd done to the Toomeys' vehicles and pot plants. When he finished Leonard looked not at Travis or Dena but at the mountains rising beyond the trees. Some of the oldest mountains in the world, geologists claimed, older than the Alps or Andes or even the Himalayas. Leonard had an almost consoling thought—that in one hundred years, a mere blink in geologic time, whatever happened in the next few hours would not matter at all, that everyone involved would be little more than dust.

"I don't want them finding you before I settle this," he told Travis. "Go up to Shelton Laurel. They wouldn't think to look for you there. I'll come get you when it's safe."

"What about Dena?"

"Take her with you."

"I ought to help settle it," the boy said. "It's my doing."

You're sure as hell right about that, Leonard thought, but it seemed useless to say so aloud.

"Go," Leonard said.

"We got to get these clothes off first," Travis said. "It's making us both sick just smelling ourselves."

"Take them off right here," Leonard said. "Use the hose and do it quick. I'll get you something clean to wear."

Leonard expected the boy or Dena to say it was too cold, but when he came back out Travis had stripped, shivering as the hose sprayed water over his hair and body, dripping like a dog as Leonard handed him a towel. Travis dressed quickly, teeth chattering as he yanked jeans on, slid his long arms into a plaid flannel shirt.

"Crank your truck and get some heat on you," Leonard told him. "I'll take care of Dena."

He helped her undress, letting the clothes puddle on the grass where they fell. The bracelet he'd won at the fair clinked softly. She had lost weight and the metal dangled loosely on her bony wrist. Loose like a handcuff, Leonard thought. The cold water waked her, Dena's eyes blinking before narrowing into focus.

"No more," she said, her teeth chattering like Travis's. Leonard threw down the hose, patted her torso and limbs with the towel. He had come to believe her incapable of crying, but now tears streaked her face.

"Just get me to the bus station in Marshall," she said.

"I will, but not just yet," Leonard said.

"Don't tell them where my sister lives." She clutched his arm now, her long fingernails digging in, leaving half-moons. "Promise me that."

Finally, he thought, believing this was what Dena had searched for much of her life, degradation even she could feel was undeserved.

"I won't tell them," he said.

"We got to get to the bus station quick," she said, still clinging to him.

"You can't go that way," Leonard told her. "You'd run right into them." He helped her into the sweatshirt and pants, but it was a slow matching of limbs and openings, clumsily accomplished, like dressing a child. She shook violently. Leonard got her in the cab and turned the vents so they blew directly on her.

"You have to go with Travis," he said, draping his coat over her shoulders. "I'll get up there soon as I can. When I do we'll get you to Asheville."

"What are you going to do?" Travis asked.

"Settle this in a way nobody gets hurt," Leonard said. "Go on. I'll come soon as I can."

Travis cranked the engine and the truck disappeared into the woods. Soon Leonard heard the pickup on the main road, gears downshifting as it rose toward the higher mountains.

He sat down on the steps and waited for the Toomeys. Fog clung to the trees, moving serpentine in the wood's understory, laying down a low smolder across the pasture. Rain by noon, lasting the rest of the day, the radio announcer had said, but rain was already settling in, letting the fog come first, transforming the landscape into a vast blank whiteness. Bringing with it what it always brought, a quietness like no other, every sound muted, more distant. Almost as though the fog loosened the world at its seams, made everything drift farther apart.

The kind of day the dampness seeped straight into your bones, Leonard thought. *Scawmy* was the word the old people used to describe this weather, and many believed that on such days the dead got restless and roamed the living world. Leonard's grandmother had seen her decade-dead husband on a morning like this. She'd looked out her kitchen window and seen him standing by the barn, dressed in the clothes he'd been buried in, the fog like a shroud unfurling around him.

Billy Revis had returned to Madison County in May of 1865 barefoot and near starved, bringing with him only a haversack and what rags of butternut still clung to his skin. But before he had set foot in his own house, he had stood on Doctor Candler's front porch. When Emily Candler came to the door, he'd opened the haversack and removed the ledger he'd carried with him for two years. He'd handed it to her and spoken a few words before leaving the porch for his cabin on Spillcorn Creek. Leonard knew there had been plenty of times the ledger could have started a much-needed fire, or perhaps been bartered for food, or simply left behind to lighten that final monthlong walk from Virginia. But Revis had brought it back, a final act of friendship for the man he'd helped bury in Tennessee.

The wooden cross Revis had placed on Doctor Candler's grave was long gone. The coffin rotted away as well, if there'd even been one, for Revis had told the widow only about the cross and where her husband was buried. Maybe a few brass buttons left. Some shards of bone. Leonard's grandfather had gone to Tennessee late in his life to visit the cemetery. He'd found only a clearing in the woods, had known at first it was a graveyard only because, as in so many old cemeteries, periwinkle skeined green and glossy over much of the ground. Nothing else remained but a few lichened creek stones smothered in a sprawl of briars and scrub pine, whatever had been scratched into the stones long ago worn into anonymity by wind and rain.

LEONARD HEARD THE TOOMEYS' TRUCK BEFORE HE SAW IT, coming fast up Highway 25 before bouncing and swerving up the washout to the trailer. Hubert drove and didn't brake until he was only a few yards from the trailer. Leonard did not move as the truck's front wheels bumped the lower step and halted, the two men's faces looming large behind the windshield as though suspended in water.

"Stay put," Carlton Toomey told his son, then got out. He wore only a white V-neck tee-shirt, faded gray pants, and work boots.

"We can settle this here and now," Leonard said, standing up.

"Can we?" Carlton said. "My car's down at the bridge, but I don't see that little pissant that slashed my tire and rooted up my money crop."

"I'd say five hundred for a slashed tire and the bother of re-planting is fair," Leonard said.

"That's your figuring, is it?" Carlton replied. "Must be some of that new math they're teaching in schools these days, for it don't buck up to the price I'd calculate."

The trailer door was open and Leonard pointed behind him at the gun rack. "The Winchester and scope are worth two hundred easy and I got a Colt pistol worth two hundred. I'll add the five hundred cash to that."

Carlton stared carefully at the fingernails of his left hand, as if they held some information he needed to consider before answering. Then he looked back up, his face expressionless.

"OK," he said. "Just don't be all day about it."

Leonard paused, expecting Carlton to follow him into the trailer.

"Go ahead," Carlton said. "Like I said before, you're smart. I know you ain't about to try nothing."

Leonard got the guns, emptying the clips before he went

back outside. As Carlton put the guns in the cab, Leonard crouched and pulled a cinder block out from behind the trailer steps. He took from its hollow center a tight-wrapped plastic grocery bag, inside a roll of bills thick as a fist.

"I don't have much truck with banks neither, professor," Carlton said, "but that's near the sorriest place to hide money I've ever seen."

Leonard stripped off five hundred-dollar bills from the roll and placed the rest back in the plastic bag.

"That's a good start," Carlton said as he took the bills. "Now where's Dena?"

"She's gone," Leonard said.

"Gone," Carlton said, placing his boot on the second step. "You best hope that's a lie."

"You don't own her."

"Yes, I do. I own her body and soul till she pays me the fourteen hundred dollars she owes me."

Carlton Toomey tilted his head slightly to the right, as though wanting to see Leonard from a different angle. He looked at Leonard the same way he might some strange creature he couldn't quite believe existed.

"You know something, Shuler. It ain't like I went out hunting for all this bother. That boy came on my land to take from me. Not just once but four times now. Dena done the same. She came because she wanted my pills. The difference between you and me is that she's going to by God pay for what she took from me."

Leonard motioned toward the Plotts.

"I'll give you them as well. They're worth a thousand easy."

Carlton Toomey snorted.

"They might of been before you turned them into pets instead of bear dogs. Now if you was to talk some real money, say the rest of what you got in that bag, we might could do us some business."

Leonard said nothing.

"I figured as much," Carlton said. "You're just like Dena and that boy, expecting something for free. But there ain't nothing in this world for free. Nothing."

He stepped closer to Leonard. Though Toomey stood on the step below they were eye to eye, making Leonard feel even smaller, as if the big man had lifted him like a child and set him on the step. Last night's whiskey soured Carlton Toomey's breath.

"Look professor, this ain't no hard thing to figure. Even if she's on a bus or train, that boy ain't. He's got nowhere to go and I'll make it my business to find him. Your choice, the boy or Dena."

One of the Plotts rattled its chain and whined. The dogs were hungry, but that would have to wait. The chain rattled again. Leonard remembered the carny telling Dena her name on the bracelet would keep her from forgetting who she was. The Toomeys had taken so much else, even her bridge, but they hadn't taken the bracelet. Leonard wished they'd taken everything, the bracelet, her name, her life. Put it all in a hole in the woods and covered it with dirt and leaves.

"OK," Leonard said. "Follow me and I'll take you to her."

"No," Carlton said, "you ride with us." His right hand latched onto Leonard's wrist, held it firm while his left took the bag. Toomey stuffed the roll of bills in his front pocket, gave the empty bag back to Leonard.

"I rechecked my math and realized I'd forgot to add a surcharge for the pain in the ass this has all been," Carlton said. "And one more thing. You make damn sure that boy *never* threatens to put the law on me again, because if he does I will kill him."

Leonard got in the truck, the Toomeys' wide shoulders hemming him in as they drove down to the blacktop. The windshield wipers had worn off their rubber coating, and they made a steady rasping that reminded Leonard of another sound he could not immediately place. Then he knew—a knife blade being stroked across a whetstone. Hubert turned left and downshifted as they began the climb toward Shelton Laurel.

"Think we ought to try and replant?" Hubert asked.

"No. That pot's more trouble than it's worth," Carlton replied. "We'll make do with the pills."

The road steepened and curved, wrapped itself tighter to the mountain, the drop-offs like falling off the world. A soft steady rain smudged the windshield, rain that was in no hurry. They turned left on White Rock Road. A car pulled out in front of them and Hubert slowed. They rode the car's bumper until the blacktop straightened. Hubert pulled into the other lane, halfway around the car before he saw a gray pickup coming from the other direction. Hubert swerved in front of the car, forcing it to brake. The pickup blared its horn.

"Damn, boy," Carlton said. "You about laid us out in our coffins for sure."

"The truck was hard to see," Hubert said. "It blended right in with the fog."

The road fishhooked left before straightening again. They drove past the house where Leonard had parked in January, beside it a freshly planted cornfield. A scarecrow, ragged black coat billowed by the wind, appeared to levitate above the broken soil. They followed the blacktop another mile until it looped back and ran beside the meadow. Hubert stopped next to the historical marker, directly behind Travis's truck.

Dena jumped out of the truck and ran toward the creek. Hubert jerked the pickup back into gear and drove into the meadow. He reached through the open window, grabbed Dena's hair, not letting go until she fell to the ground, leaving a hank of hair in his hand. Hubert braked the truck and got out as Dena slowly rose to her feet. She didn't try to run but waited in a half crouch.

When Hubert got close, Dena's right hand slashed out. The nail on her index finger broke the skin on his neck, then the necklace. A small shattered rainbow spilled off the thread. Hubert grabbed her right arm and Dena raked her left hand's nails across his face, four reddening furrows opening in his left cheek. One nail broke off, embedded in the younger Toomey's cheek like a sliver of glass.

Leonard got out of the cab and watched as Travis ran into the meadow to help her. Carlton pulled the hawkbill from his pocket, let the boy see the blade.

"Come any closer and I'll cut on you some more," he said.

Dena kept slashing at Hubert until he slapped her hard enough to knock her to the ground. She tucked her knees to her chest and did not move.

Hubert prodded her with his boot.

"Get up," he said. "We're going home."

But she didn't rise, remained instead tightly curled, letting her weight be a last resistance as the Toomeys dragged her to the truck as if she were nothing more than a feed sack.

"You lied to us," Travis shouted as he walked toward Leonard. "You said we'd be safe here."

Leonard saw that Travis had grown an inch since summer, fleshed out some as well in the shoulders and chest. His face had assumed a squarer, fuller shape. No longer a boy but a man. Leonard wondered how he hadn't noticed until this moment.

"Why did you lie?" Travis said when he stood directly in front of Leonard. "Why don't you do something?"

Because I never have any other time in my life, Leonard almost replied.

The Toomeys lifted Dena into the passenger side of the cab, then came around to where Leonard and Travis stood. The right side of Hubert's face was a red smear, several of the slashes deep enough to need stitches. Hubert touched his face and looked at the blood on his fingers as if unsure it had really happened.

Carlton closed the hawkbill and stuck it in his pocket. His eyes settled on Travis.

"You keep getting yourself ass deep in trouble and then wait for somebody else to save you. You probably figure yourself to be a cat with nine lives. Well, messing with me you've done used up eight of them."

"Let's go ahead and be done with them both," Hubert said.

"Damned if I'd need much persuading," Carlton said. "But

you pretending to be Richard Petty made sure everybody in this valley noticed our truck, and piece of shit that it is they'd likely figure it to be us." Carlton Toomey shook his head. "There'll be another time. These two can't seem to help themselves."

Travis's eyes remained on Leonard as the Toomeys spoke. The boy was shivering, his eyes wide and wild. Leonard stepped closer, reached out his right hand, and let it rest on Travis's shoulder.

"It wouldn't end up any different for her," Leonard said gently. "Only a different place, different people."

For a few moments Travis just stared at him, then broke free of Leonard's grasp and ran to his pickup. He reached behind the seat and brought out the .22. As he walked toward them, he thumbed back the safety.

"You ain't about to make it easy on yourself, are you, boy," Carlton said.

"Give me the rifle, Travis," Leonard said.

"Why didn't you tell me you were a Candler?" Travis shouted. The rifle had been aimed at the gap between Leonard and Carlton, but now it pointed in Leonard's direction.

"Because it doesn't matter."

"If that was true you wouldn't have hidden it from me," Travis said, his voice almost a sob. The rifle trembled in his hands.

"Damned if it don't look like he's going to shoot the whole covey of us," Carlton said to his son. The two men laughed.

"Because it would have changed things between us,"

Leonard said. "It shouldn't. You and I weren't here when the killing happened. But it would have."

"Take that popgun away from him, Hubert," Carlton said. "I'm tired of standing in the rain like some barnyard rooster."

Travis aimed the rifle at Hubert.

"You little prick," Hubert said. "If it had been up to me I'd of killed you last summer."

"Damned if I haven't come around to your way of thinking on that, son." Carlton turned to Leonard. "A nit always makes a louse, right professor?"

Leonard stared at Carlton Toomey. For a few moments no one spoke or moved, as if each awaited some cue from the others as to what to do next. The rain fell harder, a pale curtain that blurred everything outside the meadow.

Leonard stepped between Hubert and Travis.

"Get out of my way," Travis said, aiming the barrel at Leonard's chest.

Leonard walked straight toward him, put his hand on the barrel, and lifted the rifle from Travis's hands. The .22 felt light and flimsy compared to his Winchester, and it struck Leonard as nothing short of remarkable that such a shoddy piece of wood and steel could send lead deep enough into a man to kill him. For a few moments he held the rifle loose in his hands, thinking how the barrel was like a compass needle he could point in all sorts of directions.

"You better give that rifle to me," Carlton said.

That was easily enough done, everything back to where it had been just minutes earlier, back to what Leonard had decided an hour ago on the trailer's steps. But things were different now. He remembered words written during the Civil War, not by his ancestor but by a Union private the morning of the battle of Cold Harbor. The man's entry was one line: *June 3, Cold Harbor. I was killed.* The soldier had indeed died that day, the bloodstained diary found in his pocket after the battle. Terrible to know you were going to die, but a kind of freedom as well, Leonard believed, because you decided it before anyone or anything else could. Your life became something more than just a life, a kind of embodied language with no present or future tense.

"I'll keep it," Leonard said, and pointed the rifle at Carlton. He turned to Travis, speaking soft so the Toomeys could not overhear.

"Get Dena and drive to the nearest house. Don't call the sheriff. Call the Highway Patrol and tell them to get up here. Not Crockett, the Highway Patrol. Then take Dena straight to the bus station. Get her on a bus."

Leonard pulled out his billfold. He looked briefly at the Toomeys, who leaned against their truck, waiting. "Here," Leonard said, handing him what bills were inside. "It's enough to get her to Greensboro."

"I don't want to leave you here with them," Travis said.

"I'm fine," Leonard said. "I'm the one who's got the rifle."

Travis helped Dena into the truck and they left. Leonard knew an hour could pass before the Highway Patrol arrived. Even then they might defer to Sheriff Crockett, figure it his affair more than theirs. Nothing short of murder would force Crockett to do anything besides shrug his shoulders and look the other way. Leonard stepped a few feet into the meadow. The safety was off and six bullets filled the clip.

Carlton leaned against the truck, as if he and Leonard were friends who had stopped to banter. Hubert raised a handkerchief to his cheek and dabbed blood oozing from the slashes. The three of them stood there in silence, their hair matted, faces streaked with rain. Leonard felt goose bumps prickle his skin. The older Toomey crossed his arms, his fingers rubbing the backs of his biceps. Cold as well, Leonard knew, but not wanting to show it. Hubert alone seemed comfortable, the rain sliding off his nylon jacket.

"We got us a real fix now, ain't we, and there's no easy setting it right," Carlton said. "Though I figure giving me that rifle would be a good start."

Carlton took a pack of Camels from his pocket and a silver lighter. He shielded the flame from the rain and lit his cigarette.

"Killing a man is no easy thing," Carlton said. "If we was to rush you I doubt you'd get both of us, especially with that twenty-two."

Hubert stuffed the handkerchief in his front pocket, his eyes on Leonard now.

"You won't get away with murdering," Hubert said.

"I figure as much," Leonard said.

"A man no bigger than you would have a time of it in prison," Hubert said. "You'd likely not last six months."

Leonard said nothing, just stood there with the rifle pretending he could shoot them. He wondered how long it would take for Carlton Toomey or his son to realize he was bluffing.

"Neither of them is nowhere near worth it," Carlton said. "I had every right to kill that boy last summer."

Carlton shifted his body so he no longer touched the truck. The tee-shirt was soaked now, white skin visible under the material. Carlton's body was succumbing to gravity, Leonard realized, belly leaning over his pants like a short apron, breasts sagging. The water dripping down his flesh heightened the effect, as though his body were melting away like a candle. Except in the arms. There the muscles remained firm.

"Don't move," Leonard said, and trained the rifle on Carlton's chest.

"I'm just standing up," Carlton said, hands at his sides and open-palmed as if to show he hid no weapons.

Russian farmers still unearthed cartloads of bones in their fields each spring, bones planted outside Stalingrad in the winter of 1942. Blood-rich ground, good for growing crops. Here too, Leonard supposed. He imagined the broom sedge in this meadow the summer after the massacre, how it would have been taller and thicker, tinged a deeper gold. And now more blood to be spilled in this meadow. At least fifteen minutes had passed, a good enough head start for Dena and Travis.

"She tore into you good, boy," Leonard said to Hubert. "Your face will look like a baseball by the time they're through stitching you up." Leonard smiled. "How does it feel to have a hundred-pound woman kick your ass? I wouldn't know so I'm kind of curious."

"If you weren't holding that rifle I'd kill you," Hubert said.

"You haven't got the guts to kill anybody," Leonard said.

"Give me half a chance," Hubert said softly. "Put that rifle on the ground. Just so you'll have to pick it up before you can shoot. That's all I ask."

"I'll do better than that," Leonard said. "I'll throw it on the ground between us."

"He's baiting you, son," Carlton said. "Trying to set up some kind of self-defense."

"No, I'm not," Leonard said, "I'm just seeing if your boy's all talk."

Leonard tossed the rifle out before him, the gun was still in the air when Hubert broke for it. Leonard didn't move. He let Hubert pick it up, raise the rifle and fire. The bullet clipped his arm, just enough to draw blood. Leonard stood still as Hubert took more careful aim, but Carlton jerked the barrel downward just as his son squeezed the trigger. The second bullet made a spitting sound as it struck the soggy earth at Leonard's feet.

Carlton wrested the rifle from his son.

"Can't you see the son-of-a-bitch *wants* you to kill him?"

The elder Toomey settled his eyes on Leonard.

"I know what you're doing, and I wouldn't mind obliging you. But not right now." Carlton paused. "Where's that boy taking her?"

Leonard didn't say anything.

Carlton flicked the safety on, held the rifle in front of him as he stepped closer to Leonard. When he spoke his voice was weary.

"We're back to where we started this morning. Not a damn thing has changed except I'm more pissed off. I'm figuring you-all put Dena on the bus or the train. Get her to where we can't find her. But that boy's going to still be around. So like I said. We're back where we started."

Carlton shifted his grip so that both hands were under the gun, as if about to return the rifle to Leonard.

"Crockett ain't going to let us get away with out and out murder. But there's accidents that don't need much snooping around about, and I'd say someone lucky as that boy's been of late might be due for one."

"I'm betting they're at the bus station," Hubert said.

"Is that where they are, professor?" Carlton asked.

Leonard raised his gaze to meet Toomey's.

"I don't know."

The big man stepped closer to Leonard. "You know."

Leonard seemed to hear the crack of the rifle butt against his jaw before he saw its brown blur. Then he was on the ground, his face blossoming in pain. Blood filled his mouth but his jaw hurt so terribly he swallowed the blood instead of trying to unhinge his mouth. What he couldn't swallow oozed from his lips. A piece of tooth settled on his tongue and Leonard swallowed it as well. Carlton Toomey jerked him to his feet.

"So. Are they at the bus station or not?"

Leonard nodded.

"Amazing how a good pop to the head loosens up a man's re-callings," Carlton said. "I'll do it again if you get feisty with us."

The elder Toomey guided Leonard toward the truck and shoved him in. Hubert cranked the engine as Carlton pulled off his soggy tee-shirt and threw it on the floorboard. Toomey's bared flesh reminded Leonard of an infant's skin—

pink-tinged, loose, as if not grown into yet. The smoothness as well, smooth as polished marble, no welts or ragged stitching like Dena's. The skin of a victimizer, not a victim.

Carlton leaned forward and turned on the heater.

"Told you to wear a jacket," Hubert said.

"I didn't figure to be standing in the rain a damn hour," Carlton replied.

They drove south, past the church and then fields where tobacco had begun its slow rise toward September, the bright green glinting with rainwater. Leonard still swallowed blood but as long as he kept his lips pressed together the pain dimmed. He began to feel better, not just the jaw but something opening inside himself. His nose inhaled the fresh-turned earth so deeply he could taste its stored richness, taste in it the soaking rain as well. The black soil between the tobacco rows was almost tactile, as if his fingers rooted inside that cool earth.

They passed the store and Hubert turned right, but not before idling at the stop sign a moment. Tobacco rose mere feet from the road, and Leonard saw a bead of rain hanging tenderly on a leaf tip. Leonard knew there was a scientific explanation for how it could remain round, hang as it did on the leaf, but that had nothing to do with the wonder of this one drop on this one leaf, the further wonder that he was alive in the world to see it.

The creek widened gradually as the road began its long plunge toward Marshall, rain pooling on the roadsides now, the wipers ticktocking as they peeled water off the glass. Carlton shifted his body and his left hand flicked upward, the knuckles bone to bone against Leonard's chin. Pain surged through Leonard's jaw. The world receded beyond the cab's glass and metal.

"That's just a love tap," Carlton said. "If they ain't at that bus station, we're going to beat on you bad." Carlton placed his clenched left hand on Leonard's knee. "You telling us the truth, right?"

Leonard felt the weight of the fist through his jeans. He nodded.

"Good," Carlton said, and lifted his hand.

The road veered again, no guardrails for any vehicle that didn't stay on the asphalt, nothing beyond but an emptiness like some geometric line pointed toward infinity. Pointed toward the other way to end this. Hubert took the curve fast, and Leonard slid against Carlton, then back against Hubert.

"Don't be trying to cuddle up next to me," the elder Toomey said, then laughed.

The stream passed under the road and reappeared on the right. As the road straightened briefly, a Highway Patrol car flashed by, no siren but its blue light on. Behind it came a county police car. Leonard glimpsed enough of the driver to see Crockett's deputy, Ardy Metcalf, not Crockett himself, was the car's sole occupant. Neither vehicle slowed to turn around.

"Guess this hasn't worked out quite the way you planned it, professor," Carlton said. "But it's near over now. We got you and Dena and that boy out on a limb you can't jump off of. Like my daddy used to say, it's time to piss on the fire and call in the dogs."

The road leveled out for a quarter mile, then began the last long curve before they left Shelton Laurel. Carlton took the roll of bills from his pocket and counted them out loud. The road narrowed, cut into the mountain, the stream so far down it didn't appear to be moving, just a white ribbon draped around boulders.

They were halfway through the curve when the pickup hydroplaned, two wheels sliding off the blacktop and onto the gravel shoulder. Leonard locked his hand on Hubert's wrist and jerked down. The truck went off the shoulder and for a moment hung above the gorge, stalled midair like a ferris wheel at its apex. Hubert's hands gripped the wheel as if the vehicle might yet be steered back onto the road. Then they were falling. Leonard let go of Hubert's wrist and crouched so he'd hit the dash instead of the windshield. His last thought was that he'd never know if the truck would have gone off the cliff anyway.

He came to wedged between the seat and floorboard, the sound of water close by. Each breath was a drawer of knives prodding his right side. Broken ribs, three, maybe four of them. Something behind those ribs, spleen or stomach, was also damaged. Damaged bad. The jaw didn't hurt now, as though his body had made a choice of which pain to focus on and chose the ribs. He knew he was hurt in other places but nothing else seemed broken. He was thirsty, thirsty as he'd ever been in his life.

Leonard could see nothing but the underside of the dash. He listened, trying to hear a moan or the exhale and inhale of breath. He heard nothing but the stream. He had to know if the

Toomeys were still alive, and to do that he would have to move, and to move meant pain. Leonard slowly reached for the seat, using only his hands and arms, holding the rest of himself still because it felt as if any jarring movement or deep breath would cause the broken ribs to shatter apart like glass. The truck angled downward, making it harder to raise himself.

Leonard waited a few minutes for the pain jagging into his side to lessen, but it didn't. Moving couldn't make the pain much worse, he finally decided, and though he was wrong about that, Leonard did not stop until he'd gotten himself out from under the dash. He was turned toward the driver's side, and as he raised his head he found Hubert Toomey's legs looming before him. They were not moving and as he held his breath and lifted himself onto the seat he saw why. Hubert's shoulders and torso were inside the cab but his head broke through the windshield. Blood streaked the glass beneath his neck.

Carlton Toomey was not in the cab at all. The passenger door was flung open. Leonard turned and the broken ribs probed deeper and found more pain. He tasted blood, but this time it was not from his mouth but his stomach. A drink of water, think about that, he told himself. Don't think of anything else, just how good a palmful of water will taste once you get out of the truck. He inched across the floorboard to where the passenger door yawned open. The distance between him and the creek wasn't as far as he feared. He eased his legs off the running board, his left hand grasping the door hinge until water swirled around his feet. He let go of the metal and the drawer of knives in his side realigned. For a few moments he believed the effort to stand had taken everything he had left.

But soon his legs steadied beneath him. He worked his way around the passenger door to the hood.

Hubert's head stuck through the windshield like the masthead on a ship's prow. Blood matted his hair but much more had spilled where glass shunted the neck, sourced the rivulet dripping down the windshield and pooling on the smashed hood. The elder Toomey lay ten yards downstream, sprawled face up in the shallows. Carlton's eyes were open and his massive chest rose and fell with each slow taxing breath. The water was no more than three or four inches deep and it swirled around Carlton Toomey's body as if he were just another rock or fallen tree. He wasn't bleeding much, but something, maybe a broken back or shattered leg, pinned him to the streambed, kept his eyes focused on the sky.

Leonard moved through the shallows and then onto the bank. Toomey heard him coming and the big man's eyes shifted, revealing more white as he strained to see Leonard. Toomey's legs trembled as he slowly folded them, pushed his head and torso enough to get his head onto the sand. But that was all Carlton could do before his legs buckled, lay heavy and still as waterlogged timber.

Leonard stepped closer. When he stood directly above Carlton he saw it was the arms, both of them shattered at the elbow. On the right one a jagged bone broke the skin. The left elbow was swelled to the size of a cantaloupe. Both arms were crazy angled, like bent blades on a machine. Toomey's right hand still clutched the money.

"Hubert alive?" Toomey asked. His lips were tinged blue and he spoke through clinched teeth. Leonard thought Toomey's jaw as well as arms had been shattered, but then the teeth parted and began to chatter. Toomey clamped the teeth tight again.

Leonard shook his head.

"Figured as much," Carlton said.

The world blurred for a moment and Leonard's legs almost gave way. The feeling passed but he knew he couldn't stand much longer. He bent slowly, his right palm flat as he half leaned, half fell at the stream's edge. His stomach lurched and bright-red blood dribbled from his mouth. Arterial blood, Leonard knew.

"You ain't faring much better than me," Carlton Toomey said. Toomey's teeth chattered uncontrollably now, making the words sound not so much flowing off the tongue as bitten off in syllables. Toomey shifted his eyes toward his right hand. "Held on to the money."

Leonard dipped his hand into a stream so cold it shocked like a live fence wire, his cupped hand reddening from the cold. The fractured jaw kept him from opening his mouth very wide, so half the water dribbled down his chin.

"You better drag me out of this creek," Toomey stammered. "I'm freezing to death. Then go flag somebody down." The big man clamped his mouth shut a few moments to stop the chattering. He tried to raise his knees but they buckled again. "If you'll help stand me up I'll get to the road if you can't manage. We could be down here a long while if you don't."

Leonard kept drinking, his pursed lips sucking palmfuls of water as if through a straw, his hand going numb but too thirsty to care.

"Get me out and I'll give you your money and leave you be," Carlton said. Not just his voice but his torso shuddered now, his legs rippling the shallows. "I'll leave Dena and that boy alone too."

Toomey took a deep breath and released it, his chest and belly not so much rising as billowing, as though the stream's current ran through him now. The big man shook again, more violently this time, as if having a seizure. The shattered arms were now tinged blue as his lips. "Go over there to Hubert," Toomey said when his body quieted. "Get some of his blood. I'll swear it on my own son's blood."

Leonard coughed and a thick warmth rose again in his throat. Rain fell harder now, the fog thickening. He looked up and couldn't see where the gorge and road met. He wanted the fog to thicken even more, wrap around him like a cocoon, a warm swaddling cocoon where he could rest awhile.

After a few more minutes Toomey spoke again.

"I'm warming up," the big man said groggily, the rise and fall of his chest perceptively slower. "I'll be OK here. Just get up to the road and flag somebody down. Take some of this money and flash it. That'll make them stop."

Carlton Toomey closed his eyes and began humming "Will There Be Any Stars in My Crown." Soon the tune was barely intelligible. Then there was no sound at all, nothing but the slightest movement of lips. Finally not even that, the chest as still as the mouth.

Leonard cupped his hand and sipped again, his hand now so numb he had to watch it dip into the water and rise. He looked at the huge still body of Carlton Toomey and remembered how in the meadow Toomey had said that killing a person wasn't an easy thing to do. But killing someone was easier than a whole lot of other things in life. Appealing in its finality as well, because it only had to be done right once. Easier than love or happiness or making money or raising a child. So easy you could do it with no more than one finger pressing a small curve of metal or the jerk of a wrist. Or simply doing nothing at all, Leonard thought, just being there and letting it happen.

Easier than healing.

Joshua Candler had made the choice to side with the shooters that January morning. The journal had made clear the doctor's feelings afterward, but what of his feelings those moments after Colonel Keith slashed the air with his sword? Leonard believed he knew now. He understood why the page was blank.

What light filtered through the rain and fog dimmed briefly for a few moments and then came back. Leonard assumed a cloud had passed over the sun, then realized that the sun wouldn't be out if it was raining. He remembered how radiant the tobacco leaves had been, so green it was like something you could not only see but hear, a kind of verdant hum like the vibration of a tuning fork. He wished tobacco were on this bank, or some dogwood trees, something that could brighten like that as it held a bead of water on a leaf.

Leonard lay down on the sand, head pillowed by his right arm. Swaths of fog began overlapping. The unhurried, delicate movements reminded him of something he'd seen before, but the fog seemed to have worked into his mind, making everything harder to find. Minutes passed before he remembered Professor Heddon's last class at Chapel Hill, the motion of his teacher's maimed hand as it followed the music. The fog thickened until there were no more swirls, just one vast silence, white and depthless.

Leonard coughed, more blood filling his throat. He pushed his elbow against the sand and raised himself for a few moments, let the blood drain back down. He laid his head on the sand and closed his eyes. Soon the sound of rushing water broke through the fog and steadily increased and he knew it must be raining harder upstream. The bead on the tobacco plant was part of that water, flowing out of the field and into the creek, joining the millions of other raindrops to make this stream wide as a river. After a while water gathered beneath him, lifting the weight from his body, lifting him away from the pain as well. The water made a soothing sound as it moved around and under and he was so glad he wouldn't have to crawl out of the gorge after all, because he knew the water would take care of that, would carry him all the way down to Marshall and not only there but then into the French Broad and on west to the Ohio and the Mississippi, all the way to the ocean and then across the ocean and to the beach where Emily waited and he would have her tell him every single thing that had happened since that night he'd crawled out her window and he would not stop listening until every day and every hour had been accounted for and then they would wait for rain and only then walk above the beach where plants grew and find some frond or fern that held a bead of water and he would gently cup his hand to the plant and show her more than he could ever tell her, a pearl of rain held in his open palm.

FIFTEEN

They had spoken little on the drive from Shelton Laurel and there seemed nothing to say now, so they sat on the bench in silence. Dena held the ticket in her right hand, thumb and index finger rubbing the paper's slick surface. Travelers shuffled by, most too consumed hauling their own burdens to notice them. Those who did let their eyes pause on his rain-sogged clothes and the mud daubing her hair seemed more sympathetic than judgmental. Travis suspected that bus terminals attracted people all too familiar with catastrophe. Unpainted concrete gave the room a dreary hue. Being in the terminal reminded Travis of childhood days when a steady gray rain fell morning to evening and it felt like the sun had been forever washed from the sky. *Terminal*. The word fit this room. He reminded himself that this wasn't a place people stayed but passed through en route to other places, places they surely believed were better.

The bench's top slat pushed uncomfortably into his spine. Dena had chosen this seat while he bought the ticket, chosen the bench for reasons other than comfort. It faced the parking lot and the loading platform, so they could gaze through the wide wall of glass and see which showed up first—Leonard, the Toomeys, or the bus. Dena's face no longer registered fear, only a weary resignation. She wouldn't resist. She'd done all her fighting at Shelton Laurel. Truck or bus, Travis believed she'd walk out the terminal doors and get in, probably without a word or change of expression. She just wanted to see it coming.

The bus came first. As it unloaded Dena went to the ticket booth and borrowed a pen, wrote something on a scrap of paper she did not give him until they were outside. "This is where I'll be," she said. "At least for a while."

Travis read the address and phone number, placed it in his billfold. He did not know if he should hug her or say goodbye or merely walk away. Nothing felt right. They both seemed to want to say something but neither found the words. Dena finally just turned and boarded. The door closed and air brakes whooshed. The bus pulled out from under the awning and turned right onto Highway 25.

Travis drove back toward Shelton Laurel, watching the oncoming traffic for Leonard and the Toomeys. Mountains soon pressed closer to the road. He passed a yellow sign that warned of falling rock and soon afterward had to switch lanes to avoid a chunk of granite big as a hay bale. Rain came harder now and condensation began to cloud the windshield. He rolled the window down and the cool wet air brushed against his face. Though his mind was active nothing he thought of gave him any comfort. He finally remembered the speckled trout he'd caught last fall. The fish would be more active now that spring warmed the water. Maybe it was too early for any mayflies or grasshoppers but the rains would wash plenty of worms and grubs into the pool. Completely safe, the water too murky for it to be spotted by an otter or kingfisher.

When he got to the meadow no one was there, no vehicle either, and that was a relief. His great fear had been finding Leonard dead, one or both of the Toomeys dead as well, killed by a rifle Travis had loaded with his own hands. So at least not that, not the worst thing. He turned off the engine. Dribbles of rain streaked the windshield. Out in the meadow fog wisped. The broom sedge had not yet thickened, and he could see a mayapple's broad leaves hovering over its delicate white flower. Like the speckled trout, protected. He tried to figure what to do next and the only answer seemed go to the trailer.

Travis turned the truck around and headed down the mountain. The rain soon quit and he could see better, well enough to spot the skid marks on the blacktop. They could have been an hour old or months, but he couldn't remember them being there before so pulled onto the shoulder. Below, the pickup lay crumpled against a boulder. Hubert Toomey's head jutted through the windshield and Carlton Toomey lay half in the stream and half out, something green clutched in his right hand.

Travis made his way into the gorge, not trusting just his feet for balance but using hands as well to slide and bear-crawl to the bottom. He was almost at the creek before he saw Leonard. Travis kneeled beside him and pressed two fingers against

Leonard's wrist. The skin was cold. When he finally released the wrist, Travis's fingers left an impression, as if they'd been pressed into dough. A few tears welled in his eyes but he blinked them away. Crying seemed too easy somehow.

There was no need to check the Toomeys' wrists for pulses, but Travis stepped into the shallows where Carlton Toomey held a fistful of money like a shriveled bouquet. Travis tried to open the hand and the whole body moved. It floated a few yards downstream before lodging on a sandbar. Travis pried the fingers open one joint at a time until the bills slipped free. He stuffed the money in his front pocket before looking a last time at what surrounded him. Not that he needed to. The scene had already settled in his mind with the cold solidity of a creek stone.

Travis climbed out of the gorge and drove straight to Marshall. He called the Highway Patrol and reported the accident, then went to Franklin's Drugstore and bought a long manila envelope and stamps before crossing the street to the post office. He took the piece of paper from his billfold and wrote the address on the envelope before putting the money inside and sliding the envelope into the slot marked OUT OF TOWN. She'll just spend it on pills, Travis couldn't help thinking, but remembered what Dena told him last fall about starting to believe people could change. At the least the money wouldn't end up in Sheriff Crockett's hands or someone sorry enough to claim kin to the Toomeys. One thing done right, maybe even a kind of beginning, he told himself.

He got in the truck and leaned his head back, closed his eyes in the vain hope that he might escape, even if for just a few minutes, the knowledge that three men were dead from an accident on a rain-slick road, a road they wouldn't have been on if not for him. But an accident, he told himself, because the stalemate between Leonard and the Toomeys had been resolved, almost certainly by the money in Carlton Toomey's fist. Resolved peacefully because any real harm, any killing, would have been done in the meadow. They were just bringing him back to the trailer. An accident on a slippery road. "An accident," Travis said aloud, and opened his eyes.

The rain had started again, a sound on the pickup's roof like time quickening. He pulled out of the parking lot and soon came to the river. Rising water widened the banks, deepened the French Broad's color to the rich brown of cured tobacco. Across the river a new-plowed field covered a squared acre of bottomland like a dark wavy quilt. His life was beyond such fields, but Travis knew he would never forget this smell or the cool moist feel of broken ground. He inhaled deeply, held it in like a man savoring the taste of a last cigarette. The road curved briefly, then straightened as he began the long ascent north to Antioch.

ACKNOWLEDGMENTS

The Shelton Laurel Massacre was an actual event. Although I have taken liberties as far as geography and names of Confederate participants, the descriptions of the massacre are based on an account in the July 1863 *New York Times*. Phillip Paludan's excellent book *Victims* was also helpful.

Special thanks to my agent, Marly Rusoff, and editor, Jennifer Barth, as well as to Tom Rash, Phil Moore, James, Caroline, and Ann.